A MAGGIE O'DELL NOVEL

STRANDED

ALEX KAVA

DOUBLEDAY

NEW YORK LONDON TORONTO SYDNEY AUCKLAND

Copyright © 2013 by S. M. Kava

All rights reserved. Published in the United States by Doubleday, a division of Random House, Inc., New York, and in Canada by Random House of Canada Limited, Toronto.

www.doubleday.com

DOUBLEDAY and the portrayal of an anchor with a dolphin are registered trademarks of Random House, Inc.

Jacket design by Michael Windsor
Jacket photograph © Bruce Rolff/Shutterstock

Library of Congress Cataloging-in-Publication Data
Kava, Alex.
Stranded / Alex Kava. — First Edition.
pages cm
1. O'Dell, Maggie (Fictitious character)—Fiction. 2. Criminal profilers—Fiction. 3. Murder—Investigation—Fiction. I. Title.
PS3561.A8682F57 2012
813'.54—dc23   2013003001

ISBN 978-0-385-53554-0

MANUFACTURED IN THE UNITED STATES OF AMERICA

1 3 5 7 9 10 8 6 4 2

First Edition

FOR MY MOM, PATRICIA KAVA

He seemed to be a genuinely kind
man—when he wasn't killing.

—Helen Morrison, M.D.,
referring to Ed Gein in her book
My Life Among the Serial Killers

STRANDED

CHAPTER 1

He was still alive.

That was all he needed to think about. That, and to keep on running.

Noah could smell his own sweat, pungent and sour . . . and urine. He still couldn't believe he'd pissed himself.

Stop thinking. Just run. Run!

And vomit. He'd thrown up, splattering the front of his shirt. He had the taste in his mouth. His stomach threatened more but he couldn't afford to slow down. How could he slow down with Ethan's screams echoing inside his head?

Stop screaming. Please stop.

"I won't tell. I promise I won't tell."

Noah's lips were moving even as he ran. Without realizing it, he was chanting the words in rhythm with the pounding of his feet.

"Won't tell, won't tell. I promise."

Pathetic. So very pathetic.

How could he just run away and leave his friend? He was such a coward. But that admission didn't slow him down. Nor did it make him glimpse over his shoulder. Right this minute he was too scared to care how pathetic he was.

Suddenly his forehead slammed into a branch. A *whop* and *thump*.

Noah staggered but stayed on his feet. His vision blurred. His head pulsed with pain.

Don't fall down, damn it! Keep moving. Run, just run.

His feet obeyed despite the dizzy spiral swimming inside his head threatening to throw him off balance. It was so dark, too dark to see anything other than shades of gray and black. Moonlight flickered patches of light. It only contributed to the feeling of vertigo. This time he ran with his hands and arms thrashing in front of him, trying to clear the path. He used them as battering rams, making sure he didn't slam into another low-hanging branch.

Twigs continued to whip and slash at him. Noah felt new trickles down his face and elbows and knew it was blood. It mixed with sweat and stung his eyes. His tongue could taste it on his lips. And his stomach lurched again because he knew some of the blood was *not* his own.

Oh God, oh God. Ethan, I'm so sorry. I'm so sorry.

Don't stop. Don't look back. Can't help Ethan. It's too late. Just run.

But still, his mind replayed the events in short choppy fragments. They should never have rolled down the car window. Too much beer. Too cocky.

Too frickin' stupid!

They'd spent the first weekend of spring break partying before they went home. They hadn't been on the road long and Ethan had to take a piss. Now Ethan was dead. If he wasn't dead, he'd soon be wishing he was.

Noah's lungs burned. His legs ached. He had no clue what direction he was running. Nothing mattered except to run away as far and as fast as he could. But the woods were thick with knee-high brush. The canopy above swallowed the sky, except for those rare streaks of moonlight showing him glimpses of the rocky ground beneath his feet, jagged mounds that threatened to make him stumble.

And then he did trip.

Can't fall, can't fall. Please don't let me fall.

He tried to catch himself, arms flailing like an out of control windmill. He went down hard. His knees thudded against a rock. Elbows were next. Skin scraping. Pain shot through his limbs and still his mind was screaming at him to get up. But his legs wouldn't obey this time. And suddenly he heard a snap and rustle, soft and subtle.

No, it wasn't possible. It was just his imagination.

Now footsteps. Someone coming behind him. The crunch of leaves. More twigs and branches snapped and crackled.

No. Not possible.

He had told Noah that if he didn't tell, he'd let him go. Noah had promised. And so had the madman.

Footsteps. Close now. Too close to be his imagination.

Why isn't he letting me go? He promised.

And why in the world did he ever believe a madman?

But he seemed so ordinary when he knocked on their car window.

Somehow Noah picked himself up. Wobbled and ignored the pain. Demanded his legs move. He limped at first. Then started to jog. Pushed harder. A *chuff-chuff* exploded from his mouth. His lungs were on fire.

Faster.

Tears streaked down his face. A high-pitched whine pierced his ears. It echoed through the trees. A wounded animal or one ready to attack? It didn't matter. Nothing could hurt him as much as the animal chasing him.

Should never have rolled down the car window. Damn it, Ethan!

"Who's going first?" the madman had asked with a smile that looked almost gentle and insane at the same time. So calm but with eyes of a wolf.

Oh God, and then he cut Ethan. So much blood.

"I promise I won't tell."

"Run. Go on now. Run." The man had made it sound so natural, almost soothing.

"Go on now," he'd repeated when Noah stared like a paralyzed deer caught in the headlights.

And now he realized the high-pitched scream was coming from his own throat. He could feel it more than hear it. It came from somewhere deep and vibrated along his ribs before escaping up and out his mouth.

He had to shut up. He'd hear him. Know exactly where he was.

Run. Faster.

Mud sucked at his bare feet. Shirt, jeans, shoes, and socks—all a cheap exchange for freedom. He knew his bruised and battered soles were cut open and bleeding, scraped raw by the sharp rocks. He blinked hot tears.

Don't think about the pain. This is nothing compared to what's happened to Ethan.

He needed to concentrate on running, not the pain. Not his skin that was slashed and bruised.

How far did these woods go?

There had to be a clearing. He had run away from the interstate, away from the rest area, but there had to be something more than trees. Maybe a farmhouse? Another road?

He didn't hear the footfalls behind him anymore. No branches cracking or leaves crunching. His chest heaved and his heart jackhammered. He slowed just a fraction and held his breath.

Nothing.

Just a breeze. Even the birds had quieted. Had the madman turned back? Given up? Decided to honor his promise?

Maybe one was enough for him tonight?

Noah chanced a look back over his shoulder. That's when his foot caught on a fallen log and sent him sprawling. His elbows slammed into the rock and mud. The impact rattled his teeth. White stars flashed as his skin ripped on the palms of his hands.

He tried to stand. Fell back to his knees. The foot that had caused the fall burned with pain. He looked back at it and grimaced. His ankle was twisted and his left foot was at an unnatural angle. But it wasn't the pain that sent panic throughout his body. It was the fact that he couldn't move it.

He stopped himself. Held his breath again as best he could. Waited. Listened.

So quiet.

No sounds of traffic. No birds. No rustle of leaves. Even the breeze had been frightened to silence.

He was alone.

Relief swept over him. The madman hadn't followed after all. The last wave of adrenaline slipped away and he dropped back onto the ground. He sat up with his legs outstretched, too weak to even touch his swelling ankle. In the moonlight he didn't recognize his own foot. It was already ballooning, the bruised skin split open. His breathing still came in gasps, but his heartbeat had slowed to a steady drum.

He wiped a hand over his face before he realized he was only smearing blood with more blood. He brought down his hand in front of his eyes and saw that the skin on his palm had been peeled away.

Don't think about it. It's a small price to pay for freedom. Don't even look at it.

He glanced around. Maybe he could find a branch. A long one. He'd use it under his arm like a crutch. Take the weight off his battered foot. He could do this. He just needed to concentrate. Forget the pain. Focus.

Pain was better than dead, right?

A twig snapped.

Noah jerked in the direction of the sound.

Without warning the man stepped out from behind a tree and into the moonlight. Calm and steady like he had been standing there all night. No sign of being out of breath. No hint that he had traveled through the same thick and dark woods that Noah had just run through.

The madman didn't even bother to raise the knife in his hand. Instead he it kept at his side, still smeared with Ethan's blood.

He grinned and said, "It's your turn, Noah."

TUESDAY, MARCH 19

CHAPTER 2

So far the mud had surrendered one skull from within the dug out crater. FBI agent Maggie O'Dell had a feeling there were more. Washed clean by the morning downpour, it gleamed a brilliant white as it rested on top of the black loamy soil. Besides the skull, three long bones and a scattered assortment of smaller ones had also been uprooted. Maggie had enough medical background to identify the long bones as femurs, though she prefaced her claim to Sheriff Uniss by saying, "I'm not an anthropologist."

The sheriff blinked at the news as if she had thrown water in his face. He took a step back, wanting to distance himself, either from Maggie or from what she had just told him.

"If you're correct," and he paused while his Adam's apple danced up and down. He seemed to be having some difficulty swallowing this news. Finally he continued, "That would mean we've got two bodies here. Not one."

"Again, it's just an educated guess."

"I heard your partner say you've got like a premed background or something like that."

"Premed doesn't make me a bone expert, Sheriff. We'll know soon enough when the real experts get here."

Maggie stopped herself from telling the county sheriff that there could be even more bodies buried on this old farmstead.

Sheriff Uniss was already too jumpy and now she noticed the blinking had set off a nervous twitch at the corner of his left eye. His entire body seemed twitchy—feet shifting, long arms crossing then dangling until he hitched his thumbs into his belt, an unsuccessful effort to stop the constant motion.

His nervous energy reminded Maggie of the scarecrow from *The Wizard of Oz*. Gray strawlike hair stuck out from under his ball cap. His clothes, however, portrayed a sense of discipline. He wore blue jeans with creases that looked freshly pressed, a red-and-gray-plaid flannel shirt, and a small notebook and two pens stuck out of his vinyl-protected breast pocket. Despite the mud, his gray and black cowboy boots were shiny and polished.

Earlier Sheriff Uniss had told Maggie and her partner, R. J. Tully, that he had seen "a few mangled bodies" from car accidents. He had said it in a way that might offer the credentials needed to handle a possible murder victim. Instead, it only reinforced in Maggie's mind that this guy—no matter how organized and well intentioned—would be in way over his head with a murder investigation. Especially if there were more bodies. It was much too early to know, but Maggie had a gut feeling that this might be the site she and Tully had spent the last month searching for.

Maggie glanced at the two young sheriff's deputies leaning on their mud-caked shovels at the edges of the crater. Unlike their boss, they wore brown uniforms, shirtsleeves rolled up, hats left back in their vehicles. They eyed the chunks of dirt surrounding the bones as though expecting more to pop out from the ground.

Fifty feet behind the deputies, a crew of construction workers waited beside the Bobcat and backhoe loader that had turned up this mess. The men had taken up residence next to one of the remaining outbuildings. Late yesterday afternoon the workers had accidentally dug up what they believed might be an old cemetery. They had already leveled several buildings on the farmstead and had only just begun to dig the foundation for a new wildlife preserve's information center.

The bones made the crew stop. The accompanying smell made them back clear off. It was Maggie's understanding that the foreman called the sheriff and the sheriff—in the hopes of finding a simple explanation—called the property's previous owner, only to discover that she had been dead for almost ten years. Her executor had just sold the land to the federal government after leaving the property vacant for almost a decade. He was, according to the sheriff, now en route, despite being three hundred miles away when he received the sheriff's call and despite having no explanation for the newly discovered bones. In fact, it was the executor who suggested the federal government be notified. After all, they were now the owners of this mess.

As for Maggie and Agent Tully? It was a fluke that they were here at all.

They had flown into Omaha early that morning on an unrelated matter, an entirely different search. Their flight from D.C. had been a rough one. Maggie's stomach still roiled just at the thought of the lightning and rain that greeted their aircraft. She hated flying and the roller-coaster ride had left her white-knuckled and nauseated. When they stopped for gas and discovered fresh homemade doughnuts inside the little shop, Maggie bought only a Diet Pepsi. Tully raised an eyebrow. She rarely passed on doughnuts. Thankfully his concern dissipated after his second glazed cruller.

For weeks they had been spending a lot of time together either in cramped offices back at Quantico or on the road. Somehow they managed to remain patient with each other's habits and quirks. Maggie knew Tully was just as tired as she was of highway motels and rental cars, both of which smelled of someone else's perfume or aftershave and fast food.

Their search had started about a month ago after discovering a woman's body. She had been left in an alley next to a District warehouse that had been set on fire. But the victim, Gloria Dobson—a wife, a mother of three, a breast cancer survivor—had no connection to the warehouse fire. In fact, just days earlier, Dobson had traveled from Columbia, Missouri, to attend a sales conference in Baltimore. She never made it to the conference.

Virginia State Patrol recovered her vehicle at a rest area off the interstate. In the woods behind that rest area, Maggie and Tully found Dobson's traveling companion, a young business colleague named Zach Lester. Maggie had seen her share of gruesome scenes in her ten years as a field agent, but the viciousness of this one surprised both her and Tully. Lester's body had been left at the base of a tree. He had been decapitated, his body sliced open and his intestines strung up in the lower branches.

It wasn't just the nature of the murders but also the fact that the killer had taken on both Dobson and Lester—two apparently strong, healthy, and intelligent business travelers—and succeeded. That's what convinced Maggie and Tully that this killer had done this before. Their boss, Assistant Director Raymond Kunze, agreed and assigned them to the FBI's Highway Serial Killings Initiative.

The initiative had been started several years earlier, creating a national database that collected, assessed, and made available details of murder victims found along the United States' highways and interstates. Not a small task. There were currently more than five hundred victims logged into the system. The database allowed local law enforcement officers a way to check to see if bodies discovered in their jurisdictions could possibly be related to other murders in different states.

Maggie had easily bought into the project's core belief that many of these murders were the work of serial killers who used the interstate systems. Tully jokingly called it a serial killer's paradise. The rest areas and truck stops that provided safe havens for exhausted travelers also provided perfect targets for experienced killers. Though most were well lit, they were surrounded by woods or other isolated areas, and they provided a quick, easy escape route. In a matter of hours the killer could cross over into another jurisdiction undetected.

Bolstering the initiative, one killer had already been captured in 2007. Bruce Mendenhall, a long-haul truck driver, had been convicted of murdering a woman he picked up at a truck stop. He was suspected of killing five others from as many as four states.

The brutal murders of Gloria Dobson and Zach Lester led them to believe that they had stumbled across another highway killer. But their murders were only part of the reason Maggie and Tully had ended up in the Midwest. The killer had actually left Maggie a map. Just when they had finished solving the warehouse arsons in the District, Maggie discovered the map on the burned remnants of her kitchen counter. Her beautiful Tudor house, her sanctuary, had been set on fire. Her brother, Patrick, and her dogs had almost died inside.

But this highway killer had nothing to do with the fires. He had only taken advantage of them. The warehouse fires had been an opportunity for him to dump Gloria Dobson's body in the alley. And the blaze that almost destroyed Maggie's home was another opportunity. This one allowed him to invade her privacy. He had walked right into the ashes after everyone was gone and set the map on the granite countertop, anchoring it down with a rock from the ravine behind her backyard. The map was his invitation to a scavenger hunt.

The crude, hand-drawn diagram included wavy lines labeled "MissRiver" running parallel to more lines that looked like an interstate highway, complete with exits. Nothing else was marked other than north and south, east and west.

A young agent at the FBI's crime lab, a data genius named Antonio Alonzo, had discovered the "MissRiver" was the Missouri River after he discounted all possibilities of it being the Mississippi. Then he insisted that the stretch of highway had to be Interstate 29. That narrowed Maggie and Tully's search to seven hundred miles and thirty-two rest areas. Still a daunting amount of miles to cover.

Also on the killer's map was a rest area, drawn out in geometric shapes precisely penned to indicate the buildings, picnic shelters, and a parking lot with slots for cars and trucks. A kidney-shaped road swirled around it, connecting it to the interstate exits. Squiggle shapes—what Agent Alonzo determined were woods—separated the rest area from the river. More squiggles—supposedly more woods—stretched on the other side of the river, fading out to a series of X's, one after another, perhaps shorthand for more terrain.

That was Agent Alonzo's theory. Maggie suspected that the X's marked the spaces where he had dumped dead bodies.

Using aerial photos from truckers' websites and Google Earth,

Agent Alonzo had narrowed down the rest areas to three in Iowa, one in Kansas, and two in South Dakota. Maggie and Tully had been on the road for only a couple of hours when Agent Alonzo called. Human bones had been discovered the day before on a farmstead. The property backed to an interstate rest area. One of the rest areas on their list.

Now Maggie was anxious to see just how close the rest area was to this farmstead. Maybe this was just another detour on their wild goose chase. The skull and femurs could be an odd and unfortunate coincidence, depending on how old they were. She knew this was Indian territory once upon a time. The farm's buildings were almost a century old. It was possible they could have been built over an Indian burial ground.

Still, she wanted to see for herself. She excused herself from the sheriff and his deputies, gave a knowing look to Tully, and left them. The long driveway had been blocked off by a single black-and-white sheriff's SUV. One deputy sat bored in the driver's seat. Maggie could hear the talk radio station. She nodded at him and noticed he shifted expectantly but she didn't stop. She continued walking past a hedge of lilac bushes. Their flowers were only starting to open, but Maggie could already smell them.

Geese honked overhead. A grove thick with river maples, elms, and cottonwoods surrounded the farm on three sides, cradling it from any view of the road as well as muffling all outside noises. In fact, if she and Tully hadn't taken the interstate to get here, Maggie would never have guessed that an ongoing flow of traffic passed so close to the property.

She found an overgrown footpath behind the barn that took her into the woods. Buds had only started to appear, an eruption of bright green spots on otherwise bare and stark black branches. Last fall's pine needles and old leaves, now soggy and clumped together, covered the ground. Maggie took careful steps to keep from slipping and sliding.

The path quickly narrowed and started a gradual incline. Twigs whipped into her face even as she grabbed at the branches in front of her. Thorny vines snagged her pant legs. Sunlight filtered down in streaks. Birds provided flashes of color and song—bright yellow finches, red-winged blackbirds, a cardinal. That they were singing—continuing their spring mating calls—calmed Maggie. The last time she and Tully made their way through a thick forest like this they had been following birds that had been circling, leading them to Zach Lester's body.

Maggie climbed to a clearing at the top of the incline. Below her a shallow stream zigzagged through the brush. On the other side, the woods continued. But from above Maggie could see in the distance the ribbon of interstate traffic. And she could now hear its faint but steady hum. What attracted her attention was the rest area nestled down in the woods.

She reached in her jacket pocket and pulled out the folded map she had been carrying around with her. This was a copy. The original remained in a protective evidence bag back at Quantico's crime lab.

She had memorized the geometric shapes, the parallel and intersecting lines. She held up the eight-by-eleven sheet in front of her to one side. Then she glanced back and forth from the map to the scenery below, eyes darting, searching, and not quite believing. She felt a chill as the realization came over her. The roads around the rest area looked like the kidney-shaped sketch on the map. The inked geometric patterns matched those below: building, picnic shelters, even the parking slots had been precisely drawn.

This was it. The scavenger hunt was over. This was exactly where the killer had led them.

"Maggie."

She startled despite R. J. Tully's attempt to whisper. He was breathing hard and she knew it was from anxiety, not exertion. He was in good physical shape. She waited for him to climb the last steps and stand beside her.

She held up the map and pointed down below.

"This is it," she told him.

Tully gave it only a glance. He wiped a hand over his face and Maggie could see his jaw clenched tight when he said, "The hunt might be over but the nightmare's just beginning. We found a black garbage bag."

He met her eyes and added, "I think there's a body inside."

CHAPTER 3

Maggie could see only a section of the garbage bag that bulged out from under the chunks of dirt. The black plastic still had a glossy newness despite the mud and the smell. On their hike back, Tully had explained how he had hunted down the foul smell, which convinced him the bulging plastic bag might contain a body, although most of the bag remained underneath the pile of dirt.

The first thing Maggie noticed was that this burial plot—if it was, indeed, that—wasn't close to the crater that had produced the skull and femurs. The mound of earth was set at the edge of the woods, at least a hundred feet away from the farmhouse.

"We tore up this area yesterday morning," the construction foreman said. "We thought it was just garbage. That's what it smelled like. We didn't think much about it. A lot of country folks bury their trash instead of burning it. They sort of make their own personal landfills. We just left it alone."

"You didn't think it was odd that there wasn't any other garbage?" Tully asked.

The foreman, who had introduced himself only as Buzz, shrugged. He kept his hard hat low over his brow, and his mirrored sunglasses made it difficult to see whether he was concerned or simply impatient with the delays.

The sheriff and his deputies, along with the construction crew, now surrounded the pile of dirt that stood about seven feet tall and spread over about fifteen feet. The equipment had left tracks and gashes in the ground, including a three-foot-deep trench with claw marks. Yet, Tully seemed adamant that it was a crime scene and he even attempted to back off the men.

He asked them to stay at least ten feet away, which Maggie thought was senseless. Any evidence had already been run over, dug up, or washed away. At this point, a few more footprints wouldn't make a difference. Besides, none of the men looked anxious to poke or prod at the garbage bag. They appeared more wary of it than curious.

Tully took a pair of latex gloves out of his pocket, removed his sports jacket, and handed it to Maggie.

"What are you doing?" she asked him.

"I'm just going to check it out."

"Shouldn't we wait?" Sheriff Uniss wanted to know.

Tully glanced back at him. "Wait for who? The FBI?"

Out of the corner of her eye, Maggie saw the sheriff's face grow crimson.

"It might just be a bag of garbage," Tully said, rolling up his shirtsleeves. "You want to call a mobile crime lab out here and have them open it only to find someone's rotting leftovers?"

No one answered. The younger deputy shifted his weight and Maggie could see the discomfort on his face. She recognized that look. First murder case. First dead body. It was hard not to be excited while trying to hide the shock and a bit of nausea. He swiped at his chin and his eyes darted around.

Maggie was surprised at Tully. It wasn't like him to jump in. Of the two of them, he was the cautious one. He waited for the appropriate authorities. He played by the rules. It was Maggie who often leaped headfirst.

But she shared his impatience. That a rest area backed up to this property could be a mere coincidence, except that it matched the hand-drawn map, almost line for squiggly line. Factor in that this farm had been vacant for almost ten years. They had been searching for this highway killer's dumping grounds for more than three weeks now. Maggie could feel Tully's restlessness. The land was technically federal property. They had jurisdiction.

She didn't say a word when Tully glanced back at her. He was looking for her to stop him. But she wanted to see what was inside the plastic bag, too. She nodded her agreement.

Tully stepped carefully, gauging the best method of approach. The only two options were wading through the muddy trench and reaching up to the bag or going around the side and climbing the pile of dirt to get to the bag. Tully chose to climb.

The chunks of dirt held his weight but it looked like one wrong move and he'd start a mudslide. He'd made it within arm's length of the garbage bag when he slipped, almost losing his balance. He replanted his feet and his right shoe sank down. Maggie heard him groan but he stayed put. He was close enough to bend down and touch the bulging plastic.

He pushed up his rolled shirtsleeves. Then he reached out with a gloved hand and gently swiped off a chunk of dirt. He waited as if he expected the plastic to burst open. Maggie glanced around at the men from the construction crew and the deputies. All of them appeared to be holding their breath. No one dared fidget or shift.

Tully took another swipe and then another. A large chunk of dirt came loose and skidded down the pile, revealing more of the black bag. That's when a piece of the plastic flapped open. It had already been torn but the dirt had kept it sealed.

Tully carefully peeled it open. Suddenly he jerked away just as a foot slipped out from the plastic. An orange sock dangled from the toes.

Maggie heard several of the men gasp as they watched the pale skin change to dark red in a matter of seconds. She had seen it happen once before. A strange and eerie phenomenon that sometimes occurred when encased decaying flesh is first exposed to air and sun. It almost looked as if the body were coming back to life, trying to kick out of the sock and the bag.

"I think we can call the crime techs now," Tully said.

Then Maggie heard someone start to gag. Without looking she knew it was the poor young deputy. He finally had his first dead body.

CHAPTER 4

OUTSIDE MANHATTAN, KANSAS

OFF INTERSTATE 70

Noah had no idea how long he had been lying under the pine tree. Nor had he noticed how close he was to the back of the small brick building. Somewhere he heard the buzz of electrical machines and the hum of traffic. It all came to him muffled, like he had cotton wadded up in his ears. His breathing came in rasps and hitches. His chest hurt, as if he hadn't stopped running. His heartbeat continued to gallop and refused to slow back down to normal. Whatever normal was.

"Eleanor, there's a young man here."

Noah heard the voice, though he stayed in his fetal position, not even attempting to see if the person was close by or referring to him.

Please don't see me. Please just walk on by.

"He looks like he's bleeding."

Busted.

But he didn't have the strength to crawl out of sight. He couldn't crawl. He couldn't move. His muscles had given up. All he knew was that the last time he tried to sit up, it hurt too much.

He'd curled up into a ball, trying to make himself small. Trying to make himself disappear. Dark had turned into day. Cold into warm. But his mind had shut off. He had to shut it off.

"No, stay back, Eleanor."

The man was close but he was keeping a safe distance.

"He doesn't have any clothes on."

He took them. He took everything.

"Good God, there's so much blood. I think he's hurt pretty bad."

Noah didn't have the energy to tell the man that it wasn't his blood. It was Ethan's. Or what was left of Ethan.

Don't think about it. Can't think about it. Stop thinking about it. Just breathe.

"Go call 911, Eleanor."

No, just leave me here.

Noah tried to block out the man's voice. Somewhere above, a hawk screeched. A breeze swished through the branches. Other birds chirped and tweeted. He couldn't identify them. Leaves skittered. He wanted to fill his head with any sound as long as it might block out Ethan's screams.

CHAPTER 5

"Where's the closest FBI field office?" Tully asked Maggie.

She had joined him at the top of the dirt pile. Both of them were ankle-deep in mud. From this close, the smell was over-powering, even though they had shifted and climbed a bit higher so they could look down at the protruding garbage bag and be upwind. The sheriff, his deputies, and the construction crew kept their distance, staying on the other side of the trench. They had even backed away without being asked. It also put them out of earshot of Tully and Maggie's conversation.

"I'm guessing Minneapolis is four or five hours away," Maggie said after some thought. "I don't think we have a field office in Iowa or South Dakota."

"Omaha's probably the closest. Do you know anyone there?"

Maggie shook her head. "Not in the FBI office. But they have a regional crime lab that's first class."

They stood side by side, so close Maggie's shoulder brushed against Tully's arm. They were perched five feet above with a perfect view of the grounds. Maggie took it all in, assessing how large the property was. It would be an overwhelming task to start digging it up. And that didn't count the woods and riverbed behind the property. She knew Tully was thinking exactly what she was.

"How many other bodies do you suppose are here?" he finally asked.

"We could be wrong about this being a dumping ground."

"I'll ask Alonzo to send a canine cadaver team," Tully said as if he hadn't heard her.

"I don't think the sock belonged to the victim."

"What do you mean?"

"It looked new, too clean." She noticed that the sock still had a crease across the bottom, like it had just come out of a package. No way it had been in a shoe and still had that pronounced a crease.

"Wasn't there a body found just recently wearing orange socks?" Maggie asked.

"An FBI case?"

"No, not one of ours." Maggie tried to remember. For some reason she could see another body, orange socks, a wooded area . . . and then she realized where. "On television," she said. "There was a TV reporter who led Virginia State Patrol to a body in the woods. Do you remember seeing that?"

Tully pushed up his glasses and rubbed his temple. "I try not to watch any reality cop shows."

"It wasn't a prime-time show. It was on the news. Maybe three or four weeks ago. The reporter said he was directed to the site by a tip. I can't remember if there was an eyewitness."

"You think the two are connected?"

Maggie didn't believe in coincidences. And now she wondered if the bastard had gone out and bought orange socks? Could the socks be his signature? But she couldn't remember Gloria Dobson wearing any socks at all when her body was discovered.

"Ask Agent Alonzo to check the database for orange socks," she said. "And have him find out as much as he can about the woman found in Virginia."

He jotted notes on a scrap of paper.

"The skin looks like it hasn't even started to decompose," Tully said. "How long ago do you think this one was?"

"Standard rate of decomposition is one week in the open air. Two weeks in water. Up to eight underground."

"I hate that you know that stuff off the top of your head."

Maggie smiled. It wasn't a trait she was proud of. Not only did she remember such gruesome trivia but she could store and retrieve it at will.

Just then the ripped piece of plastic flapped open in the breeze. It was enough for Maggie to see movement inside the bag. She felt a cold sweat and she grimaced. And what was worse, Tully noticed.

"Maggots," she said through clenched teeth and it came out in almost a whisper. She hated maggots. "That speeds up the rate."

Had the killer ripped the bag on purpose, knowing that maggots would make it more difficult to identify the body?

"We need to get a mobile unit out here before dark," Tully said.

Maggie glanced at the men below. It was human nature for these guys to share today's discovery. "And some extra security," she added.

"I'm on it." Tully pulled his cell phone out of his trouser pocket as he started to skid down the pile.

Maggie stayed put. By now the smell didn't bother her and she kept from glancing at the flapping plastic. Instead she continued to survey the property. The sheriff had said the previous owner had died ten years ago. Had the property been vacant the whole time? And if so, how did the killer know? Did he just stumble upon such good fortune or did he have a connection to this place?

The sun blazed down now. All the clouds had left. The temperature stayed cool but at least they wouldn't need to worry about more rain. Something caught her eye, the sun glinting off glass. The farmhouse was about one hundred feet away but something made her look its way.

Maggie's heart skipped a beat.

She put her hand to her forehead to shield out the sunlight. Certainly she was mistaken, and yet she made her way down to ground level, keeping her eyes focused on the house.

"Sheriff," she said, coming around the trench, walking to his side to avoid raising her voice. "Does anyone have keys to the house?"

"The property's executor does. He should be here soon."

"Can you call him and see how close he is?"

"You mean right now?"

"Yes, now. And we need to move these men back over to the outbuildings. Slowly. Make sure they don't rush."

"You mean right now?"

"Yes."

She left him before he asked more questions. She was pleased that he was already getting the men to move and tapping on his cell phone. She walked over to Tully and waited for him to finish his call.

Then she calmly told him, "Someone's inside the house."

CHAPTER 6

"What are you talking about?" Tully asked and he started to turn toward the farmhouse before Maggie grabbed his elbow.

"I saw a curtain move."

"That could be anything. A breeze, a draft."

"Something moved in front of the window. Then the curtain fell back into place."

"We're both pretty wiped. When was the last time either of us got a full night's sleep?"

He didn't believe her. Before she could argue her case, she saw his fingers instinctively move up to his shoulder holster. But he didn't reach for his weapon. Instead he grabbed his sports jacket from where he had draped it carelessly over a fence post. He pulled it on casually without a hint of tension.

Maybe she was exhausted from too little sleep, but Maggie knew she had seen something or someone in the house. A house that had been vacant for ten years. Tully started walking away. With or without him she'd check it out. Still, she followed him, trying to figure out what would convince him. It was smarter to have backup. They had both been in situations before where a killer had come back to the scene just to watch law enforcement officers discover his victims. They'd also been at crime scenes where the killer had left a trap for the police.

Now it made sense to Maggie. Why had the killer given her a map? Why send them on a scavenger hunt then lead them directly to the gravesite if he didn't get to enjoy or observe it?

Tully stopped beside the backhoe, and that's when Maggie realized he had put the heavy equipment between them and the rear of the house. Then he said in a low voice, "Damn it. We should have thought about checking out the house first thing."

So he did believe her.

"The sheriff said the estate's executor is on his way here. He has a key."

"But if the house is rigged . . ."

So she and Tully were on the same page.

"It'd be doors, not windows."

"Are you sure he didn't see you notice him?"

"I'm not sure of anything right this minute," Maggie admitted.

"He's watching the excitement back here. He can't watch all sides of the house at the same time."

"We split up?"

Tully nodded.

"What do we tell Uniss and his deputies?"

"To stay put."

"You don't want them to back us up?"

Tully looked over her head at the men gathered by the barn. She stole a glance over her shoulder. Foreman Buzz had wandered into the woods and was coming back, smoking a cigarette. His crew was talking, pointing or waving at the garbage bag. The sheriff was still on his cell phone. His deputies were on their own, either talking or texting.

"I'd rather we have them stand down until they hear from one of us."

Maggie remembered the young deputy losing his lunch and she couldn't help wondering if he'd ever fired his weapon in the field.

"I'll tell them," Tully offered. "Why don't you check out those lilac bushes and take the east side of the house. I'll go behind the barn and come up on the west side."

Maggie glanced at the house again. The double-hung windows were set about four feet up off the ground. She remembered seeing a porch at the front of the house and a side door on the west side. She hadn't seen the east side that was flanked by lilac bushes. If the windows were as high, she'd have to struggle to get up and in without taking too much time and becoming a target.

"What are you thinking?" she finally asked Tully.

He took off his jacket again and draped it over the side rail of the backhoe.

"Break a window. Then take cover and wait. If someone's inside, he'll go check it out. It'll give me enough time to kick in the door on my side. From what I remember, it didn't look like much of a challenge."

"I'm not sure I like it. What if he's sitting in a corner with a semiautomatic, waiting for you? Maybe we should wait for the executor and a key."

"He could still be sitting in a corner with a semiautomatic waiting for us. Or we could put the key in the lock and the whole place explodes."

"Were we always this paranoid?"

Tully smiled. "I think you've been a bad influence on me."

Maggie took off her jacket now and draped it over Tully's.

"Just be careful," she told him. "Gwen would kill me if something bad happened to you." Then she started for the lilac bushes hoping they might find a stray cat inside.

CHAPTER 7

Noah awoke to white walls and machines humming. He startled so violently he ripped a needle from the back of his hand and beeping erupted above his head. He crawled over the bed rail in one easy, frantic move but when his feet touched the floor pain shot through his body. That's when he noticed swaddled gauze at the ends of his legs. They looked like enormous stumps and for a brief moment he panicked.

Oh my God, did they amputate my feet?

A nurse hurried into the room and her motion made him jump. *Fight or flight.*

The instinct still raw inside him.

"Stop. You'll hurt yourself."

She was small and quick and amazingly strong as she grabbed him by the shoulders. In seconds he was cradled back down into the pillows. Before he could protest and try again, he felt a wave of nausea.

"I'm gonna throw up."

She didn't flinch. Instead she helped him sit forward and placed a plastic wash basin on his lap.

There was nothing left in his stomach to vomit. His dry gags scraped his sore throat and his jaw ached. When he was finished, the nurse eased him back down and pulled the covers up over him. The flimsy hospital gown stuck to his sweat-drenched body and he started shivering so badly he was certain he must be having some sort of convulsion.

He felt the prick of a needle before he could fight it. Warm liquid flooded his veins. His body almost immediately began to relax. He melted deeper into the pillows as his head began to swim. His heartbeat quieted but his chest still hurt.

His eyes darted at every sound and every movement in the room. Blurry green and red lights flashed on equipment he didn't recognize. A face appeared at the door. Another peered down over the bed at him—the nurse. Only now he was seeing three of her.

Eyelids heavy. Don't close them.

He didn't want to see Ethan's face again.

It felt like only minutes later when Noah opened his eyes. This time his mother's face hovered over the bed and he blinked hard, trying to clear her from his view.

"Oh look, Carl, he's waking up."

Noah's head swiveled to find his father standing by the window. Another man was with him. Noah jerked up, eyes popping wide open before he realized he didn't recognize the other man.

"I'm sure there's an explanation for everything," he heard his father tell the stranger. Neither seemed as pleased or as excited as Noah's mother was that he was waking up.

"I hope so."

His father turned to Noah but stayed by the window as the other man came closer. His mother stepped aside and her smile went away, too.

"Noah, I'm Lieutenant Detective Lopez with the Riley County Police Department."

Noah could hear a slight accent and he glanced at his father. The man was shorter than Noah's dad. His face was lean, skin a bit weathered, his button-down shirt tight where his arm and chest muscles bulged.

"Do you know where you are, son?"

Noah's eyes darted to his father again to see if he would object to this man addressing him as "son." His father didn't move, didn't shift, just stared at him, waiting for Noah's answer.

"Hospital," Noah managed to say.

"Do you remember how you got here?"

Noah looked at his mother. She smiled but it was forced and nervous, a twitch at the corner of her lips.

He shook his head.

"Do you remember what happened last night?"

When Noah didn't answer, Detective Lopez prompted, "At the rest area?"

He didn't want to remember.

Don't tell. Don't tell. I promised I wouldn't tell.

Noah shook his head again, but his heart started racing.

"Do you remember being on the road last night? Stopping at the rest area?"

He shook his head. This time too quickly. He could see the detective didn't believe him.

"When they brought you here you were covered in blood."

His eyes darted to his father to be met with a hard stare. His mother's smile was gone for good now. Her hand covered her mouth. Brow furrowed. It wasn't just concern. There was some-thing else.

"It was a lot of blood," Detective Lopez continued, "too much for the injuries you sustained."

Noah heard it now plainly. Suspicion. Could the detective hear his heart banging against his rib cage?

So much blood. Ethan's blood.

"Ethan," he said, but it was barely a whisper.

"Your friend, Ethan. That's right," Detective Lopez said more gently now, coaxing Noah.

Can't tell. Don't tell.

But Noah slipped and said, "He's still out there."

By the look on his parents' faces and Detective Lopez's, Noah realized they thought he meant Ethan, when he really meant the madman. He was still out there and he'd know if Noah told. He'd know and he'd come back and do to Noah what he had done to Ethan.

CHAPTER 8

Maggie watched from behind the thick shrubs. Behind her, beyond the bushes and trees, was a freshly plowed field. The scent of lilacs and dirt surrounded her. At least it would be difficult for anyone to sneak up from the opposite direction. The afternoon shadows made it difficult to see inside the windows of the house.

She saw Tully stop to talk to the sheriff. Somehow he managed to keep the man from turning to look back at the farmhouse. In fact, even after Tully disappeared behind the barn, the group continued on as if nothing had changed.

She checked her watch and waited to give Tully enough time to get in place. Five minutes felt like twenty and the entire time she kept her eyes on the windows. There was no movement. Not even the hint of a curtain swaying. The fabric looked thin enough for someone to see through. But all Maggie could make out was a veil of gray and black.

She glanced at her watch.

Time's up.

Maggie searched the ground and found a rock as big as her fist. She picked it up in her left hand. Her right already held her Smith & Wesson. It was the revolver she had trained on, opting out when the bureau went to Glocks. Only six bullets, but she had never needed more and her Smith & Wesson had never jammed. Now she clutched the grip. She kept the muzzle down, trigger finger ready. In three steps she was close enough. She pulled back and threw despite thinking how wrong it felt to shatter glass without provocation.

Then she hunched down. She shoved her back against the side of the house. Not directly beneath the broken window but close enough that glass crunched under her mud-caked shoes. She steadied her breath. Birds had quieted. Even the breeze paused.

Maggie's pulse pounded and she strained to hear inside the house.

Something shuffled. Footsteps? There was a click. The hammer of a gun being pulled back? Or a door latch engaging? Had someone come into the room? Or left? It was killing her not to stand up and glance inside.

Come on, Tully, where are you?

Finally she heard the crack. Another crack followed by the sound of wood splintering. Then a crash.

"FBI. Step out where I can see you."

Maggie shot up. Glanced through the broken window. A bedroom. Shattered glass on a paisley comforter. The window was too high for her to climb through. She hurried along the front of the house. She could hear Tully shouting again as he made his way inside.

Slouched down under the windows, she made her way to the other side of the house until she found the door Tully had kicked in.

She paused. Listened.

"Tully?"

No answer.

Damn it.

She stopped outside the doorway, her back against the house.

Readjusted her grip on her gun. Then she ducked low and spun around into the house.

Sunlight filled the first room. Furniture covered with white drop cloths reminded her eerily of a crime scene, white covers over bloated bodies.

"Bathroom at the end of the hallway," Tully called out.

"Are you okay?"

"I'm good. Check the front rooms. I didn't get to those."

She made a careful sweep, pulled off several of the larger covers. Dust filled the air but she was relieved no one was hiding underneath. After she examined every corner and closet she made her way back down the hall.

She found Tully standing in the doorway, his Glock at his side but his finger still ready at the trigger. He shifted just enough for Maggie to see the intruder. The woman looked about forty, long dirty-blond hair, mascara-smudged raccoon eyes. She was dressed only in pink panties and a tight midriff T-shirt that hugged her emaciated figure, highlighting the lines of her rib cage.

"Who the hell do you people think you are?" she asked, swiping greasy strands of hair out of her face.

The gesture provided a better look at her pale face, which was covered in acne and sores. Several were bleeding, as if she had just scratched them open moments ago.

"She was more concerned about flushing something down the toilet," Tully said to Maggie without taking his eyes off the woman, "than she was about someone breaking in here."

"Can't a gal go to the bathroom without an audience?"

Then the woman laughed, a smoker's dry rasp, and Maggie got a glimpse of blackened teeth, a couple of gaps with only rotted nibs. It was enough for Maggie to start examining the woman's arms and legs. There were more sores on her forearms but Maggie couldn't see any needle marks. She tried to remember what she knew about methamphetamine users. Were they dangerous? Psychotic? They didn't always inject it. The crystals or "crank" were smoked. The powdered form could be snorted or eaten.

Maggie glanced across the hall into the bedroom behind her, the one with the paisley bedspread. She saw dirty white sneakers, a pair of jeans, and other clothes left in a pile on the floor where they had been taken off. Beside them was a huge leather shoulder bag surrounded by trash, mostly candy bar wrappers and soda cans.

On the dresser was an assortment of candles, melted down to different sizes. A hint of white powder blended with dust. An obvious swipe had been made quickly and recklessly through the middle. Also on the dresser top were dollar bills wadded up and discarded like trash. Maybe not dollars, Maggie realized when she noticed Benjamin Franklin on one not crushed as tightly.

"How 'bout you tell us who you are," Tully said. "And what you're doing here?"

"This is my place."

"Of course, it's your place," Tully told her. "I really like the decor. White sheets go with everything."

"Just ask the owners. They'll tell you they gave me permission to stay here anytime I want."

Maggie noticed that the woman didn't seem to be fearful, not paying attention to either Tully's or Maggie's weapon.

"Is that so?" a man, accompanied by Sheriff Uniss, said from down the hallway.

The man wore a suede jacket, blue jeans, and a ball cap. He stood as tall as the sheriff but was in better shape, lean, maybe in his early to mid-thirties. Black glasses framed probing black eyes but his face was friendly.

"Agent Tully, Agent O'Dell," the sheriff said. "This here's Howard Elliott. He's the executor of this property. In other words, the most recent owner. Do you recognize this woman, Mr. Elliott?"

"No, I don't."

"Miss," Uniss said in a polite tone, "there hasn't been anyone living here for almost ten years. If you knew the owner, what was her name?"

The woman snorted another laugh. "If she's been gone for ten years how the hell would I remember her name?"

The men just stared. Maggie caught herself feeling sorry for her.

"Maybe we should start with *your* name."

But now she seemed to be thinking, her eyes scrunched, the lines of her forehead making her look older than Maggie's earlier assessment.

"Helen."

"Your name's Helen?" Tully asked.

"No, asshole. Mine's Lily. The woman who lived here. I stayed here when I was a girl. When I was thirteen. She fostered me. She was very kind."

All eyes looked to Mr. Elliott for confirmation.

"Helen and her husband did take in a lot of kids," he admitted. "In fact, I was one of them."

"I didn't realize. She must have died the year after I left," Lily said.

Silence made Lily's eyes dart from one face to another.

"She's been gone only ten years," Tully finally said.

"Yeah, exactly. I'm twenty-four, asshole. I know you all think I look more mature and sexy."

She was greeted with more silence.

"Hey, back off," she yelled, though no one had moved.

She became so agitated Maggie thought Lily might start swinging at Tully.

"I don't like the way all you bastards are drooling over me." She was serious and now visibly angry.

"Drooling?" Sheriff Uniss said in almost a whisper of disbelief rather than sarcasm.

Maggie tapped Tully on the shoulder for him to step out of the bathroom doorway.

"Why don't you come with me, Lily," she told the woman. "You can put some clothes on. You must be chilly."

"Chilly?" She cackled and Maggie couldn't help thinking her voice sounded like the raspy wear of someone who had abused her body for decades, not years.

"It's hotter than hell in here," Lily said, and she brushed at the loose strands of hair that had fallen back into her face and were sticking to her sweaty forehead.

Maggie realized the woman was probably still high. Meth runs could last up to twenty-four hours. Heavy users sometimes kept it going for days, even weeks. Judging by the sores and rotting teeth—despite being only twenty-four—Maggie knew that Lily wasn't a novice drug user.

Lily was still agitated but seemed to welcome the opportunity to get out of the bathroom and out from under Tully's and the other two men's scrutiny. She edged around him and Maggie motioned for her to continue to the bedroom across the hall. Maggie followed but not before exchanging a look with Tully. She glanced at Howard Elliott and noticed just a hint of a smile, as though he found all of this quite amusing.

CHAPTER 9

PANHANDLE OF FLORIDA

Ryder Creed heard footsteps, a soft *tap-tap* on the hardwood floor of his loft. Someone was either sneaking up on him or didn't want to wake him. Either way, he didn't much care. His eyelids twitched enough to see sunlight but refused to open. He wanted to stay in bed. It was perfect sleeping weather. A cool breeze came through an open window bringing dampness along with the smell of a wood fire. He was too comfortable to move, yet he slid his hand underneath the mattress and let his fingers wrap around the Ruger .38 Special +P.

A dog's tongue slobbered over Creed's face. He hadn't even heard the dog. He kept one hand under the mattress and with the other made half an attempt to brush the dog away. There was something comforting about the dog's licking. That is until he began to whine.

Creed's eyes opened, blinking hard against the sunlight. It felt like gravel scraped under his eyelids. He pulled the revolver out before noticing the dog's wagging tail. Then he saw the large black woman standing on the other side of his loft apartment.

"How did you get in here?" He caught himself looking around like he wasn't quite sure where "here" was.

"You gave me a key."

"My bad," Creed said and sat up, tucking the gun back under the mattress.

"One of these days you're gonna shoot somebody."

"That's the idea."

He suddenly felt dizzy, like his head was disproportionately larger than his body. His mouth was dry, his throat scratchy. It was hard to swallow. He looked for a glass of water and saw only empty beer bottles. The woman—Hannah—had already started picking them up. There were scattered paper plates, too, filled with pizza crusts and other unidentifiable leftovers.

He'd had the loft apartment custom built over the dog kennels so he could hear if any of the dogs were distressed and sometimes when he needed their company they were close by, just like Rufus alerting him with his slobber-licks. It was the one comfort he allowed himself.

The loft's open floor plan included a gourmet kitchen, a high beamed cathedral ceiling, cherrywood floors—though you'd never know there was wood beneath the clutter he had allowed to pile up. Clothes and shoes, electronic equipment and file folders were everywhere. An assortment of maps in various sizes were spread across every major surface, anchored down with coffee mugs and dirty dishes. Truth was, he didn't like seeing the place like this. He didn't like Hannah seeing it like this either. And he didn't like her seeing *him* like this.

She wouldn't care. It would take much more than filth and disarray to send her packing. Or at least, he hoped so. Other than the dogs, she was all he had in this world.

She was quiet now, perhaps satisfied that she had sufficiently rattled him. She tossed the beer bottles into his metal wastebasket, letting each one bang against the side. The insides of his head exploded with each hit. She smiled when she noticed him wincing, as if she had scored a major point.

She continued to pick up a few pieces of clothing from the floor and toss them onto a pile. Something caught her attention. She gave him a hard look then bent down, pinched the item up by as little fabric as possible, and held it up for him. It was a pair of women's panties. A pink thong.

"Do you even remember who these belong to?" she asked.

"They're not yours?"

"Only in your dreams."

Creed smiled.

He'd known Hannah for only seven years but it felt like a lifetime. He trusted her more than anyone else in the world. She was like a big sister, only meaner. They became business partners five years ago. Creed trained and took care of the dogs. Hannah took the assignments, managed the finances, scheduled the other trainers and handlers.

"None of the women complain," he said, referring to the panties that she now tossed aside.

"That's true," she admitted. "Those I've seen, always leave here with a smile. I guess even as they're leaving their panties behind."

He thought she looked more amused than angry, but then she became serious again.

"When you drink you depreciate the business," she said, looking him square in the eyes.

"You don't need to worry. I have that all under control."

"Right. That's exactly what I was thinking when I walked in

here." She said it as she waved her hand around the room like Vanna White on *Wheel of Fortune*, showing him what he had won.

He knew he wouldn't win this argument. She was right. He was drinking too much, but he tried to defend himself anyway.

"I only drink on weekends."

"It's Tuesday."

"Are you sure?" He rubbed at his eyes. That couldn't be right. How could he lose a whole day?

She shook her head at him.

"I just took an assignment for you. Some bodies dug up in Iowa. Might be more buried."

"Maybe you can send Felix."

"Felix is on vacation."

"I thought he wasn't going until the eighteenth."

"Yesterday was the eighteenth. You sure you're okay?"

The sarcasm was gone. Now she sounded concerned. That wasn't good. Ryder would rather take the sarcasm.

She continued when he didn't respond. "This has been a bad stretch for you, Rye. I'm starting to get worried."

The truth was he wanted to tell her she was right. He wanted to tell her he couldn't do another search. Not this soon. The last one had drained the life from him. The high hopes and then the crashing low that followed nearly broke him. He couldn't stomach the smell of another rotting corpse while his adrenaline pumped and his expectations soared. Each time with each dead body he kept thinking, "Will this one be her?" Would he finally find his little sister?

This last body had been that of a child, approximately the same age Brodie was when she disappeared. But even when the bodies were those of adult females it didn't rule Brodie out. Just because she disappeared at eleven years old didn't mean she had died then. There was always the possibility that she had lived on for any part of the fifteen years she had been missing. So each child, each teenager, each young woman, each unidentified female corpse, held promise and misery. And each time a body was identified as someone else, Creed felt a sickening combination of relief and sadness. Relief because she might still be alive. Sadness because if she was, it could be a life of hell on earth.

He looked up at Hannah, met those brown eyes that could lecture as good as love. "Let me take a shower and you can tell me about the assignment."

He stood and the room swirled. He caught himself and glanced at Hannah to see if she noticed. Of course she had.

"Don't worry, okay?" he told her and this time he was serious. When that didn't seem to convince her, he added, "I promise I'll let you know when it's time to get worried."

CHAPTER 10

Maggie would rather be back in the mud instead of being stuck inside to watch from the window.

The mobile crime lab had just arrived. She saw Tully stop them in the driveway. He directed them to the site where the garbage bag waited. She knew he would make them outline their plan of how they'd remove the body before he allowed them to start.

He'd been on his cell phone since he'd left the farmhouse in between questioning the property's executor, Howard Elliott, and ordering around Sheriff Uniss and his deputies. In the past, Tully always seemed pleased to hand off jurisdiction to the local authorities. A play-by-the-rules guy, he understood and accepted his role as outside consultant. So Maggie was pleased but, again, surprised to see him taking over with such relish. Perhaps he was simply happy not to be stuck in the house with a half-naked Lily.

Maggie felt like she had gotten the short straw. For ten years she had fought to be treated no different than her male colleagues. And for the most part she was successful. One look into Tully's eyes had reminded her that dealing with Lily was a job for a woman. No discussion. No doubt about it. Which made little sense to Maggie because, despite their shared gender, there was absolutely nothing else she had in common with this woman.

She glanced back at Lily, who still hadn't put on any additional clothes, claiming it was way too hot and she needed to cool off.

"Damned bugs are crawling all over the place," she had told Maggie as she picked at the scabs already on her arms. "They're in my clothes, too."

Maggie hadn't seen any evidence of bugs in the house and wondered if they were hallucinations caused by the drugs. The house was, in fact, remarkably clean for a place that had been vacated ten years ago. Someone had been taking care of it and it certainly wasn't Lily.

Taking a break from her bug and skin-picking obsession, the woman had found a half-eaten candy bar among the scattered empty wrappers. She was now nibbling around the peanuts and nougat. She took cautious bites at the side of her mouth. Her teeth were in worse shape than Maggie had originally thought. Despite the discomfort, it sounded like the woman was grinding her teeth in between bites.

As Maggie looked around the bedroom again, she wondered if Lily had flushed her entire stash and, if so, what she'd do when she realized it.

"She was really good to me," Lily said suddenly without prompting.

It took Maggie a couple of seconds to realize she meant the farmstead's owner.

"How long did you live here?"

"I don't remember," she said, as all the nervous motion of her body lessened.

Lily's eyes darted around for the answer. Her leg stopped jerking and her fingers stopped picking. Even her teeth stopped grinding. Maggie couldn't help thinking how much her movements, her reactions, looked like those of an emaciated animal.

"Why did you leave?" Maggie asked, but when Lily's eyes met hers, Maggie realized that wasn't any easier of a question.

The woman finally shrugged her bony shoulders and said, "Everybody has to leave sometime."

"Do you come back often?" She tried to make it sound like she was only making conversation, even looking back outside the window like she couldn't care less if Lily answered.

"As long as the key's where she left it, I figure it's okay."

She was still on defense. That wasn't what Maggie wanted.

"Some strange stuff must have happened," Maggie said, waiting for Lily's eyes and then nodding out the window to emphasize she meant out in the backyard.

Another shrug. Not defensive but simply not interested.

"When you've stayed here before," Maggie tried again, "did you ever notice anything weird?"

"Weird?"

"Did you ever see anyone else on the property?"

"Just the construction guys."

"How about at night? Any vehicles? Any lights?"

"Oh yeah, there was one night I saw lights."

Maggie kept calm. This was what she suspected. Had Lily been here when the killer dumped the body in the garbage bag? Or when he dumped any other bodies? Did she see him? Could she have watched while he pulled a body from his trunk? While he dug the grave?

But Lily was silent.

"You saw headlights?"

"No, the lights were up higher."

They had long suspected the killer could be a long-haul truck driver.

"Like on the cab of an eighteen-wheeler?" she asked when it was obvious Lily needed some help remembering.

"No, higher."

"Spotlights? Floodlights?"

The woman stopped again to give this some thought and Maggie found herself on edge, patience wearing thin. If Lily had been here and saw something. Saw someone . . .

"Out of the sky," she said. "Bright like stars. Dozens of them."

Then she swatted at her leg.

"Damn bugs," she said, scratching at a scab until it started to bleed. "Sons of bitches are under my skin now."

And Maggie realized that if Lily had seen the killer, the woman probably wouldn't even remember.

CHAPTER 11

They talked in whispers. Detective Lopez was at the door with a uniformed police officer. Noah's mother and father stood by the window. It was difficult for Noah to hear what they were talking about because the sound of Ethan's screams had returned inside his head. The screams weren't loud. In fact, they were muffled, as though coming from outside his hospital room, somewhere down the hall. But they wouldn't stop. It was a constant, frenzied screech that clawed at Noah's brain like fingernails scraping a chalkboard.

At one point he sat up and clapped his hands over his ears. He rocked back and forth, moaning, wishing, begging Ethan to shut up. He didn't even realize what he was doing until he saw the horror on his mother's face. But instead of embracing him, comforting him, Noah saw her clutch his father's arm as if needing his strength to remain upright.

That's when he realized that it wasn't his odd gestures that had unnerved his mother. It was that he was actually saying the words in his head out loud, over and over again.

Ethan shut up! Shut up, shut up! Stop screaming!

And Noah shut up immediately.

He stared at his parents and knew that he looked like he had been caught doing something unspeakable. If they only knew.

"You said he's still out there." Detective Lopez was standing at his bedside now. "Where is your friend Ethan, Noah?" Then without waiting for a response, he said, "What did you do to him?"

"Do to him?"

Noah could hardly believe what the detective was asking. He looked to his parents again.

"Go ahead and tell him what happened, Noah." It was his father, but the tone was stern.

They thought he was responsible? Why?

"All that blood," Detective Lopez said. "We know it wasn't all yours."

But he *had* done something to Ethan. He left him with a madman. And it was worse than that. Much worse . . .

"We found Ethan's car." Detective Lopez seemed to wait for Noah to look at him. "It was still parked at the rest area. Doors unlocked. Keys under the seat."

He paused, studying Noah.

"We found the rest of your clothes. Folded up, neat and tidy. Right on the passenger seat. Shoes on top."

Noah just stared at him. How could he explain that his clothes were part of the bargain?

"The boys are best friends," he heard his mother explaining. "Since third grade."

"*Who goes first?*" Noah heard the madman's voice and searched the room, looking past his parents, looking past Detective Lopez, past the officer at the door. The killer wasn't anywhere to be seen. But he was still in Noah's head.

"Your cell phone was there, too," Detective Lopez was saying, without acknowledging Noah's mother. Without acknowledging the voice in Noah's head.

"There were no phone calls to 911," Detective Lopez said. "No text messages to friends or family asking for help or talking about being stranded."

Again, Noah stared at the man. Why hadn't he called for help? Why had he left his phone behind?

Then he remembered. The man had borrowed Noah's cell phone. He'd told them that his own had run down its battery. His car wouldn't start. Could they help him out?

Those eyes. That smile. They should never have rolled down the window.

Ethan's fault. I told you not to roll down the window.

"Noah." It was his father.

Had he said the words out loud again?

His father was growing impatient.

"Tell Officer Lopez what happened," he said.

Noah glanced at the detective to see if he noticed his dad had just demoted him. A silly thing for him to notice, but his father was good at that. He could disarm someone with his words before the person realized what had happened.

Like father, like son.

But then his father snapped at him. "Just tell him for Christ's sake."

None of it fazed Detective Lopez, and he continued, "Noah, if Ethan's hurt badly we might be able to still help him. Just tell us where he is."

The room became silent. Machines hummed and beeped. And amazingly, Ethan's screams had stopped for the moment.

"I don't know where Ethan is," Noah finally admitted. Then he added in a whisper that sounded embarrassingly close to a whimper, "But I know he's dead."

CHAPTER 12

Maggie had left Lily after writing her personal cell phone number on the back of her business card and handing it to the woman.

"What the hell good is this?" Lily had wanted to know.

"You can call me anytime."

Lily had laughed like it was the funniest thing she'd ever heard. She was still laughing when Maggie walked out the door. But she had taken the card.

Now the sun began to sink behind the barn. Maggie had returned to the top of the heap alongside a CSU technician named Janet. The removal of the body in the garbage bag had become a slow and tedious chore. Because almost half the bag remained within the pile of dirt, they couldn't just pull it out for fear of destroying evidence.

It had been agreed that they needed to dig out the bag from the top, removing the soil, bucket by bucket. Tully had convinced Maggie and the young CSU tech that because they weighed the least of the recovery crew, they were less likely to start a landslide. So here she was again—only this time with a hand trowel—so close to the bag she couldn't avoid the smell or avoid seeing the writhing mass of maggots every time the plastic flapped open.

She had borrowed a pair of boots from the construction crew

that swallowed her feet. Buzz, the foreman, had also offered her a ball cap, reassuring her that it was brand-new, even showing that it still had the sales tag dangling. It seemed easier than trekking all the way back to their rental to unpack their gear. So she had accepted the ball cap before she'd noticed the saying embroidered on the front: *Booty Hunter.*

It could be worse, she thought as she adjusted the cap and ignored Tully's grin.

Maggie and Janet filled their buckets, one scoop at a time. Both were cautious, sliding the trowels in slowly and ready to stop at any hint of resistance or even a faint scrape of something that didn't sound like dirt. Buzz and the three members of his construction crew, along with Sheriff Uniss's deputies—and even Howard Elliott—had formed two assembly lines, one to take and replace Maggie's bucket and the other Janet's.

Maggie and Janet handed off the blue plastic buckets full of dirt. Then the buckets made their way down the lines, each man handing it to the next without moving, to avoid stepping more than necessary in the mud.

At the end of the lines were the other two CSU technicians, Matt and Ryan, who spilled the buckets across a three-foot-by-six-foot designated area on top of the grass. At a later time the techs would be able to sift through the dirt chunks. Right now, they all just wanted to remove the garbage bag, intact, place it in a body bag, and send it on its way to a medical examiner.

"Outdoor scenes are the toughest," Janet admitted to Maggie.

She wiped a sleeve of her sweatshirt across her forehead. Her long sleek dark hair was pulled back into a ponytail and stuck out the back of her navy CSU cap. Her smooth skin showed only slight laugh lines at the eyes and Maggie guessed that she was her age—mid to late thirties.

Maggie could tell that Janet was a veteran at collecting forensic evidence, despite her age. She had taken command of the process with ease immediately after their arrival, allowing Tully to address other issues, like the flow of information. Maggie could see him still on his cell phone. At times she noticed him jotting down notes on anything he managed to pull out of his pockets. She knew that later he'd be trying to decipher his scratch marks on the backs of gas station receipts, his boarding pass, even a napkin with smudges from his chocolate doughnut.

"You have any idea who's inside?" Janet asked Maggie.

"No."

The woman looked at her and raised an eyebrow like she didn't appreciate secrecy when they were ankle-deep in mud.

"We've been tracking a killer for about a month now," Maggie said, but she wasn't willing to tell anyone about the map that had led her and Tully here. "We suspect this farm might be his dumping ground."

"Yeah, we heard about the bones."

Janet glanced around the property but Maggie saw her attention go to the woods that lined the back of the farmstead. She was thinking the same thing Maggie and Tully had.

Before she could say anything more, Maggie told her, "We have a cadaver dog team on its way."

"Don't forget to have them check if there's a storm cellar."

It was Maggie's turn to raise an eyebrow.

"Most of the old farms have them somewhere on the property for tornado shelters. Last year we found a woman and two kids. Husband claimed his wife had left him and taken the kids."

She shook her head at the memory and Maggie could see it was still fresh.

"One of them was just a baby, not even two years old."

Janet stopped digging. Shadows started devouring the last streams of daylight. They didn't have much time if they hoped to remove the garbage bag before dark, but Maggie stopped digging, too, waiting, giving the woman time to do what she needed to put the image away and return to the task at hand.

"But hopefully we got enough evidence to nail the bastard."

She offered Maggie a weak smile, more a thanks for understanding than an indictment on the weight of the evidence.

They were almost to the top of the black garbage bag when Maggie's trowel met something more solid than a clump of dirt. She set the trowel aside and with gloved fingers she raked at the dirt until she saw white.

Janet had noticed and set her trowel aside, too. She watched Maggie slowly unearth what appeared to be another plastic bag. This one was smaller. Through the smears of mud Maggie recognized the major retail store's logo. Janet helped her uncover it but both of them stopped, sitting back on their haunches when they were finished. There was definitely something inside. The bag bulged like the black garbage bag beneath it. This one was sitting upright with the top handles tied haphazardly in a loose knot. And it also smelled like rotten meat.

"We found something else," Maggie yelled to the men below, and immediately her eyes searched for Tully.

CHAPTER 13

It didn't seem like that long ago that Dr. Gwen Patterson had been to the FBI facility at Quantico. Her boyfriend and best friend worked there, so she heard about the place on a weekly basis. But when the guard at the security hut scrutinized her driver's license— eyes darting from her face to the plastic ID card—she realized it had actually been several years. The guards used to hear her name and wave her through. A few of them would recognize her and lift the gate before she'd had a chance to roll down her car window.

She was no longer a recognizable figure. And for a good reason. Gwen had purposely tried to distance herself from the place. The last time she had worked as a consultant on an FBI case, a psychotic young cult member had attempted to stab a sharp pencil into her throat.

The scrutiny started all over again at the front desk.

"I don't have a name badge for you," the receptionist said, making it sound like it was Gwen's fault. "Who are you here to see?"

"Assistant Director Raymond Kunze. In the Behavorial Science Unit."

"And what is the nature of your business?" the woman asked, holding on to Gwen's driver's license while giving her a full body search with her eyes. This was worse than the guard at the hut, and Gwen wondered how the woman thought she had made it this far if she was a threat.

She needed to calm down. She had been through tougher interrogations. This was simply more annoying than intimidating. She kept still, containing a sigh and resisting the urge to shift her weight and cross her arms. Gwen had spent most of her career compensating for her petite frame by wearing three-inch heels and fine tailored power suits—skirts, never trousers, and dark or bold colors, never pastels. She had refined her Brooklyn roots to create a classy, don't-screw-with-me attitude. She believed confidence and poise more than made up for her lack in stature. But being back at Quantico reminded her only of vulnerability and of that split second of mind-numbing fear.

The receptionist continued to stare at her, and Gwen fought the unexpected flicker of nausea in the pit of her stomach.

"It's okay, Stacy, I'll vouch for Dr. Patterson."

Gwen turned to find Detective Julia Racine coming in through the front doors.

"She's on the Highway Serial Killings Task Force," Racine told the receptionist, who was already pulling out a different stack of folders.

"I wish people would tell me these things ahead of time." The woman now seemed irritated by both Gwen and Racine as she riffled through one folder and then another.

Racine positioned her back to Stacy and rolled her eyes for Gwen to see. Gwen smiled but tried not to show the young detective how terribly relieved she was. Julia Racine was cocky enough without knowing that she had just saved the District's number-one psychologist to the politicos from launching into a panic attack over a misplaced name badge. And Gwen suddenly realized—and did not like it—how much she had changed since her last visit. What had become of her lately?

Turning fifty had sent her into a tailspin. Instead of focusing on her accomplishments, all she could think about were her physical challenges: tired, moody, uncharacteristically second-guessing herself. Not just herself, but second-guessing her choices, her career, her relationship, her life.

Focus on the here and now, damn it!

"So you're on the task force, too," Gwen said after she and Racine signed in and pinned on their badges.

She let Racine lead the way, though it hadn't been so long ago that Gwen would have forgotten how to get to the BSU conference room.

"The homicide that tipped off this investigation is my case. Remember those arsons back in February? Three warehouses and a church in Arlington?"

"Of course." The same arsonist had torched her friend Maggie O'Dell's house before he turned himself in.

"We found a body in the alley next to one of the warehouses."

Racine pulled open a door to the walkway and held it for Gwen to go through. It was a polite gesture that threw Gwen off coming from Racine. The detective was anything but polite. She'd built a reputation on being tough as nails, one she reinforced by wearing trousers and leather jackets and keeping her short hair spiked just enough to give her an edgy look. Yet the knit T-shirt beneath the bomber jacket couldn't hide full breasts and the trousers only accentuated her long slender legs.

"The body," Racine continued, "was Gloria Dobson. We're

pretty sure she and her traveling partner were murdered at a rest area in Virginia, just off the interstate."

"I remember Tully and Maggie talking about it."

But Gwen was careful not to mention just how much she knew about the case. It still unnerved her to remember how upset Tully had been when describing the crime scene he and Maggie had stumbled upon at that rest area.

R. J. Tully was a veteran FBI agent. He was one of the most centered and even-tempered men Gwen knew. He had seen and witnessed some gruesome murders, so this scene had to be horrendous to leave him shaken. And now he and Maggie were somewhere in the Midwest searching for the killer who had ripped apart that strong, healthy young man and left Gloria Dobson's bashed-in body in a District alley.

Being a part of the task force, Gwen would learn more of the details, whether she wanted to or not. That was probably Racine's thought since she continued to fill Gwen in as they made their way through the training facility and finally down to the Behavioral Science Unit. Gwen had worked on only one case with Detective Julia Racine and the detective had not been so forthcoming at the time. Actually "worked" was probably not the correct term. Racine would insist Gwen had obstructed evidence and gotten in the way.

Bottom line, the two women were acquaintances by accident and circumstance, not by choice—and by their mutual friend, Maggie O'Dell. Gwen knew it was more for Maggie's benefit than hers that Racine was even polite to her.

Three men waited for Gwen and Racine in the Behavioral Science Unit's conference room. Assistant Director Raymond Kunze waved them to take seats across the table. Kunze was a linebacker of a man, barrel-chested with a thick neck that looked strangled in his cheery yellow tie. Combined with a mauve sports jacket the colors almost looked clownish. Though there was nothing clownish about the assistant director.

Everyone else in the room appeared to know one another.

"I've asked Dr. Gwen Patterson to join our task force," Kunze explained. "As a trained forensic psychologist and a sort of outsider—" He stopped himself and turned to Gwen, quickly adding, "No offense intended."

"None taken," she answered.

Why was everyone being so damned polite? Like she was something old and fragile? She'd had her yearly physical yesterday. She was being overly sensitive. But she also trusted her instincts and she wished she had never agreed to this.

"I'm counting on Dr. Patterson to offer some fresh insights," AD Kunze told his group.

Gwen smiled, thinking that wasn't entirely true. While Kunze had, indeed, asked Gwen to be a part of this task force, it wasn't his idea. A high-ranking senator had strong-armed Kunze to include her. It was a high-profile case. The Highway Serial Killings Initiative happened to be a program that Senator Delanor-Ramos had pushed through Congress. Everything in the District was about politics these days. Gwen joining this task force may have been sold as an outsider's "fresh insights" but she knew it was really about covering the senator's professional ass. She'd be the easy scapegoat if the project didn't produce results quickly.

"Dr. Patterson has worked with the FBI on several cases," Kunze was explaining to his team. "So she already has a working relationship."

As Kunze continued his introduction, Gwen couldn't help wondering if her familiarity might be as much a hindrance as a benefit. After all, her significant other and her best friend were assigned to this task force. Gwen hated the fact that AD Kunze may have agreed so enthusiastically to her presence to use her against Tully and Maggie. The assistant director had made both his agents' lives a working hell since he took over the unit. So she couldn't help but be suspicious of Kunze's motive, of his agreeing so easily to her being foisted on his team.

"You've met Detective Julia Racine," Kunze was saying. "The District was good enough to loan her to us."

Gwen also knew Keith Ganza, the director of the FBI crime lab. The tall, skinny agent wore a white lab coat, frayed at the cuffs. His long gray hair was tied back in a ponytail, adding to his look of a reclusive scientist. Gwen had often heard Maggie claim the man to be a mild-mannered genius who could see more in a piece of lint or a clump of dirt than any trace evidence specialist she'd ever worked with.

Gwen had not, however, met Antonio Alonzo before. The handsome, young black man wore frameless rectangular glasses and a purple button-down shirt with the sleeves neatly rolled up. Kunze called Agent Alonzo a computer wizard, on loan from ViCAP (Violent Criminal Apprehension Program). The young man seemed unfazed by the praise, which made Gwen instantly like him.

For all the talk of technology, however, when Kunze finally settled in and started the session he directed their attention to the front of the room where an old-fashioned paper map of the United States—three feet tall by five feet wide—had been spread out and hung up on a poster board. Bright-colored stick pins marked prominent areas across the country, some clustered together, others alone.

"Each of these pins represents a suspected murder victim. If they're here it's because they were found along our country's interstate systems in the last ten years. Or at least part of them was found. They've been entered into a separate database under the Highway Serial Killings Initiative.

"Many of these victims are transients who lived high-risk lives—prostitutes, drug users and dealers, hitchhikers, runaway teenagers. But there are about two hundred who were ordinary folks, traveling from one place to another like Gloria Dobson and Zach Lester.

"The idea behind the initiative was to organize a way to assist local law enforcement, to help them connect some of the dots. Until now it's been tough for them to track since many of these victims disappeared from one state and their bodies showed up in another. The highway systems, by nature, create some unique challenges.

"Think of it this way—the crime scenes are also transient. The interstate system provides immediate and easy escape routes. A killer can simply get back on the road and be three hundred to four hundred miles away before the body is even discovered.

"Just since the database was created, two serial killers have been apprehended and convicted. Both long-haul truck drivers. We believe there are possibly several serial killers out on the roads using the rest areas and truck stops to supply them with easy targets."

"When you say 'several,' how many do you really suspect?" asked Gwen.

Kunze didn't hesitate. "Possibly a dozen."

Gwen glanced around the table. None of the others flinched at this number.

"You can't be serious," Gwen said. "You're saying there could be a dozen different killers—serial killers? Today? Driving the highways, undetected. Stopping at rest areas and truck stops to find their victims? And essentially getting away with murder?"

"Yes. That's exactly what I'm saying. We believe Agents O'Dell and Tully are close on the trail of one of them right now. The guy who killed Gloria Dobson and Zach Lester. We think he's killed more. This particular task force is assigned to catch this guy."

Kunze rubbed his eyes and pinched the bridge of his nose. That's when Gwen noticed the man's fatigue and his attempt to downplay his frustration.

He looked around the table at them and there was a hint of anger in his voice when he said, "He's dared us to find him, to catch him. We probably have a window of a week or two before this bastard simply changes his route. Chooses another part of the country. Revises his killing pattern. And when he does, he'll be gone again. But one thing is certain—he won't stop killing."

CHAPTER 14

IOWA

Maggie had already guessed what was inside the white plastic bag.

She and Tully let the CSU techs take charge. They stood back with the others at the bottom of the dirt pile and watched as Ryan, the taller of the two male techs, carried the small bag. Janet had handed it down to him, both as careful as though they were handling fine china.

After helping to free the bag from the dirt, Maggie had lifted and felt the contents. She could tell it was double bagged. There was a large solid mass inside and she noted the squishy mess that had pooled at the bottom. She estimated its weight at about ten to eleven pounds, and she had a good idea what it was.

With the bag free of the chunks of mud, it was easy to see the Walmart logo.

"The contents of this one might not even be related to the bigger one." It was Matt, the other tech, but even as he said it, he was spreading out and preparing a body bag, anticipating that it was human remains.

Maggie glanced around at the men. Of course no one believed it held someone's discarded impulse buy at the twenty-four-hour retail store. All of them were eager but there was a nervous quiet. The air had started to cool with dusk settling in around them. Maggie could feel their contradictory emotions—they wanted to see, but maybe they didn't want to see.

At first she had considered whether she and Tully should push back the men, not allow them access. In fact, she was surprised that Tully—who usually played by the rules—hadn't suggested it. But they had all spent an afternoon digging in the mud, sharing the significance of what might be buried here and exposing themselves to the rancid smells. Maggie wasn't going to be the one to tell these men thanks for all your help, but no, you don't get to see what you worked so hard to uncover.

In the middle of the black body bag the small white plastic one looked less sinister. Matt and Ryan waited for Janet. She knelt down after putting on a fresh pair of purple latex gloves. The plastic bags' handles had been tied in a loose knot. It would have been simple enough to untie it. Instead, Janet snipped off the knot entirely and placed it into an evidence bag that Matt held out for her.

As soon as she cut it open, a much stronger odor emerged.

Maggie stole a glimpse of the young deputy who had vomited earlier. What a difference an afternoon of smelling death made. He continued to watch without expression or a single gag.

Janet spread the top opening just enough to be able to look inside. She didn't flinch. Didn't wince. The only look on the woman's face appeared to be one of disappointment. She eased back into a squat and let her colleagues take a peek. Then she looked to Maggie and Tully.

"I'm guessing it belongs to the victim inside the black garbage bag," Maggie said without leaning in or coming any closer to see.

She had already felt the heft of the item and had recognized the smell of decomposing human flesh. A month ago in the woods behind a rest area in Virginia she and Tully had found another of this killer's victims. Not always, but often, a killer repeated certain things, developed a pattern. The body of Zach Lester had been lying at the base of a tree, the intestines strung up through the lower branches. He had been decapitated.

She heard Tully release a sigh. Out of the corner of her eye she could see his jaw tighten. He didn't, however, make a move forward either.

Janet dipped her right hand into the bag and gently, slowly brought up . . . a piece of paper. Almost in unison, several of the men expelled the breaths they had been holding. Janet handed it off to Matt, who had another evidence bag ready, but before placing it inside he took a good look at it.

He showed his colleague Ryan, and then his eyes found Maggie and Tully. "You two might want to take a look at this."

Rather than expose the paper any further, Matt slipped it into a clear plastic ziplock bag. He pulled a marker out of his jacket pocket and popped the cap off in his mouth so he didn't need to use the hand still holding the bag. He scrawled a date and number on the side of the bag, recapped the marker, then held the bag up for Maggie and Tully.

Maggie immediately understood why Matt didn't want to tell them out loud what they had found. Despite not telling the construction crew and Sheriff Uniss's men to back off or leave, *this* was information that would need to be kept quiet.

Maggie took the plastic-encased paper while Tully pushed up his glasses. It was a sales receipt, in rather good condition despite a rust-colored stain at the corner. It had been carefully placed on top of the bag's contents to be easily found. The retail store matched the logo on the white plastic bag. The first thing Maggie noticed was the bold type in the middle of the receipt that read: # ITEMS SOLD 1. Above, it clearly listed that item: SOCKS, $8.98.

She took no comfort in being right. The orange socks were obviously not the victim's. They had been added later, most likely postmortem.

Maggie searched for the store's address. There wasn't one, but the store's number (#1965) would tell them where it was. The manager and a phone number were also included. What surprised her was the date at the bottom of the receipt. The socks had been purchased just two weeks ago. Which meant the body had not been here as long as they had initially suspected. It also meant that it had been buried after she had received the hand-drawn map, the one that had started their scavenger hunt.

She gave Tully the receipt for his own closer inspection. She waited, watching him. In seconds he came to the same conclusion and when his eyes met hers she could see he was thinking the same thing she was.

There were definitely more bodies here.

CHAPTER 15

Ryder Creed sipped coffee from one of the three thermoses Hannah had prepared for the trip. He didn't bother to pour it into the thermos's cup. He had been on the road for almost eight hours now. Drinking directly out of the thermos was easier.

He glanced in the rearview mirror. Behind him, Grace sprawled on her dog bed, which took up half the back of the Jeep. Her empty kennel and their gear took up the other half. The dog lifted her head every once in a while as if to ask, "Are we there yet?" Then she'd drop it back down. But Creed hadn't heard the heavy breathing of a deep sleep, so he knew she was simply resting, still on alert. Even one of her ears stayed constantly pitched. Most of the dogs understood that a long car ride meant a job at the end of the trip. And somehow they instinctively knew to conserve their excitement and energy.

Creed wished he could tap into his dogs' instincts. He'd spent the last seven years of his life training and working with dogs, but what they had taught him made his lessons insignificant by comparison.

Grace was one of his smallest dogs, a scrappy brown-and-white Jack Russell terrier. Creed had discovered her curled up under one of the double-wide trailers he kept on the property for hired help. When he found her she was literally skin and bones but sagging where she had recently been nursing puppies. What fur hadn't fallen out from lack of nourishment was thick with an army of fleas. At the time it made him so angry he had wanted to punch something . . . or someone. It wasn't the first time he had seen a female dog dumped and punished when the owner was simply too cheap to get her spayed.

Locals had gotten into the habit of leaving their unwanted dogs at the end of Creed's driveway. They knew he'd take them in or find homes for them. In some twisted way it was their attempt at compassion. It was either leave them at Creed's back door or take them to the nearest animal shelter, where they would most certainly be put to death.

Hannah used to roll her eyes at him every time he'd bring in a half-starved or hobbling, abandoned dog. Then she'd tell him that people were just taking advantage of his soft heart.

"Good lord," she'd told him. "We could hire a vet on staff for the money we pay out in canine health services."

"You're absolutely right," he had agreed, to her surprise. And before Hannah could enjoy her victory, what she believed would be an end to his annoying habit of taking in abandoned dogs, he'd hired a full-time veterinarian.

The fact was—and this was something he could never get Hannah to appreciate the way he appreciated it—the abandoned dogs that he had rescued made some of his best air-scent dogs. Skill was only a part of the training. Bonding with the trainer was another. His rescued dogs trusted him unconditionally and were loyal beyond measure. They were eager to learn and anxious to please.

Though Grace had been dumped, she adapted quickly to her new surroundings. She didn't cower or startle easily. Once she caught up nutrition-wise, Creed recognized she possessed a drive and an investigative curiosity. She was independent but followed and looked to Creed not only for praise but also for guidance. And most important, she passed his number one test—she was ball crazy.

It was a trick Creed used to test all his potential work dogs. Did a simple tennis ball get their attention? Did their eyes follow its every movement? Did they dive for it? And last, when they caught it, did they have a good grip on it? For air-scent work, it was all about drive and Grace had passed his ball-crazy test with flying colors.

Despite all the training and harnessing the independence, Creed was always surprised by how a dog's mood and behavior could be influenced by the handler. As he started getting fidgety and looking for someplace to stop, he noticed Grace's head coming up more often.

"It's okay, girl," he told her.

Even in the dark, Creed knew this stretch of Interstate 55 and knew that in a couple more miles he'd be leaving the state of Mississippi behind and entering Tennessee. He tried to avoid stopping at Mississippi's rest areas. The state was one of the few that had security guards at their interstate rest areas 24/7. That should have been a plus, but Creed considered them a nuisance and the term "security guard" a joke. The only thing they guarded was where a dog could or couldn't pee. He liked to have his dogs stretch their legs, walk around, and sniff without a security guard following in his motorized cart telling him to stay in the designated "pet area." The area that amounted to a fifteen-by-twenty-foot patch of dead grass. So he waited until he passed the blue-and-white sign that read:

TENNESSEE

THE VOLUNTEER STATE

WELCOMES YOU

Then he started to look for the rest area he'd use before he reached Memphis.

He'd rather drive straight through the night. Grace wouldn't mind. His dogs always needed fewer bathroom stops than he did. The coffee made that difficult. But stopping wasn't about losing travel time. The truth was, he didn't like rest areas or truck stops.

Actually, they called them truck plazas now. They'd become miniature towns with cafés, small grocery stores, and what was called "convenience retail." Some even had a twenty-four-hour, full-service barber shop. There were places for truckers to shower, watch TV, use the Internet, and rent a bed by the hour to catch some sleep outside of their trucks. There were also places to buy drugs, if you knew where to look. And late at night there were women who went from truck to truck, knocking on the cabs.

Unlike the rest areas, the truck plazas were busy night and day, big rigs pulling in and out, motors constantly humming, brakes screeching.

Creed avoided the truck plazas.

Rest areas, however, were no less a challenge. No matter how many years had passed since his sister had gone missing from one, he couldn't stop—especially in the middle of the night—without memories of *that* night. All it took was the smell of diesel and the sound of hydraulic brakes.

Creed knew subsequent panic attacks could be triggered by a slight reminder of the original one. Something as simple as a smell or a sound. He hadn't experienced a full-blown attack in years but lately he felt one simmering close to the surface. Exhaustion, stress, anxiety—all were contributing factors. He had worked three homicide scenes just this month. All young women. And each time the assignment came in, Creed had insisted on taking it himself rather than sending one of his crew.

Maybe he needed to avoid these cases for a while. Take only search-and-rescue requests. Focus on some drug cases. Devote his time to training. He had a way with dogs. He could train them to sniff out just about anything from lost children to cocaine to bombs. Dogs, he understood. People, not so much.

What had started as a desperate search for his missing eleven-year-old sister's body had turned into a successful business, success beyond his expectations. He had a waiting list of law enforcement agencies across the country that wanted his dogs or his services. He could afford to hire more handlers and scale back or redirect his time and energies. Most important, he knew he needed to take a break, rest, and rejuvenate, and do it soon, for his own peace of mind. The panic attacks weren't the only feelings he kept at bay. There was a hollowness inside of him that threatened to suffocate him if it continued to grow.

As soon as Creed left the interstate, Grace sat up. The exit ramp to the rest area curved down and around, taking them into a wooded area that immediately shielded them from the interstate's traffic. The road forked: right for cars, left for trucks.

Creed was familiar with this one. He'd stopped here on several other trips. But he'd barely pulled into a parking lot when he saw something that made his skin prickle. Beyond the one-story brick building Creed could see a big man holding hands with a little girl, leading her to the truck parking lot, where big rigs filled every slot.

Creed sat back, tried to control his breathing. His palms were sweaty and his hands fisted around the steering wheel. If he could just breathe, he could ward off the panic. But he didn't stop watching.

Was the man leading her? Or dragging her?

How could he tell in the dark?

The pair walked from shadow to shadow, illuminated only now and again by a shot of light from the pole lamps. And those got fewer and fewer as they headed toward a rig at the back of the lot.

Creed told himself that he needed to settle down. He couldn't afford to interfere every time he saw something that he didn't think looked right. And yet, his heart wouldn't stop racing.

That's when he noticed the little girl wore only socks—bright white against the black asphalt. No shoes.

CHAPTER 16

Maggie and Tully had offered to buy dinner and drinks for everyone. Even Lily.

The CSU techs had collected the skull and three long bones. They had loaded up the body and head, zipping them into separate body bags and keeping them in their respective plastic bags. Janet had insisted they not open the black plastic one in the field and Maggie agreed. The tear had already shown them enough. Opening it any farther might disrupt evidence. And certainly disrupt the maggots. As much as Maggie hated the disgusting insects, they played an important role in determining time of death. It was best to leave them undisturbed for the techs to process back at their lab, and let the human remains stay intact for the medical examiner.

The techs passed on the dinner invitation. They were on their way back to Omaha, about a two-hour drive.

Sheriff Uniss had assigned new deputies to secure the farmstead. Two of his deputies chose to go on home. The sheriff and the young deputy joined them, as did Howard Elliott and Buzz, the construction crew foreman, along with his men.

The person Maggie thought definitely needed a meal passed. Lily had accepted the ride to the truck stop but said she wasn't hungry. Maggie suspected that Lily's meth run was winding down. As soon as they arrived Lily seemed to know exactly where she wanted to go. This was her haven and before Maggie even noticed, Lily had disappeared from sight.

They had been at the truck stop's bar and grill for almost two hours and yet Maggie and Tully were the only two eating. Also, Maggie and Tully hadn't bought a single thing. The men took turns buying rounds of drinks. Several truck drivers had joined them, shoving together four tables in the middle of the restaurant. The truck drivers were having fun educating Maggie and Tully on trucker lingo, which helped lighten the mood.

Although they had warned the deputies and construction crew not to discuss what they had seen at the farm for at least twenty-four hours, Maggie knew after several drinks the men wouldn't remember their request. As odd as it sounded, she hoped their shock and awe remained on the decapitation and that they would forget about the orange socks. As insignificant as the socks seemed to be, they might play a crucial role in the case.

Now as they sat back, Maggie noticed that Tully had fallen behind, accumulating bottles of Sam Adams. And it looked like he hadn't touched his fries. Yes, the burgers were huge and loaded with extras but that didn't usually stop Tully from stealing her fries by now. They sat side by side, Maggie crammed between Tully and Sheriff Uniss, so close that they had been bumping elbows. Sheriff Uniss was in a discussion with one of the truckers about the price of gas and the politics that came with it.

Maggie plucked one of the fries from Tully's plate to get his attention.

"You doing okay?" she asked and waved a hand at the three bottles of beer in front of him, only one of which had been touched.

The others were still full. He had the corner of the table and plenty of room, unlike the rest of them. In fact, Maggie had set her *Booty Hunter* cap there on the edge, out of the way.

"I keep telling them not to bring me any more."

"And you're just not hungry?"

He pulled a ziplock plastic bag from his trouser pocket to show her about a dozen white pills.

"Sinus infection. I need to be taking these antibiotics, but I keep forgetting."

Maggie stopped a smile. It was so like Tully to empty the whole container into his pants pocket and carry them around with him as a reminder. But he did look a little miserable, his eyes watery, his face flushed and damp with sweat. Suddenly she understood that was probably why he had been acting so odd earlier.

"We should get you out of your wet, muddy clothes and into a bed," she told him.

Immediately she realized she had spoken too loudly when she saw Howard Elliott and the young deputy across the table look over at her. Even one of the truck drivers standing at the corner of the table smiled at her.

Instead of being embarrassed, Maggie leaned in closer to Tully and he reciprocated by leaning down into her.

"This would be a good time to leave," she said. "They all think I just made a pass at you."

Tully's eyes flashed up and around and he grinned.

"I reserved us a couple of rooms at the Super 8 just up the road," he told her.

"Sounds romantic. Can I have the rest of your fries? Then we can go."

He grinned again and nodded. Then he watched her squeeze a

pool of ketchup onto his plate and begin her ritual of dipping and munching. He even joined her.

"I'll give you the details later," he said in a low tone, almost a whisper, as if keeping up their charade. "Triple A made a hit on the hosiery."

The orange socks. She refrained from saying it out loud and reminding any of the men. But she asked, "Triple A?"

"Oh sorry, that's what I've started calling Agent Alonzo. His first name's Antonio."

"Was the hit a recent case?"

"Within the last month. You were right. Woman victim. Wooded area not far from a rest area."

"Did he find any other cases?"

"Just the one so far."

Tully yawned and it reminded her how exhausted she was. It had been a long day for both of them.

"How about we excuse ourselves?" she asked, and he agreed.

Maggie nodded at Sheriff Uniss. They had already decided on a strategy for the next day. Tully promised to call first thing in the morning. Then they said their good nights and started to leave. Maggie went to grab her cap from the corner of the table. It wasn't there. She glanced around, checking the floor and under the table. The cap was gone. Someone had probably picked it up by mistake. It didn't really matter. She shrugged and followed Tully out.

They were getting into their rental car when Maggie saw Lily across the plaza. She wandered the lot where the trucks were parked for the night. She had left the farm dressed in tight jeans and a clinging knit blouse that highlighted her ribs and bony shoulders more than anything else. She had the big, awkward handbag around her neck and under her arm and she was knocking on the door of one of the cabs. The trucker inside shook his head, hanging out the window and telling her something. Lily didn't wait to hear what he was saying and instead headed for the next truck.

Tully noticed, too, and as they settled into the car, he said, "I offered to take her to a women's shelter."

"This place is her shelter. Didn't you notice how relieved she was to get back here?"

"Do you think she saw anything out at the farm?"

"I don't know," Maggie said. "But the meth's probably fried it out of her brain."

CHAPTER 17

Creed snapped a fresh cylinder of UDAP pepper spray onto his belt. He left his revolver in its case under his seat.

"Come on, Grace," he said to the dog as he grabbed her leash and stepped out of the Jeep.

In seconds they were hurrying up a path, a shortcut that took them around the rest area's bathrooms and welcome center and gave them a straight shot to the other parking lot, where semi-trailers filled the slots.

Grace understood they were on a mission. She kept a steady pace beside him, sniffing the air and looking up at him for instruction.

The man and the little girl had been walking slowly but soon they'd be at their destination, an eighteen-wheeler at the corner of the parking lot. The truck's amber running lights lit up the length of the trailer. The cab's engine had been left humming. Creed saw motion inside behind the windshield. There would be two of them he'd have to contend with. His fingers instinctively reached inside his jacket and found the canister of pepper spray attached to his belt. He hoped he wouldn't regret not bringing his gun.

From this close, Creed realized the little girl was crying. The man held her right hand but her left was at her face, wiping at her nose. And he was right—she wore only white socks. No shoes.

Creed's pulse continued to race. There was no longer panic as much as urgency that pressed him and caused his heart to bang against his ribs.

Grace scampered alongside him, constantly looking up, then forward and back up for a signal from her master. Never once did she whine or hesitate. Even after she saw that they were headed toward a child Grace didn't show any additional excitement. Somehow dogs always seemed to react differently to children. Grace remained focused on Creed.

He still wasn't sure what he should look for. He didn't know many children or spend time around them. His experience extended only to the memory of his sister and Hannah's two boys, who were too young for Creed to compare to this girl. He guessed she was nine or ten. Maybe eleven, at the most. Brodie had been eleven. Yes, this girl looked about Brodie's age. Was that it? Was that the only reason an alarm seemed to have gone off inside his head, inside his chest? Was it only that she reminded him of Brodie?

He was counting on Grace's instincts.

As he approached, Creed tried to assess the man. He was Creed's height but outweighed him by about a hundred pounds and none of it looked like fat.

Creed stood an inch over six feet, and had broad shoulders but a thin waist, long arms and legs—a lean swimmer's build. Several years ago when Hannah declared their business solvent and making a steady profit, Creed had added an enclosed (heated and air-conditioned) Olympic-size swimming pool to their complex. It allowed him to include water rescue and water tracking on their list, but it also ensured his own physical health and mental sanity.

Since he was a kid, swimming had been the one escape, the one retreat that he enjoyed. No, it was stronger than that. There was something about diving into water and feeling it surround his body that rejuvenated all of his senses. But Creed was well aware that swimming wasn't exactly a sport that prepared him for a brawl.

"Excuse me, sir," Creed said before he knew what he was going to say to the trucker.

The man stopped but glanced over his shoulder as if he thought Creed might be addressing someone else. Creed watched his eyes dart to Grace and there was something there that told Creed the man didn't like dogs. Maybe was even fearful of them.

He looked younger than Creed originally thought. Probably no older than Creed, which meant late twenties. Thirty at the most.

"My dog loves kids," Creed lied. "She's been pulling on me to come see your little girl. I think she's missing my daughter."

He squatted down to pet Grace and in doing so he pointed to the little girl. Grace took the signal and started wagging, finally relieved to have some instruction. She focused her attention on the little girl, leaning toward her and sniffing.

"See, she's smiling already," Creed said, only this time he said it to the little girl, who was staring at Grace in awe. And the little girl was smiling, too.

Creed stayed on his haunches next to Grace and watched the man. From this angle he appeared less threatening but also from this angle if he shot the man in the face with the pepper spray he would be shooting upward and miss getting any on the little girl's face. As he kept a hand on Grace he kept his other tucked inside his jacket, fingers ready on the canister.

"Can I pet her, Daddy?"

Creed didn't need to know much about kids to hear the little girl's voice was genuine. Nothing sounded forced, including calling the man Daddy. But the man still seemed wary of Grace. Was it just dogs or was there something else he was hiding?

Before Creed could figure it out he heard the truck's cab door open and slam behind him. He stayed in position but his nerves were firing, his fingers itching.

"Bonnie loves puppy dogs, don't you, sweetie," a woman said.

Creed glanced back to see her.

The young woman came over. She was in jeans and a denim jacket.

"Is it okay for her to pet your dog?" she asked Creed.

"Absolutely."

The woman waved the little girl over and she started to rush. "Slow down. Don't spook her. And be gentle. Like this."

The woman gave Grace her hand for Grace to sniff it, waiting for permission. Then she stroked Grace's back. The little girl mirrored the woman's gestures, giggling when she finally touched Grace.

"Bonnie adores dogs," she said to Creed.

"No school this week?" Creed asked casually.

"Spring break. We thought it would be a treat to join Rodney. Show Bonnie what it is he does all week when he's away."

The man was actually smiling now, watching the little girl.

"See Rodney, just because you're scared of dogs—"

"I'm not scared."

"He had a dog attack him when he was a little boy, so he doesn't trust them." Then to her husband, she said, "I can't believe you took her to the bathroom without putting her shoes on."

"She didn't want them on, then she was crying that she was getting her socks dirty."

The more the couple bickered, the more Creed relaxed.

They sounded like a normal family.

CHAPTER 18

He slipped two receipts into the back-cover pocket of his log book, then turned to a new page and jotted down:

Tuesday, March 19
10:47 p.m.
Pilot Plaza #354, Sioux City, IA

He had just filled his gas tank and had done a quick maintenance check. He was ready to head out on the road again. He was still flying high on adrenaline. Not only had he been able to hear what everyone thought about his handiwork back at the farm, but he had also been able to finally meet Maggie O'Dell face-to-face.

Magpie: even more exquisite up close

He'd even bought her a beer . . . well, a round of beers for all of them. But it gave him surprising pleasure to watch her drink it. He cataloged the details now on the flip page of his log book:

Sam Adams lager

He liked that she waved off a frosted mug, choosing to sip directly from the bottle. He took note of what and how she ordered her food, too, adding to his page:

Cheeseburger, medium-well
cheddar cheese, bacon, extra pickles
side of fries (lots of ketchup)

She thanked the waitress whenever she brought Maggie something, taking the time to notice that her name was Rita and using it, glancing up and making eye contact. No one else paid attention to the woman as she served them, reaching over and around again and again all evening long.

He saw that Maggie left her a nice tip, too, even though someone else had picked up the tab. He should have been quicker. He could have bought her meal, too, but someone beat him to it and he didn't want to make a fuss.

Until today he had observed Agent Margaret O'Dell only from a distance, but he felt like he'd known her for years. From the first time he saw her he realized they were kindred spirits. And no, he wasn't easily attracted to pretty women. It took more than a pretty face to grab his attention these days. Besides, he was a professional, just like Maggie.

Last month he had watched her at a crime scene, a warehouse in D.C. that had been gutted by fire. He had also watched the asshole who set it on fire. Same asshole who later torched Maggie's house. If he had seen him doing it, the guy would be maggot food right now. He never really understood the fascination with fire.

The only reason he had been at that warehouse that night was because he was dumping a body in the alley. Sometimes he liked to do that. Then stick around so he could be there when people discovered his handiwork. Once he even called 911 to report a body so he could observe the first responders. It wasn't just to get off on it like some stupid sons of bitches. He actually learned a lot by watching the investigators, getting close enough to overhear their conversations and see what they collected.

There had been times like tonight when he frequented cop bars, just to listen to them. Buy them a few drinks and they started talking about all sorts of things. The time he spent hanging around cops and watching and listening had proven invaluable. It helped him change things up, perfect his methods, alternate patterns. He liked new challenges.

When he first saw Maggie—back at that D.C. crime scene—he could tell she liked challenges, too. Watching a CNN profile on her he'd learned that her mother sometimes called her "magpie" and that's when he knew they were kindred spirits. His own mother had often spoken of the magpie bird and considered it a good omen. It was the only bird that refused to go aboard Noah's Ark and instead perched on the roof. So spirited, just like him. Curious and constantly questioning, searching, learning, testing. What would it be like to take on a magpie?

That's why he left the map for her. That's why he included the socks—though he really hated repeating such an obvious pattern. He wanted her to find him so he could share his handiwork with her. Challenge her. See what she was made of. Poke and prod and prepare her for what he had planned. He hoped she wouldn't disappoint him.

He saw Lily crossing the parking lot, her hair still a tangled mess, her handbag making her slouch as she walked. What a pathetic creature. She had knocked on almost all of the truckers' cabs, even daring to knock on one that had a sign posted on the windshield: NO LOT LIZARDS! She was headed back to the main building of the truck plaza.

He started his engine. He'd offer her a ride. She'd recognize him from the farm and not give it a second thought. If she didn't want a ride, he'd offer her twenty bucks to get in, though he didn't want her touching him. Her sunken cheeks and rat-nest hair disgusted him. Already he was thinking it wouldn't be much of a challenge to kill her. That's why he didn't bother with women like her. He didn't imagine she was capable of putting up a good fight, let alone the psychological interplay he so enjoyed. She'd probably welcome death. He hated that kind of attitude. But he needed to look at this as a necessity.

He grabbed the ball cap he had taken from the bar and grill. He sniffed the inside, filling his lungs with the scent of Maggie's hair. He slipped it on and immediately liked how close it made him feel to her.

Then he pulled up next to the lot lizard and rolled down his window.

CHAPTER 19

Maggie had gotten used to the interstate hotels and motels. Most of them offered the basics, some added free Internet service. Maggie didn't care as long as the room was clean. Tully's eyes lit up— despite not being hungry enough to finish his burger—when he saw a sign in the lobby for a free continental breakfast that the Super 8 Hotel called the SuperStart.

Tully hadn't been able to reserve two rooms close to each other. And from the looks of the back parking lot it was no wonder. It was already packed with trucks and buses, a variety of sizes from eighteen-wheelers to cargo vans and service panel trucks. Earlier at the bar and grill their friendly lesson from the truckers who had joined them included a list of what truckers hauled. Maggie saw that this hotel parking lot displayed just some of those goods, from timber to automobiles. And obviously many truckers didn't sleep in their trucks back at the truck plaza.

Tully gave her the room on the third floor and took the one on the first. He hadn't been feeling good, so she was surprised to have him knocking on her door less than twenty minutes after she had gotten to her room. She had already peeled off her muddy clothes and was wearing only a nightshirt and panties. She opened the door a crack, hoping he'd just forgotten to tell her something—until she saw his face. He looked worried.

"Is Gwen okay?" she asked.

"I haven't talked to her tonight, but I'm sure she's fine. Were you already in bed?" His eyes fell to her bare legs as if he hadn't considered that possibility.

"Not yet, but close. Hold on a minute."

She closed the door and went to her overnight case where she had left it on the second double bed. She dug out a pair of jeans and pulled them on. Skipped socks and shoes. She started for the door again and stopped, contemplating a bra. The nightshirt was mid-thigh length and baggy, a Packers jersey. Nothing revealing or suggestive. Besides, it was Tully. She opened the door.

This time he came in without hesitating. He had his cell phone in one hand and a notepad in the other. A quick glance and she could see that it was a Super 8 notepad. He'd already been on the phone. The results weren't just noteworthy, they had Tully wired.

"You found something out?"

"Janet, the CSU tech, is starting to process the contents of the garbage bag."

He paced to the other side of the room, pulled the curtain enough to peek out. Maggie had already checked out the back parking lot below. Tully wasn't interested in anything out the window. His nervous energy had him on edge and the room was too small. Maggie sat on the corner of the bed farthest away.

"He left the woman's driver's license inside the bag," Tully said. "The body's mutilated, not to mention decapitated, but the son of a bitch left the victim's driver's license for us."

"That is weird. He already left us the orange socks and the receipt."

"Oh, that's not the weird part. Wendi Conroy disappeared last month. Her car was found at a rest area off I-95. In Virginia." He paused. "A rest area just south of Dale City."

He turned from the window and met her eyes, waiting for her reaction. They both knew that rest area. It was less than five miles away from her house—or rather what was left of her house—in Newburgh Heights, Virginia.

"This is Albert Stucky all over again," Tully said.

"It's not like Stucky." Maggie hated that the mention of his name could still make her skin crawl. She had crossed her arms and was rubbing them before she even realized it. "I don't know a Wendi Conroy. And I didn't know Gloria Dobson or Zach Lester."

Albert Stucky had targeted women Maggie had come in contact with: a girl who had delivered a pizza, a waitress, her real estate agent. Of those he killed, he left a piece of them in takeout containers usually someplace obvious to be easily found and to shock the finder.

"This is not like Stucky," Maggie repeated, almost as if she needed to convince herself. Then wanting Tully to lighten up, she added, "He hasn't left us any takeout containers."

"No, just garbage bags and a couple of mutilated bodies."

He started pacing the narrow lane between the beds and the TV stand, from the window to the door.

"When he left you the map I thought it was just because he saw you on that CNN profile and he knew that you were working the arsons along with the Dobson case. It made as much sense as his bizarre scavenger hunt makes. But that's not it." He stopped mid-stride and looked at her. "He's obsessed with you. Just like Stucky."

"Stucky wanted to hurt me."

"How do we know this guy doesn't want to hurt you?"

"Because he's had plenty of opportunities." She thought about that for a second or two. The whole time they'd been searching for this killer she'd never once felt threatened. "It seems like he's more interested in showing us his handiwork than he is in hurting either of us. Maybe he wants to be caught."

"He left you the map about the same time that he took Wendi Conroy from that rest area. A rest area that's five miles away from your house. In Virginia. But instead of leaving her body somewhere close by, he brought her twelve hundred miles to Iowa to bury her so she'd be here for you to find. Oh, and on the way he stopped and bought a pair of orange socks to put on her and left the receipt for you to find, too. In a separate bag with the woman's head. Does that sound like a guy who wants to be caught?"

Tully was right. Both of them had studied and experienced killers who had played "catch me if you can."

"Now that you put it that way," she said, "no, it doesn't. It sounds like a killer who's showing off."

CHAPTER 20

Gwen stumbled in the dark to find her ringing cell phone. Usually she left it on her nightstand. She didn't stop to put on a light in her living room as she hurried from her bed and her deep sleep.

"This is Gwen Patterson."

"I woke you. I'm sorry."

It was Maggie.

"Is everything okay? Is R.J. okay?"

"He's fine. Everything's fine. I forgot we're an hour behind you. I can call back in the morning."

"No, this is okay. I'm awake."

She ran a hand through her tangled hair and snapped on a lamp. She looked to the clock on the mantel. It was after midnight. She'd been asleep for only a half hour but it felt like half the night. She rubbed at her eyes and sank into a leather recliner.

"Where are you two tonight?"

"Just outside of Sioux City, Iowa. We found it."

Gwen sat up. Maggie didn't need to explain what "it" was.

"A farm behind an interstate rest area," Maggie continued. "There's a lot of ground to cover. Some of it's wooded and along a river. I'm not even sure if we can discount the fields and pastures. There're literally hundreds of acres that he's had access to. The perfect hideaway. Several abandoned buildings and a vacant farmhouse to crash in as long as he avoided the meth-using lot lizard."

"The meth-using what?"

"Prostitute. Lot lizard is what the truckers call them. We found her crashing inside the farmhouse. Long story."

Gwen could hear the exhaustion in her friend's voice.

"Her name's Lily. Tully and I were hoping she might have seen something. But no such luck. At least, not that she can remember right now."

"Lily the lot lizard."

"The body we found was in a black plastic garbage bag," Maggie continued. "Well, most of it. The head was in a separate bag, a smaller one close by. And he left us another puzzle piece to our scavenger hunt."

Gwen felt nauseated at the mention of the head. The last time she had worked on a homicide case, it also involved a decapitated victim. The victim was someone Gwen knew—a receptionist who had worked in her office.

Gwen was beginning to second-guess joining this task force. She had a successful practice listening to the District's elite— generals and politicos and their wives or husbands rehashing their emotional instabilities, their addictions, and their dysfunctional childhoods. Sometimes it wore her down but rarely did it scare or nauseate her. Did she really want to delve back into criminal behavior? Sort through its psychotic motives and view their bloody aftermath? Maybe she just wasn't cut out for this anymore.

"Gwen?"

She suddenly realized she hadn't heard the last of what Maggie had said.

"Gwen, are you okay?"

"I'm fine." Then because she knew Maggie would worry, she added, "I guess maybe I'm not quite as awake as I thought. What were you saying? He left you something?"

"He used the same retailer's bag where he bought the orange socks. Even left the receipt for us."

She realized she had missed more than she thought.

"Orange socks?" Gwen asked.

"The victim's wearing orange socks. I knew they looked too new. We think the killer bought them and put them on the corpse before he stuffed her in the garbage bag and buried her. I'm sure the socks are simply for our benefit. Like I said, another puzzle piece for the scavenger hunt."

Gwen stood and walked around her Georgetown condo now, turning on more lights. As she passed the front door she checked the locks. Working these cases brought on a whole slew of obsessive-compulsive habits. Oh sure, she double-checked security, but suddenly she wanted the room filled with light. She wanted the shadows and dark corners gone.

She opened the refrigerator. Grabbed a bottle of water. Twisted off the cap with too much urgency and swigged almost half the bottle while Maggie told her about the significance of the orange socks.

"Tully's been talking to Agent Antonio Alonzo. Have you met him yet?"

"We had a long meeting today. He's impressive."

"He's a data whiz. He can put together information in a remarkably short amount of time." Maggie paused before continuing. "I remembered a recent case that involved orange socks. Last month. In Virginia. They discovered a woman's remains that had been stuffed in a culvert. She had gone missing more than a year ago and no one had found her. The culvert was on a remote gravel road just off the interstate."

"A year? How did they find her?"

"A prisoner tipped off a television news reporter."

"Possibly the killer?"

"No, this guy's in for arson," Maggie said. "As far as Agent Alonzo can tell, Otis P. Dodd hasn't killed anyone. In fact, it sounds like he's gone out of his way to not kill. He's in prison for setting more than thirty fires across Virginia. The last one was a retirement home and yet he managed to do it without any of the residents getting hurt."

"Okay. If he's been in prison how did he know about the woman in the culvert?"

"According to Alonzo, Otis claims he had an interesting evening throwing back a few too many drinks with a guy who confessed to murdering a woman. He told the television crew that the conversation happened before Otis got arrested and went to prison."

"And he was convincing enough for them to search?"

"Sounds like they didn't need to search too hard. Otis was able to tell them exactly where to look."

"Coincidence?"

"Otis also said the guy left her in orange socks. Not exactly something he could take a wild guess at."

Gwen wandered back to her bedroom, snatched a robe and pulled it on, suddenly chilled.

Great.

She was still nauseated and now her skin felt clammy and cold. The refrigerated water certainly didn't help. She needed hot tea instead. Maybe with a splash of bourbon in it.

"So Otis may have met the highway killer. Well, this is definitely something the task force needs to look at," she told Maggie.

"I'm glad you agree. There's no way we'll be able to keep the orange socks out of the news. Too many helpers on the site saw them. So we need to move quickly on this. I already talked to Kunze and he's arranging the interview for tomorrow. I'd do it myself but I can't get back yet. Tully and I are meeting a canine cadaver team tomorrow at the farm."

"Wait a minute. An interview? What exactly is it that Kunze is arranging?"

"For you to interview Otis P. Dodd."

"Me?"

"I can't think of anyone who'd do a better job."

Gwen caught a glimpse of herself in her bedroom mirror. Her pink fleece robe was cinched tight. Her strawberry blond hair had a tangled knot on one side and flat bedhead on the other. She had dribbled water down her chin and missed a spot when she had wiped at it.

Oh, yes, she definitely looked like the person to take on a serial arsonist who palled around with a slice-and-dice killer.

CHAPTER 21

Lily had more spunk than he realized.

Looking back, he should have noticed right from the beginning. She was mouthing off even as she climbed into the passenger seat, pointing at his head and telling him, "That's not your cap."

But it hadn't stopped her from slamming the door behind her.

"You know she's with the FBI," Lily said. "Stealing from her's probably like a big-time felony or something."

"Maybe she gave it to me."

She pushed back in the seat to give him an exaggerated look-over.

"Yeah, right. You look exactly like her type. That's why you're picking me up, because she was so into you."

Then she had hacked up a laugh. "Hacked up" being the perfect phrase since the raspy sound came with a fair amount of phlegm sprayed onto his windshield.

Which reminded him—he'd need to clean that, too. He didn't want the whore's DNA splattered anywhere on him or his vehicle. Now, as he stood in the back of his truck, he shook his head at his miscalculation. He liked challenges, but he liked to choose them.

Not have them foisted on him. And Lily, the whore, had foisted this challenge on him.

But it was over. It was done. He considered it simply a detour.

And it had been a small bonus to see the surprise and confusion flash behind those drug-blurred eyes when he told her that Helen would be really disappointed in her.

Lily putting up a fight made him think about Maggie O'Dell and he smiled. He had been learning about her for about a month. Back in Washington, he had followed her around but was never able to get close enough. The closest was walking around the burned-out remains of her formerly beautiful home. Even then, he hadn't poked and pried into her belongings, though he certainly could have. He simply left the map on the granite countertop in what used to be her kitchen.

After spending a day observing Maggie up close he felt a restlessness. He couldn't wait to put her to his test. See what she was capable of doing. Unlike Lily, Maggie would be a worthy adversary. She would fight him wit for wit. She wouldn't give up as easily as Noah or any of the others.

He looked forward to finally catching her. There would be fear in her eyes but there would also be respect and admiration. He wondered if she would plead with him to kill her quickly or would she bargain with him for a few extra hours of life. Yes, Maggie O'Dell would be the ultimate challenge. He had to be patient just a little longer.

Now he dipped the iron tire thumper into the vat and watched the acid eat off Lily's blood and hair. In seconds it'd be clean without a hint of the damage it had done to her skull.

He peeled off his gloves and blood-splattered clothes, stuffing them in a black plastic garbage bag. He'd toss them in a trash receptacle at the next rest area, somewhere miles from this one, so if someone found them they'd never find a body anywhere in that area. He'd figured that out long ago. No reason to change the process.

Likewise, he had built and customized the back half of his truck into a workshop with everything he needed, not only for his job but also for his hobby. So if anyone checked it out there was no reason to question the array of tools, cleaning solutions, saws, and knives. And because he was on the road so much, he also had all the personal comforts he needed. That included a week's worth of clothing, shoes, and other accessories.

Some of those accessories served as disguises and included a hearing aid, a cane, an arm sling, Coke-bottle-thick glasses, a neck brace, and a dog leash. It was amazing the simple things that brought people's guards down. The thought that a stranded motorist might be even more vulnerable because his arm was in a sling or perhaps because he'd lost his dog. He kept a list in his log book of those that worked the best. He observed and studied the things people didn't seem to notice when they were exhausted from traveling. He kept a list of these as well.

He had already replaced the magnetic sign on the outside of his truck. He had several, all of them creative names of businesses that exuded integrity and trust. The one he just put on read: COM-MUNITY RESCUE UNIT. Actually he'd gotten the idea from listening to a group of cops at a truck stop café outside Toledo, Ohio. They had just caught a killer using a public works department uniform. Homeowners let him in without question. Almost as good as a uniform was his idea of converting the outside of his truck into a vehicle that people automatically trusted.

Finally finished cleaning up, he pulled out his log book and recorded the date, time, and place in the corner. Then he added the details he wanted to remember:

Even drug whores fight for life.
Two bashes in the head and still crawling.
Rolled into the river.
Skin and bones. Not much of a floater.
Wrapped the strap of her bag around her neck.
Bag should weight her down.

He paused to roll up his shirtsleeves and only then noticed that the bitch had managed to scratch his arm. Immediately he grabbed a bottle of alcohol from one of the cabinets. He remembered her fingernails had been chipped and broken, and for the short time she sat in his passenger seat she couldn't stop clawing at her scabs.

Seeing the damage she'd done made him angry and sick to his stomach. What if the bitch had given him some disease? He poured half the bottle over the open wound despite the sting. He didn't mind the pain. Pain made you feel alive. Then he searched through his stash of pharmaceuticals until he found the antibiotic he wanted. He popped one into his mouth and washed it down with a can of Coke from the large ice chest he kept well stocked.

The whole incident was beginning to remind him that small mistakes had tripped up many killers and landed them in prison. Ted Bundy, Edmund Kemper, Henry Lee Lucas, Jeffery Dahmer—all of them had done something stupid that ended up getting them caught. Wouldn't happen to him.

Along with talking and listening to cops, he prided himself on being an expert on serial killers, their patterns, fetishes, weaknesses, and even those mistakes that got them caught. But he was more careful and smarter. Besides, he could control when and where he chose to kill. He wasn't driven by voices or impulses. Tonight was a rare exception. Tonight he killed out of necessity rather than challenge and hobby. There hadn't been much pleasure in it. He just wanted Lily dead.

He had no idea if the woman had seen anything. He'd had no idea she had been staying in the farmhouse. How many times had he dumped a body and she was there? He couldn't take the chance that she might have seen him. Although she didn't seem to recognize or know him beyond meeting him earlier today. He wondered if she really had been one of Helen's foster kids, though he knew there had been dozens over decades. So it was possible. And if she had been one of Helen's then he was right—Helen would have been disappointed in her.

He bandaged his arm. It would be easier to make up what had happened if people didn't see the claw marks. In fact, it would gain him sympathy. As he exited the back of his truck and moved to the driver's seat, he found himself scanning the cars parked on the other side of the rest area. Only two vehicles.

He climbed behind the steering wheel and watched. A small SUV had two middle-aged women. One went up the incline to the restrooms. The other stayed to clean out their car. He pulled out his pair of binoculars from the console and watched her throw their garbage into the trash receptacle. Most of it was empty junk food containers and cups with sip lids—which probably meant coffee. Tired and exhausted. He saw the license plate was Texas. Lots of miles on the road. Long way from home.

Easy targets.

The second vehicle was a four-door sedan. A man and a little boy. The boy looked ten or eleven, an age the man had evidently determined was old enough that the boy could go up the short walk to the building by himself to use the restroom. Meanwhile the man went to the trunk and started pulling what looked like sweatshirts out of a huge duffel bag. The entire time he would not be able to see the door to the restroom. In those few minutes the boy was an easy target. So was his father.

Both vehicles presented excellent opportunities. In either case he'd be able to do doubles if he chose. What would a father be willing to do? Would he insist he go first? Would he bribe or fight or plead?

Unfortunately Lily had fought more than he'd expected and he was too exhausted to enjoy the challenge. Maybe another time. He had a long trip ahead. He was quite certain other opportunities would be available.

CHAPTER 22

Lily clung to the straps of her leather handbag.

Cold, so freaking cold.

She was used to the opposite. Usually her body was burning up from the inside.

The straps had gotten snagged on a tree branch that hung over the river. She knew she was bleeding. The pain inside her head made it difficult to think, to move, to react. Her normally feverish body was submerged in freezing water. She no longer felt bugs crawling all over her. Instead she was quite certain they had now burrowed down deep into her skin. She could feel the prickling sensation and the tingle of them gnawing their way into her veins.

Her bravery had started to wear thin. At first the asshole had made her angry. And she fought him. When he hit her she became more angry. She lashed out at him, pleased to gouge some of his skin. But now, in the dark, surrounded by night sounds that she didn't recognize and feeling dizzy with pain, she was no longer angry. She was scared.

She waited. She had to wait, she told herself, until he was gone. She had to convince him that he was leaving her exactly the way the bastard wanted to leave her—dead.

WEDNESDAY, MARCH 20

CHAPTER 23

Gwen had a bone to pick with Maggie. When her friend told her that Assistant Director Raymond Kunze was arranging for Gwen to interview convicted arsonist Otis P. Dodd, she hadn't mentioned that Kunze would be escorting her there. It was bad enough that her nerves were already frayed. An hour and a half trapped with Kunze threatened to unravel her completely. To make matters worse, he was being polite, which made it harder for Gwen to take out her frustration on him.

Frustration was putting it mildly. Her last interview with a convicted felon had left her with a freshly sharpened pencil almost impaled in her throat. Maggie had tried to assure her that Otis P.— as he liked to be called—was not violent. Out of the thirty-seven fires he had started, no one had ever been hurt or killed.

Gwen had wanted to ask Maggie last night how she could say such a thing about a serial arsonist? The simple act of torching building after building was quite violent. She wanted to remind her friend that many serial killers started as arsonists. But to do so would alert Maggie that perhaps Gwen wasn't up for this assignment. And Gwen would much rather tamp down her ridiculous fear and struggle through this interview than admit to Maggie that she might not be capable of doing it.

Gwen was fifteen years older and she knew that Maggie considered her a mentor even as the two of them became friends. In fact, Gwen had a strong maternal instinct when it came to Maggie, wanting to shield and protect her, concerned to the point of nagging. Maggie's dysfunctional childhood and failed marriage had closed off her heart in ways that even Gwen hadn't been able to pierce. But she knew she was the only person Maggie trusted unconditionally. That should have been a triumph for Gwen, but in some ways it felt like a burden. Gwen didn't want to give up the façade of being the older, wiser, reliable, unshakable mentor. She didn't want to let Maggie down.

So here Gwen was, getting patted down by a prison guard with bad breath and clumsy hands. Or at least he pretended they were clumsy while he groped exactly where he wanted. The warden stood less than three feet away watching and enjoying so openly that Kunze stepped in between. She had purposely worn slacks with her suit instead of her trademark skirts. And pantyhose, knowing the control top and added layer around her thighs would make it more difficult to slip fingers where they didn't belong.

Gwen also knew that if she complained she could lose the interview. She knew enough about prison politics. Warden Demarcus didn't care that they were FBI. If they wanted entrance into his house, they had to play by his rules.

"You'll need to remove your high heels," Demarcus told her when his man was finished.

"Why is that?" she asked, trying to sound curious instead of stunned.

"Too provocative. What are those, three inches?"

"And what would you have me wear instead?"

The guard pulled out paper shoe covers that were about twice the size of Gwen's feet.

"She's not taking off her shoes," Kunze said before Gwen could respond.

She watched the two men stare each other down.

Outside the prison walls Warden Demarcus might be mistaken for a high-paid lawyer. His shirt and trousers looked tailored, his tie an expensive silk. Gwen recognized Italian leather shoes when she saw them, though she thought the tassels were a bit much. He had a handsome face and a thick head of dark-brown hair with a peppering of gray at the temples that made him look distinguished. But it wasn't the clothes that made the man intimidating. There was something about the way he carried himself. His back was ramrod straight. He held his square chin slightly up as though he were looking down at everyone he met. Gwen decided it was the man's eyes that made him so intimidating. They were narrow set with a hawkish nose that made him look like a predator.

Demarcus stood several inches shorter than the assistant director. Gwen had heard that Raymond Kunze had played linebacker in college and had even been drafted into the NFL. But he chose the FBI instead. He still looked like he could level half of an offensive line and he certainly could pick up Demarcus quite easily and throw him across the room. But he didn't need to do that. His stare telegraphed that fact quite well.

Gwen got to keep her shoes.

Now, as she waited alone in the interview room, she actually felt better knowing Kunze sat somewhere behind the one-way tinted window that took up most of the wall to Gwen's left. She made herself as comfortable as was possible in the metal folding chair. She had bypassed the opportunity to take notes. Her last experience proved how easily pen and pencil became weapons. It even made her question how the wire in a spiral notebook could be used.

Gwen heard the door open and she sat up straight. Otis P. Dodd came into the room and instantly filled it, a giant of a man with a lopsided grin. As the guard attached Otis's shackles to the iron rings in the floor beside his chair, Gwen couldn't help thinking how silly it was for her to worry about pens and pencils. Otis P. Dodd's hands looked big enough to snap her neck in seconds.

CHAPTER 24

"What do you like about starting fires?" Gwen asked him.

After their short introductions, she delivered her first question exactly like she had practiced it in her head during the long drive from the District to the prison. It was a gamble. She didn't want to put him on defense but she wanted to learn about him. She wanted to find out a little something about Otis before she asked about his friend, the killer who left his victims in orange socks.

Otis seemed pleased with the question, but it was actually difficult to tell. He hadn't stopped grinning since he sat down.

"Some people like to call me a pyromaniac." He licked his lips and Gwen already recognized it to be a nervous tic. "I'm really a powermaniac." Then he smiled more broadly, crinkling the crow's-feet at the corners of his eyes.

Despite his size and Gwen's initial reaction, she realized she didn't find him as frightening as she had expected. He had almost a childlike demeanor about him. His Southern drawl came out soft and gentle, slow and thoughtful. Even as he claimed to be a "powermaniac," there was nothing threatening in his tone or manner.

"You like the power it gives you?"

"Absolutely. Nothing quite like it."

Before Gwen could ask another question, Otis offered, "I'd like to see a whole city burn down. That'd be somethin', wouldn't it?"

Still grinning, his tongue darted out the corner of his mouth.

Gwen would quickly learn that the grin was a permanent fixture, no matter what Otis was talking about. Perhaps another nervous tic, just like licking his lips. There was nothing salacious about either. In fact, he reminded Gwen of a teenager, a bit awkward and uncomfortable in his own body.

Then he added, "But I know you didn't come all this way out here to ask about me." He tilted his head and squinted, looking her directly in the eyes, as if gauging what she was after. "You wanna know about Jack."

"You know his name?"

"Don't know if that's his real name, but that's what he was going by."

"He told you about a woman he murdered. Is that right?"

"Actually he told me about quite a few."

Gwen tried to hide her surprise. She held his gaze. Criminals were good liars. Was Otis playing with her?

"He told you he murdered more than one person?"

"That's right."

The lopsided grin didn't budge.

"How many people did he claim to have murdered?"

Otis looked up at the ceiling as though he might find the answer there. He thought about it for a few seconds then said, "Probably about thirteen or fourteen. Course it's been more than a year since me and him talked."

Gwen swallowed, hard. Maggie and Tully believed this killer had murdered others, but more than a dozen? This wasn't what she had expected.

"Did you find another one of 'em?" Otis asked. He sat forward, his brow furrowed, not just curious now but offering her his confidentiality.

"Yes. We think so. She had on orange socks."

This time Otis's smile flickered and he raised one of his eyebrows, as if all of a sudden he had tasted something bad but he didn't really want to complain. Finally he shook his head.

"I don't think it's one of Jack's."

"Why do you say that?"

"You see, Jack said he did all kinds of things. Different ways, what have you. So there wouldn't be no pattern." His tongue poked out and wet his lips.

Gwen waited.

"Last time that pretty little thing with the orange socks . . . you see, she had those on. Or that's what Jack said. She was wearing those. He didn't plan that."

"What if he put orange socks on this one?"

Otis looked to the ceiling again and when his eyes came back down he was shaking his head. "Why'd you think he'd do that? That don't make no sense at all. See, Jack likes to change things up. That's why he sometimes does doubles."

"Doubles?"

"I guess he travels a bit. Said he gets bored. Likes a challenge or what have you."

Gwen's mind raced over what she knew about Gloria Dobson and Zach Lester. She couldn't remember anyone saying that they believed the killer took on both intentionally. Lester's body had been so viciously decimated it had been presumed that he had gotten in the way of the killer's real target: Gloria Dobson. Was it possible he had planned it that way? That he wanted to take on two victims at the same time?

"So where'd you find this one?"

Gwen hesitated. In a day or so the location would be all over the news, so there wasn't a reason to keep it secret. But she knew criminals could draw facts out of their interviewers, lead them to drop enough details that they could cleverly manipulate and spin them back. She hadn't gotten anything out of Otis that would help Maggie and Tully. And she sure as hell wasn't going to give Otis anything more than he had given her.

Instead of telling him where they had found the last victim, she simply said, "We believe we've found his dumping ground."

She watched his reaction, trying to see beyond the silly grin.

"Which one?" he asked.

Gwen's stomach flipped. Again, was it boyish charm or was he just a very good liar?

"Are you saying he has more than one?"

She showed him her doubt, even a little impatience. And she saw that he noticed.

He laughed but it was a nervous laugh. Then he sat back, putting some distance between them, like perhaps she no longer deserved his confidentiality. He tilted his head again to look at her, studying her.

"That first reporter I told about the girl in the orange socks, he didn't believe me. Warden Demon—that's what we call him and I know he's probably watching and listening behind that glass and I don't even care if he makes me pay for telling you that—he didn't believe me either. You decide you believe me, you come back and maybe we'll talk some more."

The entire time he said this, his tone remained gentle and polite. He didn't sound angry, though his words certainly were. The grin hadn't left either. Then Otis pushed away from the table as far as his shackles allowed and he stood up, finished with her. Immediately a guard came through the door.

"The dumping ground is someplace in the Midwest," Gwen told him, calling his bluff, giving him just enough rope to hang himself. She didn't want to come back here and put herself through Demarcus's full-body searches. If Otis was lying, she wanted to trip him up now and be done with it.

Otis nodded and squinted again like he needed to give it some thought.

"That'd be the one off I-29. Sioux City, Iowa."

She stared at him. Was it simply a lucky guess?

"You should check the barn," he told her. "I think that's where he buried the biker guy with all the tattoos."

Then he offered his hands to the guard to release his shackles from the iron rings in the floor. And Otis P. Dodd shuffled away without looking back at her.

CHAPTER 25

"He was pretty convincing," Gwen told Maggie.

She called Maggie as soon as she got back to her office. She had been anxious to get back, asking for a rain check on lunch when AD Kunze offered. Now as she stood looking out the window and at the Potomac in the distance, now that she was back in familiar territory, she felt comfortable and—she hated to admit it—she felt *safe*. She also knew she could give Maggie a more objective assessment of Otis P. Dodd and what he had told her. And what he had *not* told her.

"But there's something very odd about him," Gwen added.

"Agent Alonzo said he's mentally slow."

"No, I don't think he is. He's like a giant hulk, only with a receding hairline and thick sideburns and a crazy lopsided grin that doesn't go away. He speaks in this slow and easy Southern drawl that can easily disarm you. He actually comes off as polite and . . . God, I hate to admit this, but he's almost charming."

"But not mentally challenged?"

"Socially he's stunted and that's probably what causes people to think he might be slow. Also, he's not well educated. He talks very simply. Double negatives, poor grammar in general. He may not be the sharpest, but he's definitely not dumb. In fact, I think he's quite manipulative."

"He wants people to believe he's not smart?"

"Yes," Gwen said, relieved that Maggie understood despite Gwen's difficulty in explaining.

"So is he making this all up?"

Gwen let out a sigh and raked her fingers through her hair before she admitted, "That I don't know. There were some things about him that were quite genuine. Things I don't think he could have faked.

"For example, he genuinely appears to be uncomfortable in his own skin. He has the mannerisms of a thirteen-year-old boy. Awkward. Almost gawky. Facial tics that I don't think he's aware of. He reminded me of a teenager who woke up one day to find that he had grown six inches in the last month but in his mind he still wasn't that tall."

"Are you saying he has the maturity of a thirteen-year-old? Or just the physicality?"

"That's a good question. I'm not sure I have an answer."

"Well, he's serving a twenty-five-year sentence for arson. From what I understand, he's set more than thirty fires in the state of Virginia. It takes a certain maturity to get away with that many, even for a pyromaniac."

"Oh, that reminds me. He said people call him a pyromaniac, but he says he's a powermaniac." As soon as she repeated his line Gwen realized she had been fooled. Before Maggie could respond, she said, "He's playing me, isn't he?"

"If he is, how did he know about the woman in the culvert? The first one in orange socks? He told them exactly where the body could be found."

"And he couldn't have randomly chosen Iowa along with Interstate 29 as a lucky guess, could he? I did prompt him by telling him it was in the Midwest." Now Gwen wished she hadn't even given him that much.

"No, I don't think he could. That would be too big of a coincidence. Tully and I know how hard this has been to pinpoint and we had a map. That we found this killer's dumping ground so quickly was dumb luck. It's just started to leak out to the media so he couldn't have heard about it on the news."

There was a pause. Gwen realized neither of them knew what to think. She took the opportunity to talk about personal things for a few minutes. Gwen wanted to know how Tully was doing. He hadn't been feeling well when he left yesterday morning. And Maggie wanted to know how the contractors were progressing on her house. A good deal of her two-story Tudor had been damaged in the fire. There was no connection to Otis. He had already been in prison.

Gwen tried to keep positive, constantly reminding Maggie that now she could rebuild her house exactly how she wanted it. But the contractors were already behind schedule and she knew it was driving Maggie crazy to not be able to check up on them. Gwen promised to do a drop-by.

As they wound down their conversation, Maggie suddenly asked, "Are you doing okay?"

"Yes, of course," Gwen said too quickly and immediately wondered what tell she may have unconsciously given Maggie.

"You seem . . . I don't know, tired?"

"Maybe a little."

Maggie was quiet and Gwen knew she owed her more than that.

"I just had my yearly physical on Monday," she added. "So I'm fine." She hadn't heard back on any of the lab results but they were always good. She took care of herself. She didn't feel ill. Truth was, she didn't want to admit to Maggie that being back out at Quantico and interviewing criminals—all of it was having an adverse effect on her. Silly, but she didn't want to admit that perhaps she had lost her edge . . . or worse, her nerve.

So she changed the subject. "Do you think Otis made that up about a body in the barn? Is there even a barn? When I talked to Tully this morning he said some of the buildings had already been bulldozed."

"I would have sooner believed it if the barn had been bulldozed. Then a body could have been buried where it once stood. But the barn's still there," Maggie said. "And I'm not sure how easy it would be to bury someone under its floor."

Then she added as an afterthought, "I guess we'll see if Otis likes to serve up his facts mixed with a little fiction."

CHAPTER 26

Ryder Creed had stopped at a Drury Inn just outside Kansas City. He and Grace had gotten a couple of hours of sleep. He didn't need much. As Hannah had reminded him, he had slept through an entire day. But he wanted a shower and a hot breakfast and he was even able to add some scrambled eggs to Grace's meal, too.

Creed was particular about where he stopped and more so about where he stayed. He always used this hotel chain whenever he could because it treated pets as family and provided a large grassed area for his dogs, as well as a nice clean room that didn't smell like an ashtray. He never understood interstate motels and hotels that put pet owners in smoking rooms, like the two were even related. Even after a long day's work, his dogs never smelled as bad as a smoker's room.

His GPS had them arriving at the site in a few minutes. Creed had already begun observing and assessing the terrain, determining what he and Grace would deal with. Lots of foliage just starting to bloom, but this far north he knew it had still been chilly at night. The cold and snow of winter usually preserved much more than what they had to deal with in the South. A real winter with cold temperatures for weeks, if not months, of frozen earth slowed down decomposition.

It was only March. In these parts that meant fewer insects, another slowdown. Most investigators would prefer those conditions. After all, they wanted to find as much of the remains intact as possible. But cold temperatures made it more challenging for an air-scent dog that depended on finding bodies by smelling all the by-products of the decaying process—the gases, liquids, and acids.

Creed took in the blue sky, not a cloud as far as he could see. The weather forecast called for more of the same later today and tomorrow. It was a gorgeous spring day, already close to seventy degrees, with no wind.

A perfect day for decay.

He caught himself smiling at that and wondered when he had started measuring the success of each day by his ability to find dead people. Maybe he really did need Hannah to schedule a search and rescue for him. Or even a bomb or drug search assignment. At least there was a fifty-fifty chance there'd be living people at the end of the search.

Grace had been watching all morning from the back of the Jeep. As soon as Creed turned into the long driveway she started getting excited.

"Sit back down," he told her. "You know the rules."

She wagged and squatted, pushing the envelope.

"All the way down."

Finally, down went her butt. Her head stayed up, looking out at the surroundings. Halfway up the driveway a black-and-white sheriff's department SUV blocked the gravel road. Creed still couldn't see the farm buildings. Trees blocked his view. Before he stopped his Jeep a sheriff's deputy was already walking down the middle of the road to head him off.

"Be good," Creed told Grace. He grabbed his ID from the console and opened the driver's window.

"You need to turn around," the deputy said, stopping in front of the Jeep's grill and motioning with one hand while keeping the other on his gun belt.

It looked like he wasn't going to bother coming to the window, so Creed held up his ID to the windshield.

"My name's Ryder Creed. I'm with CrimeScent K-9."

The deputy looked young and nervous. He also didn't seem to expect anyone who wasn't in official law enforcement gear. He pulled out his cell phone and was punching in a number, trying to do it while not taking his eyes or his attention away from Creed.

He heard the deputy say, "Some guy with a dog," not even bothering with Creed's name or his business's name. It didn't matter. In seconds his face turned a bright red and he slipped the phone back into his uniform's shirt pocket without saying anything.

He pulled his wide-brimmed hat low over his brow before he yelled to Creed, "You're good to go." And he waved his thumb over his shoulder. Then he headed back to his SUV to move it so Creed could pass by.

Creed shook his head. "Amateurs, Grace," he said to the dog, glancing back at her in the rearview mirror. She was wagging her tail again but still sitting, still obeying despite her excitement. "They've got us working with a bunch of amateurs, girl."

CHAPTER 27

Maggie shook her head at Tully while he opened the last Hostess Honey Bun that he had taken from the hotel's complimentary breakfast bar. She hoped it meant that his appetite had returned and he was feeling better.

By the time they arrived at the farm, Sheriff Uniss and his men had set up a perimeter with security posts at three places where they believed the property might be vulnerable to intruders. And by intruders they knew he meant media.

As far as the sheriff was concerned, this was a crime scene that still needed to be protected and processed. He knew Tully had called for a K-9 unit, but neither Maggie nor Tully had shared with him the killer's map or their suspicions about this being his dumping ground. Assuming most of the excitement was over, the sheriff had left, grumbling that he had to go deal with the governor's press secretary. For his sake, Maggie hoped they didn't find anything . . . or anyone . . . else.

Earlier when Maggie relayed Gwen's prison visit she tried to ignore the pained look on Tully's face. She knew he'd be remembering the last time Gwen had interviewed a convicted prisoner. He had been there. She went through the information quickly and prompted him to share what he had. Agent Alonzo was becoming their right-hand man despite being twelve hundred miles away. Now, as they walked along the grove of trees, out of earshot of the deputies, and toward the barn, Tully filled her in on what he knew.

"The receipt was for a Walmart outside of Council Bluffs, Iowa, just off Interstate 29."

"Council Bluffs is next door to Omaha, right?" Maggie remembered from their own road trip yesterday morning. They had landed in Omaha and drove that same stretch of interstate highway.

Tully was trying to decipher the notes he'd taken while talking to Agent Alonzo. The crosshatch marks didn't even resemble words but rather looked like someone had tried to test whether a pen still had ink.

"Alonzo said the Walmart does have security cameras in the parking lot. He's checking but he said it's doubtful they have anything. He said most of these places don't store more than a week's worth of footage. He's got someone from the Omaha bureau checking on it. Sounds like a long shot that we'd even see this guy. He strikes me as someone who'd be conscious of where cameras would be and try to avoid them."

"Were the CSU techs able to pull any fingerprints off the receipt?"

"No, and I doubt they will. My gut tells me that's gonna be a dead end. We found the receipt because he wanted us to find it. Just like the driver's license."

"Was there anything else in either bag?"

Tully shrugged. "You mean other than a head in one and a decapitated body in the other?"

"Anything under the fingernails?"

Tully fished another scrap of paper out of his pocket and

searched through more chicken scratches. "They did preliminary scrapings. Chunks of dirt."

"Chunks of dirt?"

"Janet said it looked like—" Tully flipped the paper over, then frowned like the words left a bad taste in his mouth. "She said it looked like the woman had clawed at the mud."

They both were silent. Neither stopped walking. They were almost at the barn when Tully finally continued, "ME's trying to schedule in the autopsy."

"So he brings us all the way here and we're no closer to knowing who he is."

"Part of the game. It's like I told you last night. He's obsessed with you." He pointed at the barn. "But maybe we get lucky and find something he doesn't want us to find."

The outside of the barn was faded red and the front doors sagged on ancient hinges. "Doesn't seem likely that he'd just leave a body in here." But Tully had already started to open the rusted latch.

"Otis P. Dodd told Gwen that his friend Jack buried one of his victims in the barn. A tattooed biker."

"He told him all this over a couple of drinks?"

"I know it sounds strange. Only problem, Otis was correct about the woman's body stuffed in a culvert, right down to the orange socks. Who knows how he called that one. Could have been dumb luck. Maybe he heard about it inside the prison. But my guess is Otis P. Dodd likes to make up stories to get attention."

"What about I-29 and Iowa?"

"Gwen told him it was in the Midwest."

"A lucky guess?"

"You don't really believe a killer named Jack told Otis about all the people he murdered and where he dumped bodies?"

Tully shrugged again and pulled open the barn doors.

Truth was, Maggie wasn't quite sure what she believed. It wasn't unheard of that a killer would share his exploits. Others had, but usually anonymously. In fact, this killer was sort of doing it with Maggie by leaving her the map and then the receipt as well as the socks. But again, that was anonymously. But sharing with someone who could identify him? Why would he do that?

They were in the doorway of the barn when Tully pointed at the Jeep coming in through the tree-lined driveway. "Looks like our K-9 team is here. Alonzo says this guy is one of the best dog trainers and trackers in the country. If there's another body out here, he should be able to find it."

Tully turned to head back and meet the man, but Maggie paused. When she glanced inside the barn, she noticed something and felt an instant dread. A chill slid down her back. She took a few steps into the barn and, with her foot, she swept aside a patch of the straw scattered over the floor.

That's when she saw that the barn didn't have a cement foundation or even wood floorboards. Beneath the straw was only dirt.

CHAPTER 28

Neither Maggie nor Tully had ever worked with a cadaver K-9 team. Maggie wasn't sure what to expect, but she definitely hadn't imagined a nationally known expert to look like the man who got out of the Jeep.

First of all, he looked too young. Thirty, at the most. He was tall, broad-shouldered, and wore a white T-shirt that stretched over a lean and muscular torso with arms to match. His Levi's telegraphed more of the same. Leather hiking boots and wrap-around sunglasses finished off the outfit. Once outside the Jeep, he put on a light blue oxford shirt but kept the shirttails out and the buttons undone.

No, this was definitely not what she had expected.

He was rolling up the sleeves when he saw Maggie and Tully. He reached in the opened Jeep window and brought all of the windows down halfway. As they approached the vehicle Maggie could see the dog inside and it didn't look anything like she had expected either—too small and too white.

"I'm R. J. Tully and this is Agent Maggie O'Dell."

"Ryder Creed."

He pulled off his sunglasses to meet their eyes as he offered his hand, first to Maggie, then to Tully. She noticed a silver chain bracelet with a small engraved plate but couldn't make out the words. A diver's watch on the other wrist, no wedding band. She caught herself and wondered why she had checked.

His eyes were deep blue, almost the same color as the sky, bright against tanned skin. A confident, self-assured smile started in his eyes and triggered the corner of his mouth, a subtle but genuine smile that belied his age. His short dark hair looked like he had towel-dried it that morning and not bothered to comb it. Nor had he bothered to shave. But on closer inspection, Maggie realized his bristled jaw had been trimmed, leaving sharp and precise lines that gave order to a face that perhaps fought a five o'clock shadow too early every day.

"This is Grace," Creed told them, pointing inside the Jeep but making no effort to free the dog.

"You just have the one?" Tully asked and Maggie immediately heard his skepticism.

"She's probably my best air-scent dog."

"It's just that there's a lot of ground to cover." Tully waved his hand to include the fields behind the trees.

"Working multiple dogs at the same time can present problems. Competition between the dogs. False alerts. Overlapping grids. Believe me, one dog will be more than efficient." He said it matter of fact without sounding offended or defensive.

"She seems kinda small." Tully still wasn't convinced. He leaned down to take a better look through the window.

Creed already had the liftgate up and was sorting through his gear. Grace met him at the back but didn't attempt to leave the vehicle, sitting, wagging, and watching her master instead of paying attention to Maggie or Tully. Maggie got a good look at the dog. She was a Jack Russell terrier, a surprising pick for a tracker.

"I don't think size matters," she said to Tully as she watched

Creed. "Harvey's twice Grace's size—maybe three times—and I doubt he'd focus long enough to find his favorite Frisbee if I hid it."

Creed didn't look up as he transferred items from a duffel bag to a small backpack, but she saw his corner-of-the-mouth smile again and she liked that she was able to provoke it.

"What kind of dog is Harvey?" he asked.

"Labrador."

"You're right. Size or breed isn't as important as drive."

Tully was standing with his hands on his hips, watching the dog, watching Creed, and doing a poor job of hiding his disappointment. At one point when he caught Maggie's eyes, he rolled his as if to say, "Not much of an expert."

The two men were almost the same height, but that's where the comparison stopped. Tully was wiry and lanky, dressed in trousers and a button-down shirt, wrinkled but neatly tucked in. Today he wore wire-rimmed glasses, a staple on the road, because he didn't like packing all "the stuff" that went with his contacts. Tully was a conscientious do-gooder, a corny but romantic everyman whose coffee stains and absentmindedness could easily be forgiven because when he told you he had your back, you could count on it. He did.

Grace had nudged her way to the open liftgate, still sitting, but now able to lean out. She was sniffing in Maggie's direction.

"Are we allowed to pet her?" Maggie asked.

"Sure. She's just not allowed to leave the Jeep until I tell her it's okay."

Maggie reached her hand in slowly for the dog to sniff. Then she scratched Grace's neck, keeping her hand where the dog could still see it. She felt Creed watching her from the corner of his eye. Of course, he had to be protective of his dog.

Finally finished, he slipped on the backpack. To Maggie he

said, "Would you mind taking Grace to stretch her legs while I check around?"

"Sure."

And to Tully, "Can you fill me in while I take a look?"

Tully simply nodded.

Creed handed Maggie a small, soft, pink elephant. The dog toy was plastic, but squishy and squeaky, and as soon as it came out of Creed's pocket Grace could barely contain herself. Her entire hindquarter wiggled, excited and impatient, but she still sat waiting for her master's permission. She watched Creed but also watched as he handed off her toy to Maggie, eyes darting back and forth, wagging, listening, ears perched and haunches ready to run.

"Toss it around for her, but she might just want to carry it in her mouth. Tap your hand against the side of your leg like this"—and he demonstrated—"if she strays." Then he looked into Maggie's eyes and asked, "Is it okay if I call you Maggie?"

"Yes, of course."

But immediately she realized he wasn't asking for himself. He turned back to Grace and said, "Okay, Grace, go with Maggie."

The dog leaped into Creed's arms—obviously something they did without either of them thinking—and in one fluid motion he swung her to the ground. Immediately all her attention was focused on Maggie and the pink elephant.

She seemed so playful, so spirited, so ordinary. As Maggie led Grace to the soft grass closer to the house it was hard for her to imagine that this little energetic dog spent a good deal of her time hunting dead people.

CHAPTER 29

Creed tried to concentrate on what Agent Tully was telling him. As they walked, Creed kept Agent O'Dell and Grace in his line of vision. To Agent Tully it probably looked like he wanted to make sure Grace was okay. That was only half the truth. He couldn't get Agent O'Dell—Maggie—off his mind.

God, she had gorgeous eyes, rich brown with flecks of caramel.

Hannah would be laughing at him about now, telling him, "Since when have you ever noticed a woman's eyes, let alone what color they are?"

She was right. This was stupid.

Agent Tully pointed at the crater left by a backhoe and was telling Creed about the construction project that had uprooted a skull and other bones along with a garbage bag containing a body.

"Was it male or female?" Creed asked.

"That's information we haven't released yet," Tully said.

Creed didn't need to know. Grace didn't care what gender the corpse was. They all smelled alike to her. But Creed wanted to know. The only reason he put himself through so many of these recoveries was in the hope of finding his sister, Brodie. Hannah had told him that when Agent Alonzo at Quantico called, he mentioned that the farmstead was behind an interstate rest area.

"Does it make a difference?"

Tully must have seen something in Creed's face. Hannah had said that these two—O'Dell and Tully—were profilers and that Creed should "behave" himself. If they really did have antennae for someone's psychological wellbeing they should have already sent him packing back to Florida.

"It doesn't matter to Grace," Creed confessed. "But it helps me to know as much about the situation as possible. For instance, if you suspect it's a crime of passion the body might not be hidden or buried as deep."

"That makes sense."

"How many others do you think there are?" Now Creed just wanted to cut to the chase.

"We really don't know. There might be a dozen or there might not be any more than what we've found."

The details that helped Creed and Grace weren't necessarily the same ones that law enforcement was interested in. And sometimes it was better to *not* know everything law enforcement suspected, or even what their expectations were.

Creed knew Hannah had also gone over with Agent Alonzo what Creed and Grace could offer, what they would do, and what that meant. She always spelled it out before she ever accepted an assignment so that there were no misperceptions, no misunderstandings, and so the client knew there were no guarantees. At least no family members were here. Creed hated when the officials allowed family to wait somewhere in clear sight.

"If you can't tell me the gender, can you give me an idea of how old the remains were in the garbage bag?" Creed asked.

"About three weeks."

"And the skull and bones? What kind of shape were they in?"

"There wasn't any flesh. No residue of decomp. They definitely had been in the ground for a while. This property has been vacant for almost ten years. We don't know if the killer has had access to it for that long, but we can't discount it either."

Creed pulled a GPS monitor out of his pack and turned it on. He started tapping into the gadget's memory some baselines to define the search corridor. It was a large area, and overwhelming if the woods behind the property were to be a part of the grid.

"I imagine it must make a difference," Agent Tully continued when Creed had no more questions, "whether a body's been buried a couple months or a couple of years."

"Grace has a remarkable ability to work through multiple targets, but yeah, it can be difficult if those targets are in different stages of decay. Cadaver scent is not one single scent. There's a whole range of scents that the body gives off at different stages. And there are a variety of things—as you know—that affect decomp. For instance, how deep the body is buried. If it's enclosed in a garbage bag or just underneath the dirt. The composition of the soil and what the air exchange might be. When we're searching in water, it makes a difference how warm or cold the water is."

Creed glanced at the agent and realized he may have given him too much information to decipher. He found that often law enforcement just wanted him to find the dead bodies. They didn't care how it was done. As far as they were concerned it was magic. If he tried to explain the science of it, he usually lost them.

"Your dog can smell a body underwater?"

Creed smiled, pleased that Agent Tully appeared fascinated rather than lost.

"The scents can carry up to the surface," he told him. "If you teach a dog to recognize certain scents, the dog doesn't care whether it's underground, under water, or up in a tree."

Suddenly Creed heard Agent O'Dell calling to Grace. He turned to see the agent trying to get the dog to come back to her side. He also saw Grace, nose in the air, her ears pricked forward. She was circling and her tail stood straight up, wagging rapidly.

Grace had started without him.

CHAPTER 30

"Do you keep her off lead?" Maggie asked. "Doesn't she need a collar or leash? Something for you to keep track of her?"

She hated that she sounded out of breath, that she felt like she had done something wrong. Maybe she shouldn't have thrown the dog's toy so far.

"She's okay. We don't use collars or leashes for free range. I don't like to risk that she'll get tangled up in the brush. Especially if we get separated."

Maggie had picked up Grace's pink elephant and didn't realize until now that she was squeezing it in her fisted hand.

Creed didn't seem angry or worried. He'd come over to Grace and without any urgency in his voice simply told her, "Show me."

The dog had been straining, almost as if she had been on a leash, struggling to leave Maggie but knowing she wasn't allowed. She kept circling farther and farther away until Creed came over and gave her the command.

Maggie watched him tap coordinates into a handheld GPS. He kept an eye on Grace and followed her, but he wasn't in a hurry. He walked as Grace trotted. Maggie and Tully stayed a couple of steps behind.

"Why does she keep circling?" Tully asked in almost a whisper, as if afraid to interrupt the process.

"She's in the scent cone. Barriers can create secondary scent pools, even secondary scent cones. Like I told you before, there're a number of reasons she might not be able to zero in on the primary scent yet."

"Barriers?" Maggie said and just then noticed that despite Grace's erratic circling, she was headed for the opened doorway of the barn.

"If there are other bones scattered or even . . ." Creed hesitated. "Is there any possibility of pieces buried in several spots?"

Maggie shot a look at Tully. Creed noticed.

"The body in the garbage bag was decapitated," Tully told him. "The head was in a separate bag, but close by. Practically on top of the other bag."

Maggie realized it was ridiculous for them to keep information from Creed. It would only impede the search. This wasn't like holding back details to see if Grace was the real deal, like some initiation rite for her to prove something to them.

"We do have information that there could be a body buried in the barn."

Grace was already at the doorway but she paused and looked back at Creed, waiting for his permission to enter.

"What's the floor like in there?" he asked as he pulled a rod out of his backpack and started unfolding it until it became a spear with sharp prongs at one end.

"Hard dirt," Maggie answered, and Tully raised an eyebrow, surprised that she knew. "I checked," she said to Tully. "It looks like there's old straw scattered and matted on top."

"Any chance the place is booby trapped?"

"Holy crap," Tully muttered. "We didn't really think about that."

Neither of them had considered it when they recklessly unlatched and swung open the doors earlier.

"If it's any consolation," Maggie said, "The house wasn't."

The three of them stood silently as Grace wagged and whined, excited and ready to enter.

Finally Creed said, "You two stay right here. I'll make Grace sit outside until I'm sure it's safe."

"We'll check it out with you," Maggie said, looking at Tully. They had taken over this crime scene. It was theirs to protect.

"Maggie's right. This site, including the barn, is our responsibility." And Tully started leading the way.

"Actually it'll be easier if I go in alone," Creed said, walking along with the two of them.

They kept a slow steady pace and Maggie suddenly felt conscious of every step, of what could be underfoot.

"We train bomb dogs, too," Creed continued, "for law enforcement, the military. Even Homeland Security. I have an idea of what to look for."

"An idea doesn't sound convincing," Tully said.

Ten feet away from the open barn doors Creed stepped ahead, turned, and stood in front of them as if to make his case.

"It's not going do much good if all three of us get blown up. Seriously, I'm not questioning your authority or jurisdiction. I'm just saying I have a better idea of what to look for if the place is rigged."

Creed's eyes went from Tully to Maggie, back to Tully. If he were being cocky this would be easier, but he was sincere. He made it sound like this was just another part of his job. But Maggie didn't like it. She was more comfortable taking a risk than letting someone else do it. Most of all, she hated that she and Tully hadn't thought about this killer ambushing them. After all, he'd left them a map. They had gone by the premise that he simply wanted to show off his talent and his dumping ground. But they knew plenty of killers who enjoyed setting up his pursuers, of besting them just to make them squirm, or worse—to watch them die.

She found herself looking around the property again, glancing back at the house, studying the windows and watching for movement. Beyond the grove of trees she couldn't even see the deputies Sheriff Uniss had stationed. It would be easy for someone to hole up in one of the other buildings and keep an eye on them without ever being detected.

"Maybe we should call in experts to check all the buildings," she said to Tully.

"That construction crew was ripping down and digging up stuff all last week," Tully said, but now he was looking around, too. "Chances are pretty slim that he'd rig one structure and none of the others."

"It's probably fine," Creed said. "I'm always overly cautious. But I need to protect my dogs from as many unforeseen hazards as possible. Sometimes farmers put down rat traps. So let me just do a check."

Maggie could feel Tully's eyes on her. She knew he'd made his decision to let Creed go ahead but he wouldn't say so unless they were in agreement. Maggie was watching Creed, waiting for him to meet her eyes. When he did, he didn't blink. There was an intensity, a maturity beyond his young age, but there was something else—a reckless disregard for his own safety. That realization jolted her. Usually in risky situations she was used to seeing the kick of adrenaline, sometimes a healthy dose of fear or passion.

But in Ryder Creed's eyes Maggie saw a hint of resolve, that if he happened to get blown up in the next few minutes, so be it.

She hated that the two men had put her in this position. She wanted to believe that Tully was right. If the killer had wanted to blow them up he'd already had a half dozen chances. Then she thought about him planting the orange socks. He wanted his handiwork to be found, not destroyed, not blown up.

Without taking her eyes away from him, she said to Creed, "If you see anything at all that doesn't look right you back out immediately and we get the experts."

"Absolutely," he agreed.

He started to turn but stopped as if he'd forgotten something. He dug in his jeans pocket and handed his Jeep keys to Tully.

"Just in case," he said with that subtle smile that hitched up the corner of his mouth and painfully reminded Maggie how right she was about what she had seen in his eyes. And it also surprised her how much she didn't want something bad to happen to this man.

They watched him instruct a wiggling, excited Grace to sit outside the open doorway. Then he went inside holding the collapsible rod-turned-into-spear.

"We've got nothing that says this killer would set up booby traps, do we?" Tully asked, still needing reassurance.

"He strung up Zach Lester's intestines in a tree. He left us a map." Maggie was thinking her way through it. "But the orange socks," she told him, "he put them on a victim who was already dead just for our benefit. If there's another body inside, I'm hoping he wants us to find it and not join it."

She stared at the barn's doorway and only then did she realize that she had unsnapped her holster and her right hand was now inside her jacket, gripping her revolver.

CHAPTER 31

Noah's mother had brought him a clean set of clothes. The detectives had confiscated his overnight bag with Ethan's car and everything else that was inside. It had been towed in to their crime lab. He was told that they were going through it right now, examining every single thing for clues. Detective Lopez told Noah this in a tone that sounded like a threat. But Noah knew they wouldn't find anything that would tell them what had happened. No one would believe what had happened. In the light of day, Noah wasn't even sure he believed what had happened.

When he told them that Ethan was dead, his mother had gasped but Detective Lopez and his father looked at him like he was either lying or delirious. Now they talked around him like he wasn't there. People came and went, in and out of the hospital room.

The doctor was the only one who had spoken to Noah without looking at him as though he were crazy. When he came to examine Noah he had been kind and gentle with him, and Noah wanted to tell him about the voices in his head. Did the doctor have anything he could give him? Any medication that would help. Maybe Noah should have complained. Maybe then the doctor wouldn't have dismissed him from the hospital.

Detective Lopez told Noah he was lucky. That for now he was sending him home with his parents instead of holding him in a jail cell. Noah wanted to tell the detective that he would be safer in a jail cell. That he didn't want to go home with his parents. He needed to tell them that the madman had taken his driver's license. That he knew his home address—his parents' home address.

But how could Noah explain when he had promised the killer he wouldn't tell anything about what had happened?

"What would they all think?" Noah could still hear the madman's voice. *"What would your parents say if they knew you begged me to kill your friend first?"*

Noah glanced around the room, making sure no one else could hear the voice, too. That's how convincing it was inside his head. But no one else seemed to notice. Not his father or Detective Lopez as they talked in hushed tones right outside the door. Not the nurse or his mother as they went over his dismissal papers.

Yet that voice sounded so real. And so did Ethan's screams.

Don't think about it. Stop thinking about any of it. Just stop it!

This time when he looked up, the others were all staring at him and Noah realized immediately that he had spoken some of the words out loud, again. He was still sitting on the corner of the bed but he turned his back to them and continued putting on his shirt as if he were okay, as if he hadn't just shouted strange things.

He concentrated, instead, on how good the shirt smelled. Fresh out of his mother's dryer, it felt soft against his battered skin. Next he tried to pull his socks on. His ankle wasn't broken—thank goodness. The swelling had gone down but his entire foot was black and blue.

"Take off your shoes," he heard the madman say. This time he kept his head down and fought the instinct, the urgency of his eyes wanting to dart around.

"What are you willing to do?" The voice wouldn't shut off. *"What are you willing to do to survive?"*

Noah bit his lip and tried to ignore the voice. He worked the sock up over his ankle, wincing from the pain. This was nothing, he told himself. Then he saw blood drip down. He saw the bright red fall onto the white bedsheet and panic fluttered inside his stomach. A second drop joined it before he realized it was his own. He was biting his lip so hard he had made it bleed.

There was a commotion in the hallway and Noah turned. A uniformed officer had joined Detective Lopez. They were looking at something, trying to keep it away from Noah's father.

Then suddenly he heard his father say, "Oh my dear God!"

And Noah felt the panic surge from his stomach to his heart and lungs. He didn't want to know what had shocked his father. But he saw Detective Lopez look at him and even from the doorway Noah could sense the detective's repulsion and his anger.

He saw Detective Lopez grab the item out of the officer's hand. It was something inside a plastic ziplock bag. He marched into the room to stand in front of Noah.

"They found this inside your friend's trunk," Detective Lopez said. "All neat and tucked into a plastic bag. What kind of sick game are you playing?"

He held the plastic bag up for Noah and everyone else in the room to see.

Noah heard his father tell his mother, "Don't look at it." Then he instructed Noah, "Don't answer that, Noah. Detective Lopez, my son will not be answering any more questions without his attorney present."

Noah stared at the blood-stained sheet of paper that filled the plastic bag. The numbers written on it looked like a phone number. There was only one other thing in the plastic bag and that was what Noah's father had reacted to. Without needing to look closely, Noah knew exactly what it was. At the bottom of the bag was Ethan's severed index finger.

CHAPTER 32

The minutes felt excruciatingly long to Maggie but every one that went by without an explosion was a relief. Then suddenly without warning Ryder Creed emerged from the barn. He gave them a thumbs-up and a smile, then immediately went to Grace. The dog was still sitting, obviously trained to do so until Creed gave the release command, but her entire hind end was wagging. Creed tapped his right open palm to his chest like he was tapping his heart and Grace came rushing to him.

"I checked all doors and gates, glanced in the stalls and the hayloft," he told them, brushing cobwebs from his hair. "I think we're good to go."

Then to Grace, he said, "Go find." And the dog scampered into the barn, nose in the air.

Maggie found the search fascinating. Her own dogs had come into her life unexpectedly. Harvey, a white Lab, had belonged to a neighbor whom Maggie had never met. The woman had been brutally taken from her home despite Harvey's bloodied effort to protect her. Jake, a black German shepherd, had rescued Maggie in the Sandhills of Nebraska. He'd been a stray, refusing to belong to anyone—even to Maggie when she first brought him into her home, digging his way out of the sanctuary she thought she was providing. The two dogs continued to teach her hard lessons about herself, about trust, about life. But she'd never seen a team, dog and master, work so closely together, so in sync, each recognizing the other's movements, reactions, and expectations.

She and Tully stayed in the corner where they wouldn't be in the way. They watched while Creed used the spearlike rod to pierce the dirt of the barn's floor. He called it "venting" and explained that poking holes into the hard-packed dirt allowed air to circulate and help release any scents, making it easier for Grace. The dog didn't seem to need it. With her nose in the air she walked the barn like she was breaking up the area into a grid. She didn't rush around erratically, but instead went up and down, along the side, and worked back and forth in almost perfect parallel lines.

With each sweep Grace appeared to get more and more animated. At one point she stopped and pawed at the straw and dirt. She sniffed it again, turned, and urinated on the spot. Then she moved on.

Creed had been right beside her. He bent down to take a closer look and said to Maggie and Tully, "Dead mouse."

"You think that's all she's been smelling?" Tully asked.

"No, she's trained for human remains."

"But maybe this confused her?" This time Tully sounded like he thought this was all a waste of time.

"Dead animals are just a distraction. That's why she peed on it. It's her way of marking over that scent."

And Grace had, indeed, moved on. Maggie noticed her breathing was more rapid. Her ears pricked forward. Suddenly her tail went straight out and started wagging. She was scratching under one of the stall doors. There were three stalls side by side at the back of the barn. The wooden doors didn't come all the way to the floor, leaving about three inches. The doors were about chest-high, making it difficult to see into the stalls.

Creed shot a nervous look at Maggie and Tully.

"I checked the doors but I didn't go into the stalls."

To Grace, he said, "Just a minute, girl," and he ran a hand over the hinges, rechecked the latch, and leaned over the top of the door to look inside the stall.

In the meantime, Grace had become more animated, her nose up and sniffing. She was impatient, hackles raised and ready. But when Creed pulled up the latch and opened the stall door, the dog hesitated. She took a few steps in and backed out. Then she turned and looked up at Creed.

The look actually sent a chill down Maggie's back. The dog stared directly into her master's eyes and held that stance like she was telling him, "Here's what we've been looking for."

"Good girl, Grace." Without looking away, Creed put out his hand in Maggie's direction and said, "Could I have the elephant, please?"

At first Maggie had no idea what he was talking about. Then she realized she still had Grace's pink toy gripped in her left hand. She walked over slowly and gently placed the elephant in Creed's outstretched hand. He, in turn, held it up for Grace to see. She immediately relaxed, started wagging again, only not at the frantic pace as moments earlier. She was back to being a dog wanting to have her reward.

"Good girl, Grace," Creed said again and tossed her the toy.

Grace caught it, making it squeak. Maggie couldn't help thinking how contradictory that playful sound seemed after finding what could be yet another grave.

Creed let Grace romp around but he didn't attempt to enter the stall. Finally he backed away from the open stall door and looked at Maggie and Tully.

"I'm not trained to be part of the dig," he told them.

Tully still didn't look convinced that there was anything to be dug up. Maggie walked over to take a look. The area inside was about ten feet wide by ten feet deep. From what she could see in the dim light, the floor looked no different from that in the rest of the barn. She couldn't see any mounds or depressions in the dirt. The straw on top matched the straw in the rest of the barn and it didn't look as though it had been disturbed. There was no trace, no hint of blood or residue, from a putrefied corpse. The wooden trough had been left filled up and covered with an old horse blanket. The five-gallon metal bucket beside it had a dusty lid still tightly in place.

She glanced behind her and saw that Creed had taken Grace out of the barn. She could see him tossing the pink elephant and Grace racing after it. Tully had stayed on the other side of the barn but he had his cell phone to his ear now. He was telling someone—most likely the sheriff—to bring a digging crew. Even as he explained the situation she could hear the skepticism in his voice despite his best effort to disguise it.

Maggie stepped farther into the stall and wondered if Grace could be mistaken. Now inside, she could smell a strong rancid odor that she suspected was horse manure. Then she remembered what Creed had said when Grace had found the dead mouse. Any other scent was a mere distraction. Grace had been trained to find human remains, not dead animals and certainly not animal manure. Just then Maggie realized what she was smelling.

Her eyes darted to the bucket. Five gallons, metal, and sealed.

The smell couldn't be coming from it and yet just the thought of what could be inside made her mouth go dry and her stomach do a flip.

She pulled a pair of latex gloves out of her jacket pocket and slipped them on as she approached the wooden trough. With an index finger she poked the middle of the heap under the thick wool blanket.

Something solid. Definitely not horse feed.

She found a corner of the blanket and started to peel it back but stopped when it resisted and sounded like separating Velcro. That small effort had already leaked more of the rancid odor.

Maggie glanced over her shoulder again. Tully was still on the phone. Creed and Grace were out far enough that the squeaky sounds were in the distance.

She tugged at the corner of the wool blanket again, wincing at the sound and smell but continuing, slowly, inch by inch. The putrefied flesh had melted into the weave of the blanket and as she pulled it back, she was also pulling away a layer of skin. The thick wool had attempted to mummify the body, but peeling it off had started to release the gases.

Maggie had to step away. Her pulse had begun racing. She needed to get her bearings. She turned and took a few gulps of air from outside the stall. It helped to settle her nerves. Then she went back to work. Again, carefully and slowly, she teased the wool away until she identified a forearm. That was enough. She was certain it was a dead body. She would leave it for the forensic investigators.

Before she stepped away, she saw bright red and blue. Because she had peeled away a layer of skin the tattoo had become even brighter. She knew that was true of tattoos since the ink pooled down below the top layer of skin. They were valuable in IDing bodies. It made sense *not* to wait. She was this close already. At least she could take a look at it.

She tugged the wool away until she could see the entire image—an eagle head with piercing eyes over a prominent beak. Stenciled above on two lines was STURGIS 2000.

Maggie stopped. Stood back.

The son of a bitch was telling the truth.

Otis P. Dodd was right about there being a body in the barn. And it looked like he was right about it being a tattooed biker.

CHAPTER 33

By late afternoon the quiet farmstead was no longer quiet. Maggie's and Tully's roles were quickly reduced to traffic control and site management. The crime scene techs, Janet, Matt, and Ryan, had arrived again from Omaha with their mobile lab. Agent Alonzo had told them that an FBI agent from the Omaha field office would also be making his way up, but so far they hadn't seen or heard from him.

Grace had alerted to five other sites: one behind an old laundry house, another behind the barn, and three in the woods. Creed had given her a rest after each find, along with her pink elephant and some water. They were walking the pasture now but hadn't gotten any more hits in the last hour. Creed insisted this would be their last grid of the property.

Sheriff Uniss had brought an anthropology professor from a nearby university to help direct his deputies on how to dig the places that Grace had alerted. Creed had warned them that the three in the woods could be surrounded by what he called secondary scatter; in other words, pieces of the primary targets. He had marked the primary not only according to Grace's alerts, but also to his visual observations, pointing out one spot in particular where the wild grasses were only half as tall as those surrounding it.

Maggie didn't envy the digging crew. There were at least a dozen of Creed's fluorescent flags telegraphing sites and some were in hard to reach areas, way off the beaten path.

The sheriff had sent one of his men to fetch sandwiches for everyone. Maggie and Tully were only getting to theirs. Tully went to get them some bottled waters and sodas while Maggie found them a quiet place at an old picnic table.

The sun wasn't quite as warm today but it was another beautiful day, and Maggie was struck by the absurdity—such beauty alongside the macabre. Watching Grace had reminded Maggie of her dogs and she pulled out her cell phone. She pressed the contact number before thinking what time it was or what she might be interrupting. She heard it ring only twice, then was sent to voice mail. She listened to Benjamin Platt's smooth, deep voice ask her to leave a message at the beep.

"Hey, it's Maggie," she said. "Just checking on my boys. Looks like we'll be stuck here for a few days. I'll try and catch you later. Bye."

It seemed too casual, almost too abrupt. This was a man she had considered having a serious relationship with only a few months ago. They had become friends so quickly that the next step seemed not just natural, but inevitable. Then they both put the skids on. No, that wasn't true—Maggie put the skids on. Ben wanted something more permanent. He wanted a family. And kids. She knew he still hurt deeply from losing his little girl despite it being almost five years ago. But Maggie wasn't sure she'd be able to replace the void Allie's death had left in Ben's heart and in his life. And she wasn't sure she wanted children.

"I snagged the last Diet Pepsis," Tully said, coming back with sodas in his hands and bottled waters sticking out from each of his jacket pockets.

He popped the tabs while Maggie spread out napkins and unwrapped the sandwiches. There was a certain rhythm to their daily rituals, a sure sign they had been spending a lot of time together.

"Don't forget to take your antibiotic," she told him. "And drink water with it. Lots of water." She uncapped and slid a bottle in front of him.

"I actually feel better today."

"You still have to take it."

"You've been talking to Gwen." But he was already digging the plastic bag with the pills out of his trousers pocket. "I hate that she's going back to talk to Dodd. I don't care if she insists he's harmless. I just don't like her going back there."

"Otis is the only one who can tell us who this killer is."

"Do you think his name really is Jack?"

"Doubtful." She took a bite. The lunch deputy had done good—turkey, provolone, and spicy mustard.

"Alonzo said that the Sturgis Motorcycle Rally was in August," Tully said. "Sturgis, South Dakota, is about six to seven hours away from here. I-29 north then I-90 west. Alonzo also said attendance was around a half million. Can you believe that?"

Maggie shook her head. "August seems too long ago." She pointed to his discarded wrappings. "Aren't you going to eat your pickle?"

"Knock yourself out." He slid the pickle atop the waxed paper to her.

"Just because he was one of the faithful doesn't mean that's when Jack got a hold of him."

"How long ago do you think?"

"The wool blanket makes it tough to say."

"He didn't even bother to bury this one. Is he just getting sloppy?"

The CSU tech, Ryan, came out of the barn carrying the metal bucket. The picnic table was beside the house about a hundred feet away. When he noticed Maggie, he pointed to the bucket and gave an exaggerated nod, then continued to the mobile lab parked next to the barn.

"What was that about?" Tully asked.

"I told him our biker friend's head might be in the bucket. Guess I was right."

"Jack's starting to be very predictable."

Maggie's cell phone rang. She didn't recognize the number or the 785 area code.

"This is Maggie O'Dell."

"Ms. O'Dell, my name is Lieutenant Detective Lopez. I'm with the Riley County Police Department in Manhattan, Kansas. Can you please tell me who you are and what the hell your phone number is doing in a plastic bag alongside a missing college student's finger?"

CHAPTER 34

"Just when we thought this scavenger hunt couldn't get any stranger," Tully had told Maggie as they started yet another road trip.

"It might not have anything to do with our guy Jack."

"Your guy Jack," Tully corrected her.

Detective Lopez had shared very little, though he seemed to welcome Maggie's offer of assistance. Actually, Maggie thought the man sounded relieved. What he had told them was that a nineteen-year-old college student named Ethan Ames was still missing. A search team had scoured the woods surrounding the rest area where he had vanished. His friend Noah Waters, who had been with him, was only babbling what amounted to nonsense. But because Detective Lopez believed the boy might be involved in his friend's disappearance, the father refused to let him answer their questions without a lawyer.

Lopez explained that Maggie's cell phone number had been scribbled on a piece of paper and enclosed in a plastic ziplock bag. Also in the bag was what they believed to be the right index finger of Ethan Ames. They had found it when processing the trunk of the teenager's car. The car had been confiscated from the rest area.

The last thing the detective said to Maggie before ending their phone conversation was, "So is this some crazy satanic cult?"

Maggie and Tully had left the Iowa farmstead in the hands of a very young field agent from the Omaha FBI office and the CSU techs. The drive from Sioux City, Iowa, to Manhattan, Kansas, was five to six hours. Maggie took over driving the last half when she noticed Tully fading. They stopped only twice: once for gas and coffee and again for more coffee and to use the restroom. Each time they pulled off the interstate to a truck plaza, Maggie found herself watching and listening and searching.

It was late and the last 136 miles from Lincoln, Nebraska, was four-lane highway, then two-lane instead of interstate. Lots of small towns slowing them down and long, dark stretches of blacktop lit only by the moon and their headlights. There were few other vehicles on the road.

By the time they entered Manhattan, Kansas, and passed by the university's campus, both of them were bleary-eyed and exhausted.

Detective Lopez had reserved two rooms for them at the Holiday Inn. They were to meet him in the morning. Because Ethan Ames was still missing, Creed had agreed to join them the next day. Grace was trained for live search and rescue as well. However, Creed insisted that Grace rest after her busy day. They had been on the road for eighteen hours before arriving in Iowa. He admitted that he needed the sleep, too. But he promised to make the drive early the next morning and meet them in Manhattan.

Maggie knew they had to be totally exhausted for Tully to get excited about their hotel. But these rooms were luxurious by their most recent standards. Best of all, they had adjoining rooms at the end of the hallway on the third floor.

Immediately they opened the connecting doors between their rooms. The configuration of the walls still left them a great deal of privacy. They couldn't see into each other's rooms or beyond the entryway but they could talk and go back and forth.

"They have room service until midnight." Tully came into her room with the hotel's menu along with his laptop computer.

"Tully, it's almost midnight now." She ignored him and started unpacking her nightshirt and toiletries.

"All we had were those sandwiches and that was almost ten hours ago. You gotta take a look. Their room service menu is from Houlihan's. When we were checking in I noticed the restaurant is connected to the lobby."

He left the menu on her bed while he set his computer on her desk and started punching keys. Maybe adjoining rooms weren't such a good idea. They had another long day ahead of them and she was wiped out.

"Alonzo sent me a satellite photo of the rest area."

Maggie glanced over as it came up and filled his computer screen. The last miles of driving she had noticed the increased elevation on their SUV's GPS as well as a glimpse of the limestone bluffs. Much of the landscape was covered with evergreens and hardwoods in full bloom.

When she didn't respond, Tully picked up the menu from the corner of the bed and said, "Real food. Not truck stop burgers or deli sandwiches. They have sliders and something called chicken avocado eggrolls."

"Okay, now you have my attention," she joked while her eyes stayed on the computer screen.

Tully obviously had gotten his second wind. Of course he had—she was the one who had driven the last three hours. But now that they were here Tully was ready to get to work.

"Lopez believes these two teenagers did something to each other," Maggie said. "He thinks it may have started out as a game and gotten out of hand."

"And one of them cuts the other's finger off?"

"He told me Manhattan, Kansas, is a university town. Said he's seen stranger things."

"Well, we both know that's true. Kids are capable of doing stupid and cruel things to each other. That's one of the reasons I'd like to lock Emma up in her room until she's thirty."

Tully's daughter was a college freshman. Since she was fourteen, he'd raised her alone, with very little help from Emma's mother.

"He thinks because Noah won't talk that he must be guilty of something."

"But you think his friend was killed by our guy?" Tully asked.

He tapped a couple of keys and zoomed the photo in on the rest area. Thick canopies of trees. Rock ledges. Acres and acres of both, surrounding the small brick building and parking lots.

"One kid missing," Tully said. "Probably dead. But a survivor. We've seen what Jack can do—letting someone get away doesn't quite fit his MO. Just doesn't sound right."

"How do we explain my cell phone number?"

"That part does sound like him. So what's your gut instinct?"

Maggie thought about it. She rubbed at the exhaustion in her eyes. Unfortunately, it wasn't difficult to get her cell phone number. It could be some prank not even related to Jack, their highway killer. But ever since Tully compared this killer's obsession with her to that of Albert Stucky, her anxiety had been turned up a notch.

If she really thought about it, this guy had been keeping tabs on her for at least a month. He had physically stalked her back in the District. Now here they were halfway across the country, brought here by his directive. He was playing them, toying with them, showing off what he was capable of doing.

"It's him," Maggie finally said. "But I think he may have messed up this time."

"How's that?"

"Noah Waters can tell us what he looks like."

THURSDAY, MARCH 21

CHAPTER 35

MANHATTAN, KANSAS

Noah tried not to meet the eyes of the woman sitting across from him in his parents' living room. Detective Lopez had introduced her as Agent O'Dell with the FBI. Introduced her and then left.

Oh God . . . not the FBI!

Noah didn't hear half of what the detective had said after that because the panic had begun thumping in his chest.

He had gotten very little sleep last night. Up in his old bedroom the windows rattled when there was no wind. At one point he swore he heard something—or someone—scratching at the glass. His bedroom was on the second floor with no tree close enough to scrape against his window or the house. And certainly not close enough to cast the shadows that had woken him.

That's not true.

It wasn't the shadows or the scratching that had woken him. It was Ethan's screams.

"Detective Lopez told me what happened," the agent was saying.

Noah almost laughed. His nerves were raw. His emotions played to extremes. But it was funny—how could the detective tell her anything when Noah had told him nothing? He glanced at the woman. Was she trying to trick him? He realized she was studying him. Would she be able to see what he couldn't tell?

She was younger than his mother and reminded him of his English professor. He liked Ms. Gilbert. But what would she think of him if she found out what he'd done?

"We need your help," the FBI agent said. "We need to find your friend Ethan."

He shook his head. It wouldn't do any good. But he didn't say anything.

"Even if Ethan's dead," she added as if she could read his mind.

That got Noah's attention and he stared at her, looking directly into her eyes for as long as he could stand it. Then he glanced away, let his eyes flick back and forth from her face to the new painting his mother had hung over their mantel. Horses, wild horses. His mother had decorated their home with sculptures and paintings, many of them—he only now noticed—of animals or birds fleeing.

"Detective Lopez seems to think you and Ethan were involved in a satanic ritual of some sort."

This time Noah did laugh out loud, a nervous sputter that he quickly shut down. The madman who had attacked him and Ethan was definitely some kind of Satan.

"*What are you willing to do?*" Noah could still hear the man's voice. He put his head down, chin to his chest. He resisted the urge to look behind him.

Don't think about it. Stop thinking about it. I won't tell. I promise I won't tell.

Too late. He could smell urine and vomit and blood. The scent so strong that he pulled up his hands to look and make sure they didn't still have bloodstains. Without warning he could hear bones snap, flesh being cut. Suddenly he was nauseated. He could already taste bile.

"One bite and I'll let you go."

Noah started gagging. His eyes shot up to the FBI woman's as he bolted for the closest bathroom.

CHAPTER 36

- - - - - - - - - - - - - - - - - - -

Maggie waited patiently. From where she sat she could hear Noah vomiting in the bathroom. She hadn't even started her interview. The teenager was obviously experiencing post-traumatic shock.

What Detective Lopez had labeled as guilt ran much deeper and was much more disturbing. He thought it was Noah's guilt that caused this erratic and uncooperative behavior. Maggie was quickly beginning to question whether it wasn't what Noah had done, but what he had seen.

He seemed surprised to find her where he had left her when he came out of the bathroom. Embarrassment flushed his cheeks. However, he took his seat on the sofa across from her.

She had convinced Tully to let her interview the boy alone. Whatever he had been through deserved a softer approach than Detective Lopez's. But time wasn't on their side. It was over forty-eight hours. If there was the slightest chance that Ethan was still alive, he was losing blood. The window of opportunity was rapidly closing. If Jack had attacked these two teenagers two nights ago then he could still be in the area. But wouldn't be for long.

"Noah, let me tell you about a case I'm working on."

His eyes met hers and stayed put this time. She thought she saw relief in his face but the distrust hadn't been dislodged.

"My partner and I have been tracking a serial killer."

He looked surprised and worried. She could see that he hadn't considered the madman who had attacked him could be a serial killer.

"We know he gets his victims from truck stops and interstate rest areas."

Again she paused, giving him time to take it all in. She kept her tone gentle and conversational while she examined his face and his mannerisms and his posture. His hands were in his lap. Earlier they had flexed almost constantly. Now one was a tight fist held inside the other's palm.

"We think he takes advantage of them. Plays on his victims' vulnerabilities. Perhaps the person's car has stalled. Maybe they've run out of gas and are stranded for one reason or another. These are places where travelers let down their guard. They're tired. Sometimes they've been on the road for hours, maybe days. It's late at night. All they want to do is use the restroom, get a soda, something to snack on before they get back on the road again. That's probably why you and Ethan stopped, right?"

He nodded. "Ethan had to pee." His eyes darted away for a second or two. "We were almost home."

"You were coming home from college? Spring break."

Another nod.

"Where do you go to school?"

"University of Missouri."

"Mizzou Tigers."

He looked surprised but pleased. It was the first genuine feeling he allowed her to see.

"That's right."

"I love college football," Maggie said. "Do you play?"

"Naw."

"You didn't want to go to K-State?"

"Didn't want to stay at home."

The statement delivered, Maggie thought, exactly like a regular teenager.

"This killer," he said, without prompting. "How many people has he killed?"

"We've found five," Maggie said, continuing to keep her tone gentle. She had him talking. "We know there are more."

His eyes flashed. He seemed surprised by the number. His brow furrowed as though he was trying to remember, or maybe trying *not* to remember. Detective Lopez had told them that Noah had been found wearing only his underwear and had been covered with blood. Most of it not his own.

Then in a whisper that Maggie could barely hear, Noah asked, "What did he do to them?"

She hesitated but only for a second or two before she said, "Probably the same things he did to Ethan."

CHAPTER 37

Gwen hated being back at the prison. This time AD Kunze tried to abbreviate the full-body search that Warden Demarcus ordered. Demarcus knew he had something they wanted or they wouldn't be back here this soon. He had the upper hand and he was going to use it to his full extent. For his effort, Kunze ended up getting groped as well.

This time, however, Gwen had worn sensible shoes and her control-top pantyhose again, along with what she called her best "old lady" bra. Still, the guard managed to grope and paw, not even pretending that any of it was accidental.

As soon as Otis sat down across from her—even as the guard finished clasping his shackles to the floor—Gwen noticed the bruise on Otis's face. It looked fresh and swollen, deep purple, the size of a golf ball above his left temple. Maybe larger because part of it blended into his sideburn.

She waited for the guard to leave.

"How did you get that bruise?"

"Oh this?" Otis smiled, uncharacteristically wide and toothy, his signal that he wasn't going to tell. His fingertips brushed over the area. "That's just a love tap."

She saw his eyes dart over to the wall of tinted glass that kept Kunze and Demarcus invisible as they sat and watched and listened.

Had Demarcus struck a prisoner? No, he probably wouldn't have done it himself. Just like his full-body searches, he would have had one of his men do it. But why? She tried to remember what Otis may have said the last time. Of course, it might not have been related to her visit. It could have been something else. Some other disciplinary action that had been well deserved.

"I hoped you'd come back," Otis said.

He was watching her. His lopsided grin firmly in place. He was sitting back with his arms crossed—that is, crossed in an awkward manner because of the shackle and short length of chain. Again, he reminded her of an overgrown teenager, uncomfortable and not knowing what to do with his hands.

Then without waiting for her to speak, he said, "You found something." A statement, not a question.

"Yes." It was silly to say anything else.

"And now you believe me." His tongue flicked over his lips. He was pleased.

"Yes."

His face lit up like a little boy's on Christmas morning. Obviously pleased, so much so that even the crow's-feet at the corners of his eyes smiled.

"I'm hoping," she continued slowly, deliberately, "that you'll share with me more of what Jack told you."

"Oh, I don't know," he said, then paused, head now tilted, watching her, gauging her body language. He still didn't trust her. "Why would I wanna do that?"

She wondered the same thing. Why would he want to share?

If he had wanted a deal to reduce his sentence or one that gave him any perks, he would have brought it up last month when he shared the first information about the victim in the culvert with the orange socks.

Gwen suspected Otis had shared Jack's stories with her and with the news reporter last month simply because he enjoyed the attention. Even he had pronounced himself a "powermaniac." She knew that arsonists—especially serial arsonists like Otis—set fires not just because of the power they felt through destruction but also the power they gained from the attention. But now he was looking at her expectantly, like there was something tangible he wanted from her.

"Depending on what else you offer," she said, "I would certainly consider personally testifying to your parole board about how you've helped us."

She had absolutely no authority to make that offer and she imagined Kunze jumping out of his chair and screaming at her through the soundproof wall. Whatever the repercussions, she saw immediately that the payoff would be worth it.

There was something that swept across Otis's face, an emotion so strong he couldn't hide it behind one of his silly grins. Gwen recognized that they were his coping mechanism, an internal leveler that he used even when they didn't match his words or moods. But in the seconds that followed Gwen's offer, Otis slipped. His eyes flashed disbelief. The smile waned—but just for a couple of seconds, at most. And in that brief momentary lapse, Gwen saw that Otis P. Dodd was surprised—maybe "flabbergasted" was a better word—that someone like her would sincerely offer to speak on his behalf.

"You'd do that?" The smile returned, along with the poke of the tongue.

Finally he sat up and leaned forward, but only slightly. Trust was such a delicate thing, so fragile, not easily earned and harder to repair.

"If you provide us with more information that helps us find Jack, yes, I would do that."

"Find Jack?"

He slipped back in his seat. He hadn't seen that one coming and he shook his head as if she had sucker-punched him.

So much for trust. She had shattered it before she could claim it.

"Perhaps you can help me understand him. You know, learn about him and why he does what he does."

Would he notice how much she was backtracking? If they wanted someone who was good at sucking up to criminals they should have hired a hostage negotiator. She never pretended to understand how to relate to the criminal mind even as she studied it and hoped to dissect it.

"Maybe I will tell you about Jack just because I like your company. And I think you're pretty."

Her turn—she had not seen that one coming. It was definitely becoming a battle of wits. And Otis was certainly not a dim one.

"You like older women?" She produced a laugh to make it sound like she thought he was putting her on.

"Why now, you can't be a day past what's old enough for me."

It sounded sweet and charming and only reinforced her image of him as a teenage boy. Even Otis's neck flushed red.

"Tell me about meeting Jack. You said you spent an evening drinking with him. It sounds like you had an opportunity to get to know him."

Otis leaned forward. Was he finally ready to confide in her?

"Funny thing about Jack. Just when you might think you're getting to know him and what not, you sorta realize you don't know Jack. I think there ain't nobody that knows Jack."

"But he told you things."

"Yep, that's right. He told me a whole bunch of stuff."

"Why do you suppose he did that?"

"Oh, I don't know," Otis said, but he wasn't rattled or defensive. He leaned back and did his search of the ceiling, like he'd find the answers there. "I supposed he saw that me and him have something in common, you know. Both of us kinda got messed up when we were kids."

"He talked to you about when he was a boy?"

"No, he doesn't really like to talk about it. I could just tell. Like there was something there. But Jack could see that me and him, we ain't like normal people."

"What's normal? Does anyone know?"

Otis laughed, a genuine chuckle this time. Gwen should have been pleased that she'd made him laugh. Then he squinted at her as if he were trying to determine if she was serious, or if she was playing him.

"Whatever it is, I'm not sure I can get back to normal," he said.

She met his eyes and knew there was nothing dimwitted about this man. He was too good at throwing out simple remarks that cut deeper.

Gwen shrugged, trying to encourage him to continue. She could see that he wanted to.

"And Jack?"

"Oh, he's not normal." He laughed again. But this time it didn't sound genuine or joyful. It sounded nervous and forced.

"So what makes him kill?"

He shrugged with both shoulders, practically bringing them up to his huge earlobes, an exaggerated gesture. Gwen realized Otis knew much more than he was willing to share.

"I suppose you'd have to ask Jack. But he does seem to enjoy it quite a bit."

"He told you that?"

Another shrug. "I guess he likes the challenge or what have you. He likes to study them."

"By killing them?"

He was watching her. His tongue darted out the corner of his mouth. Gwen was starting to recognize the mannerism as a tell, a nervous twitch when he was trying to decide if he should confide or reveal what was evidently on the tip of his tongue.

"Well, it's not just the killing." His voice was so quiet and soft, Gwen found herself leaning over the table between them so she could hear him.

Otis hesitated, either struggling to find words or measuring them. Gwen wasn't sure which.

"He said he enjoys seeing what they're made of, you know. What they're willing to do, what kinds of things they'll say just to stay alive. What they'll tell him and what not, just so he won't kill them."

He paused. Eyes darted up to the ceiling, again, for a moment. Back to Gwen.

"And he said he likes to . . . oh, I don't know . . . he likes to feel what they're made of, too. Their skin and their blood, what have you. He really enjoys cutting them. Cutting up a person isn't really any different from butchering a hog." Another pause, but now he was watching Gwen to see her reaction. "At least that's what he said."

The room felt hot. Gwen's blouse stuck to her back. She resisted the urge to wipe her forehead. She didn't want Otis to see that she was uncomfortable. That she was sweating. She had forgotten her mission. Somehow they had verged way off the path. She didn't need to know all this. She needed to focus. She needed to get what she came for.

"It's been over a year since you talked to Jack. You think you'd still be able to recognize him?"

"Oh, I don't know. He's pretty ordinary looking."

"Did he tell you where he lived or worked?"

Otis's smile grew wider but he twisted up his face, then shook his head. He knew exactly what she was doing and he wasn't playing.

"You found one of his dumping grounds." He said it like the discovery should mean something more.

"Does he live close by?"

Still shaking his head. Gwen wasn't sure it meant "no," or if he just couldn't believe she was asking.

"I can't give you Jack."

She stifled a sigh and shifted in her chair. This was a big waste of time.

"But I can give you another one of his dumping grounds."

"There really is another one?"

"Oh yeah. Several."

Gwen reminded herself that everything he had told her so far had been true.

"Okay." She nodded.

"But this time there's something I want. I want to go along and show you."

"Excuse me?"

"I'm not gonna tell anything more unless I get to go along."

And sure enough he pushed his chair away and stood up as

best he could with the limitations of the shackles. He was finished with her.

"Otis, I don't know that I can arrange that."

The guard came in and Otis lifted his hands to him.

"You let me know. I'll be waiting. I'm not going anywhere."

CHAPTER 38

"He's afraid," Maggie told Detective Lopez and Tully.

"That this so-called madman will come back and get him?" Lopez wasn't buying it. "Then why not give us a description? Why not tell us where we can find his friend?"

"This killer is not just confident and efficient, he's . . ." Tully paused to search for the right word. "To put it mildly, he's brutal."

Lopez shook his head.

They were waiting at the rest area for Ryder Creed and Grace. Lopez had brought two of his uniformed officers to assist, but he'd already explained how he had a crew of a dozen men search the woods for ten straight hours the day before. They hadn't found anything valuable for their efforts.

"And it's mushroom season," Lopez said.

"Mushroom season?" Maggie asked, glancing at Tully to see if he had any idea what that meant.

"As soon as the redbuds bloom, wild mushrooms sprout up," Lopez explained. "They're a delicacy. People hunt for them. Which means there's been a bunch of people traipsing around these hills and bluffs and nobody's reported finding a lost teenager. Or a body.

"You want to know what I think," Lopez continued. "I think Noah Waters is afraid, all right. I think he's afraid I'll arrest his ass. You say this killer you two are looking for is confident and efficient? Pretty sloppy to let one of his victims go. This case obviously doesn't have anything to do with your guy."

"You still think Noah did something to Ethan?"

"Hell yes. Why else would that kid be throwing up every time we want to discuss the details? Maybe he can't even believe what he did. I've seen how a guilty person acts and Noah Waters is guilty."

"So what did he do with Ethan?" Tully asked.

The detective shrugged. "I've checked hospitals in a hundred-mile radius. Just in case someone found him and picked him up. His parents have called all of his friends. I put out an APB. If he's injured he could be delirious. Maybe a trucker picked him up. He could be in another state by now."

Maggie took a good look at Lopez. Mid to late forties, military buzz cut, a short but compact body, eyebrows that were perpetually knitted with worry. He projected a serious, experienced, and tough demeanor, yet he still didn't appear to believe her or Tully that this case could possibly be related to their hunt for a serial killer. She couldn't decide if he really did believe that Ethan was still alive or if he simply wanted to believe it.

"But your men didn't find the knife?" Tully again, playing the skeptic.

"What knife?"

"You have a severed finger," Tully said. "You haven't looked for the weapon that may have cut it off?"

For the first time Lopez looked like he had been caught off guard.

Just as Creed's Jeep appeared on the interstate ramp coming down to the rest area, Maggie noticed the garbage truck, its hydraulic brakes hissing. It was finished collecting at the far end of the other parking lot and was heading for the ramp to get on the interstate.

She turned to Lopez and asked, "Your men didn't check the trash receptacles?"

"My men were busy doing a search and rescue." He seemed annoyed and defensive.

"How often is garbage collected here?"

"What? Once a week maybe. I have no idea."

Maggie motioned to Tully to give her their rental's keys.

"We have to stop that truck."

"I've got it," Tully said as he took off running for their SUV.

It was parked clear on the other side of the winding road in the cars' parking lot.

Maggie gauged the distance. The garbage truck hiccupped and belched diesel. Tully would never make it in time. She sprinted over the lawn and sidewalk, dodging travelers. Through the trees she could see the road that wound around the rest area. The truck would need to follow it to get to the interstate's entrance ramp. It was shorter for her to race through the trees that surrounded the small brick building. She ran at a diagonal, pumping, pushing, willing her legs to go faster. The truck had started up the road. She'd need to intercept it before it got to the ramp.

She didn't, however, give it much thought as to how she'd stop it.

As she ran toward the road she pulled out her badge and waved it, but she was on the wrong side and too close for the driver to see her running alongside him on the passenger side. The truck started to accelerate and so did Maggie.

She raced ahead. Beat the truck by less than a hundred yards. Then she jumped into the middle of the road waving her badge. The clutch and gears ground. Hydraulic brakes screeched. The truck's front lift claws jolted to a stop within three feet of her, so close her nostrils instantly filled with the scent of garbage.

"Jesus, lady," the driver yelled as he stuck his head out the window. "What the hell's wrong with you?"

"FBI. We need to take a look at your garbage."

CHAPTER 39

Creed watched from inside his Jeep. He'd just parked when he saw
Maggie jump in front of the garbage truck. Now he shook his head
and smiled. Even Grace stepped onto the console beside him, wagging her tail and raising her head to watch as she stood between
the front seats.

"Stop it," he told the dog. "I already know you like her."

Work colleagues were off limits. Despite what Hannah
thought, he did have some standards and limitations. But damn,
this woman had, indeed, sparked something inside of him. He
should have been headed back home. He didn't like putting Grace
through another grueling search on an entirely different terrain
and making her shift from cadaver to live rescue in such a short
time. Grace could do it, no problem. And she'd be more than willing. But Creed didn't like that the only reason he agreed so quickly
was because he wanted to spend more time with Maggie O'Dell.
That wasn't his style. He didn't mix business with pleasure.

He had worked to separate the two so that there was never any
overlap. Often the women he slept with didn't even understand
what he did for a living, nor did they usually care. He liked keeping it that way. His work could bring on too many emotions, too

many memories. It was complicated, for sure, but he had learned long ago that it was best to keep it all separate.

His women friends understood. No, that wasn't true. They didn't understand it. They accepted it.

Now that Maggie had stopped the garbage truck it looked as if she was handing over her catch to a couple of uniformed police officers. Before Creed realized the officers were with Maggie he thought it looked like they might arrest and cart *her* away. But they were already directing the garbage truck driver to back up, as soon as they could move the two cars and one eighteen-wheeler that were behind it on the exit ramp.

What a mess, Creed thought. But the local cops should have thought about going through the trash. He patted Grace's head and said to her, "More amateurs, Grace. God help us."

His cell phone started ringing. He went to shut it off when he noticed the caller's ID.

"You missing me?" he asked in place of a greeting.

"Something awful," Hannah said without missing a beat. "What part of 'please check in with me' do you not understand?"

"Actually I don't remember there being a 'please.' "

"Everything going okay?"

She was still worried about him. He could hear it in her voice and he didn't like it. He could tell her he hadn't had a drink since Sunday, but he knew she didn't expect any kind of a report.

"Grace was amazing as always." Concentrate on the things that matter, he told himself.

The dog licked his hand at the sound of her name but she continued to watch the commotion outside.

"Was it bad?"

"Grace gave six alerts."

"Holy mother of God."

Creed smiled. He could almost see Hannah making the sign of the cross. He never understood how she was able to keep such faith with the evil they witnessed every week. But he admired the hell out of her for trying.

"Two cadavers. We didn't stick around to see what the other sites produced. There were a couple in the woods that might have been scatter."

"So you're on your way home?"

"Not exactly."

He told her about the missing teenager and the possible connection. Hannah, being all businesslike, said she'd call Agent Alonzo to make sure there would be an official request put in and processed.

"You'd just go do these searches without even thinking about being paid, wouldn't you?"

"Guess that's why I have you."

"There's something else going on," she said, catching him by surprise. "I can hear it in your voice."

"What are you talking about?"

"Five, maybe six possible cadavers and yet you sound . . . cheerful."

"Cheerful? That's something nobody's ever accused me of before."

"I know it sounds ridiculous. So what's going on?"

Creed's eyes found Maggie O'Dell. "Don't be silly, Hannah," he said. "I assure you, I'm just as miserable as I always am."

CHAPTER 40

Maggie watched Creed dress Grace in a bright yellow vest and harness with a lead. The rocky terrain here in Kansas looked much more dangerous than the wooded slopes around the Iowa farm, and Maggie questioned the reasoning.

"This is her search and rescue gear," he told her as he swung the backpack onto his shoulders. He attached to his belt a water container with a pop-out bowl that he used for Grace.

"Usually I don't train dogs for multiple searches. Grace is an exception. But when I make a switch of what I want her to search for, I also need something that tells her that we're switching. I'll use different words, but using different gear prepares her."

"You said it was better she not have a collar or leash that would tangle her in the brush. This landscape looks more challenging than the last."

"Exactly. That's why I'll keep her on a lead right beside me. She won't be able to run free here. I don't want her running off on her own."

Finished and ready to start, he hesitated, his eyes on Maggie.

"Is everything okay?" he asked, looking over at Detective Lopez and Tully. Both men were bent over a map that was spread out over the hood of Lopez's cruiser. "Locals don't seem too keen on having us join their party."

"It's not that." Maggie wasn't sure what Lopez's problem was. Yesterday on the phone he'd sounded relieved to find that the number he had called belonged to an FBI agent. "He doesn't believe our highway killer is involved in this. He thinks the boys were playing some weird game with each other that went too far."

"Occam's razor," Creed offered.

Maggie looked at him in surprise.

"The easiest explanation is often the correct one," he said and smiled. "You think that just because I use a dog instead of a gun that I don't know stuff?"

"That's not true," she protested too quickly, most certainly helping indict herself. She could feel a flush of embarrassment and tried to turn it around. "I know you know stuff."

That made him smile. He wiped the back of his hand over his jaw as if he were trying to wipe the smile off or keep it from taking over his face. That small gesture made her realize how much she liked that he was here, and the realization caught her off guard.

"So how does he explain your phone number?" Creed asked, getting back to business.

"He has no answer for that. He also thinks the teenager we're looking for might still be alive."

"Thus the search and rescue." Creed waved a hand over Grace's new uniform.

"And that might be a mistake."

"Because you think he's dead?"

"Yes."

"That's important for Grace and me to know."

"You're right. I didn't realize that until you were putting her gear on. If you instruct Grace to search for a live person, will she miss finding his corpse?"

"He's been missing, what? Twenty-four hours?"

"More like forty-eight."

Creed looked like he was calculating it in his mind. He rubbed his fingertips over his right temple and his eyes scanned the landscape beyond the rest area where they would start their search.

"They know a finger's been cut off, right?" Creed asked.

"Yes."

"But the surviving boy . . ."

"Noah."

"He had lots of blood on him when he was found?"

"That's right. Most of it not his."

"Weather's cool. Even if the body's been disarticulated, decomp should be minimal. That much blood and it's about forty-eight hours fresh, she'll scent it." Then he bent down to pat the dog's head. "Won't you, Grace?"

CHAPTER 41

Creed didn't like this.

Not even a half hour into the search and Grace was already leading him up into the rocky limestone bluffs behind the rest area. Pebbles replaced dirt underfoot. Patches of grass, wildflowers, scraggly pines, and short redbuds with purple blossoms sprouted out of the cracks and crevices. And the wind was picking up.

The farther away they got from the rest area and the higher they climbed, the more rugged the terrain became. Grace hadn't experienced anything like this and Creed was starting to question his own judgment. But already the dog's nose was high in the air. She was breathing more rapidly. Both were signs that she was in a scent cone.

Maggie, Tully, and Detective Lopez followed. Creed asked them to stay back ten feet and a few minutes ago he'd asked them to please keep conversation to a minimum. He heard Lopez mumble under his breath, but Creed didn't care as long as he shut up. The detective had found it necessary to tell Creed every step of the way that his men had already gone over all of these same paths. Lopez claimed they had found nothing the day before. It was a waste of time to do it again.

Creed was surprised that Grace could smell something this

soon. He couldn't see any rust smears or smudges. No dark-colored droplets. The light color of the limestone would certainly show bloodstains. He tried to pay closer attention to the foliage, looking for broken branches, a swatch of fabric, maybe a thread or two.

Suddenly he stopped Grace. He held out his hand to stop the others. Then he made Grace sit. She obeyed reluctantly, her haunches waggling all the way into a sitting position. Then Creed took a few steps forward into the path. He squatted down to examine a thorny vine that sprawled over the rock. Touched it. Poked a finger and jerked back his hand. It had drawn blood. He sucked the injured finger.

"What is it?" Maggie asked.

He waved them forward while he told Grace to stay put. He leaned down for a better look. All the way down until he was braced on one elbow.

"This vine is crossing the path."

"Wow! We would have never found that without your help."

Creed ignored the detective's sarcasm. He carefully pinched the vine between thorns and lifted a section.

"Looks like it was pulled from the side where it was growing and looped over the path."

"On purpose?" Maggie asked.

Creed couldn't be certain, but on the side of the path where the plant originated, it climbed up into the brush. It didn't appear to climb rock. Not only that, it looped back and forth over the narrow pathway, one strand over another. It didn't look natural.

"Noah was barefoot, right?"

"Yeah, and his feet were in bad shape," Lopez said.

Creed sat back in a squatting position. He looked up at Tully and pointed to where several strings of the vine had tangled. "I think there's some blood and skin."

Earlier he had seen Agent Tully fill his jacket pockets with latex gloves and plastic evidence bags. Without hesitation, he pulled one out now and bent over the area that Creed had pointed out.

"It could be anything," Lopez said. But he didn't push it. Instead he leaned in, curious, and watched as Tully clipped and bagged the section of vine.

"If there are scattered pieces of both teenagers, Grace might be trying to track in two different scent cones," Creed explained.

"One that's alive and one that's not," Maggie said, as if reading his mind.

He nodded. "It might be confusing." He glanced at Lopez. Maggie had said that the detective didn't want to believe that the missing boy was dead. He was staring at the vine and probably wondering how his men had missed that the previous day.

In the meantime, Grace's tail was wagging as she sat, swatting the pebbles from side to side. She couldn't wait to get back to work. Her nose hadn't stopped sniffing even when Creed had made her pause.

"Okay, Grace. Let's search," he said, continuing to give her the command for a live rescue.

They climbed the rocky ridge top. Below on their right, a river valley stretched for miles. Grace was getting more and more animated. Creed had to clutch her lead tight. Unlike a collar, the harness allowed him to slow her down without choking her. She was a small dog—twenty pounds, at the most—but she was strong and strained against the end of the lead.

She had taken them off the path. Rubble made it difficult to go at a quicker pace. They found what looked like a smeared handprint, five lines of rust on the side of a limestone wall. The hair on Grace's back went up and Creed felt it on the back of his neck, too.

He allowed Grace to keep going. They were climbing slabs of limestone now, a rugged staircase. Some of the slabs jutted out at odd shapes, threatening to trip dog and man. Grace had to jump up twice to make a step. What had been cracks alongside them were now becoming ravines.

The sun beat down on them. Geese honked overhead but nothing seemed to distract Grace. She was definitely on a mission.

Creed wasn't sure how it happened. Later in the weeks that followed when he tried to explain it, it would be a blur. That moment in slow motion, three or four seconds. A flash of bright yellow sliding out of his grasp. Falling down into the cracks as if Grace had been swallowed whole.

She had gotten ahead of him, straining, pulling him down a rocky incline. He felt her slip and he grabbed the lead with both hands. He saw her body disappear down into a crack. He held on tight to the lead, trying to pull himself to her, hand over hand. He almost succeeded when he heard something snap and the weight of Grace was gone. Followed by a sickening thump and one last yelp from Grace.

CHAPTER 42

Maggie clawed at Creed's backpack. He had thrown it off his shoulders trying to wedge his body into the crack where Grace had fallen. Maggie ripped open the pack and rummaged through the side pouches until she found the nylon rope and flashlight. She handed the flashlight to Tully, who joined Creed, belly down on the rock.

Detective Lopez was radioing for help, trying to direct a unit to where they were.

She could hear Grace whimpering. She was alive, but Creed was frantic.

He called down to the dog in a soothing, gentle voice, "It's okay, Grace. Stay calm, girl. I'm coming right down." Then he shoved his shoulder into the crack, slamming himself against the rock and groaning when he wasn't able to squeeze through. His shirt was damp with blood where the jagged rock cut him.

Tully pulled him back and told him, "It's too narrow. You're not going to fit no matter how much you slam against it."

Then Tully shined the flashlight down.

"Jesus, it's about ten, twelve feet down." He moved the light from side to side then stopped. "Hey, Grace."

"You can see her?" Creed rolled back into position. "Hey, Grace, how you doing? You're gonna be okay."

Maggie heard him whisper to Tully, "Oh God, she doesn't look okay."

"I've got an emergency unit on its way," Lopez said.

Creed started to wedge his shoulder in again, only to have Tully stop him. "Don't waste your energy. We can't fit."

Maggie glanced at her watch. It'd taken them thirty-five to forty minutes to get up here. It might take another hour before the emergency unit reached them. She started tying the nylon rope around her waist, making a knot that would hold her.

"You guys can't fit, but I should be able to."

Both of them looked up at her as though they had forgotten she was there. In seconds they were helping to secure the other end of the nylon rope. As soon as Maggie swung her legs over the edge of the crack she felt the familiar cold sweat. Her mouth went dry and her pulse started to race. Tully handed her the flashlight and she shoved it into a pocket.

She held on to the rock edge as the men grasped the nylon rope. She took in greedy gulps of fresh air as if they would be her last, and she hadn't even squeezed through the hole. Then she wiggled her torso between the cracked edges. Sharp rock stabbed her back. As she twisted to get away from it, she felt it cut through her shirt and her skin.

"Wait a minute," Tully said. "You okay?"

"I'm fine." And she continued, letting her body's weight and gravity pull her down. The whole time she couldn't stop thinking, *How the hell am I going to get back out of here, let alone with an injured dog?*

As much as Maggie hated to admit it, she was claustrophobic. An occupational hazard—ever since a madman stuffed her in a chest freezer and left her there to die. This was not as bad, she told herself as her head left the surface and the men slowly lowered her down. A musty scent of earth and damp rock immediately engulfed her. Her breathing became labored and triggered a fresh panic. Her heart galloped and she started to feel a bit dizzy.

She looked up and watched the sky spin and disappear, now only a sliver of blue. The cavern around her looked and felt like a tomb. And as she descended, she realized it even sounded as quiet as one. The men's voices became muffled.

Her heartbeat echoed in her head. Sweat slithered down her back. The space grew darker and darker and it became harder to breathe. By the time her feet found the floor of the ravine she felt so weak-kneed that she wobbled to stand.

Then she heard Grace whimper a greeting somewhere behind her.

Maggie fumbled for the flashlight, turned it on, and avoided pointing it directly into Grace's face. The dog was lying on the rock floor, but she raised her head, excited to see Maggie. Grace's eyes found Maggie's and held them, intense and unrelenting.

"Stay, Grace. Don't move." She didn't know whether the dog was able to move but she didn't want her bounding up out of instinct. That she could raise her head was hopefully a good sign.

There wasn't any blood surrounding or under Grace. That was another good sign. But Maggie could see that her left hind leg was stretched out at an awkward angle. The other hind leg was tucked under so Maggie couldn't see.

"How does she look?"

Maggie glanced up, startled to see Creed's head hanging over the edge.

"No blood. I can't tell if there are internal injuries. Both back legs might be broken."

She heard his intake of air and the attempt to hold back his emotion. Instead of swearing he called out to Grace, "Hey girl. We're gonna get you out of there." Then added to Maggie, "Do you think we can move her?"

Maggie watched Grace as she walked closer to her. She squatted down beside her and the dog attempted a slow wag of her tail but ended up whimpering. Maggie ran a hand over the dog's back as she told her what a good girl she was.

Grace licked her hand and again, stared directly into Maggie's eyes. That's when Maggie suddenly realized Grace was looking at her the same way she looked at Creed. It was her way to alert him—to tell him—that she'd found their target.

Maggie felt a new chill crawl over her body. She gripped the flashlight and slowly swiped the light over the rock walls. Then she turned around to do the same on the other side of the long and narrow ravine.

The beam found what looked like a heap of rags. That is, until she saw hands sticking out from under the pile. Two hands. Only nine fingers.

CHAPTER 43

Gwen convinced Kunze and the others to come to her George-town condo for their task force meeting. Yes, it was totally uncon-ventional and bordering on unprofessional, but after spending so much time breathing prison air, she didn't want to go back to Quantico and be stuck in that BSU conference room sixty feet belowground.

She had played on Kunze's vulnerability—probably also unprofessional of her. She knew he still felt guilty about putting her through yet another full-body search. But she had decided that if she was the outsider, she could make them meet on her terms. When she told Kunze she'd fix them all dinner, instead of arguing, he simply asked her what time she'd like them to be there.

Racine arrived early, of course, because she wasn't coming from Quantico. As a District homicide detective, her precinct was less than fifteen minutes away. Gwen put her to work in the kitchen. For some crazy reason, preparing, experimenting, and creating gourmet meals had always been a stress reliever for Gwen. Her kitchen was her sanctuary. She often forgot that one woman's sanctuary could be another's hell. Julia Racine could not look more uncomfortable. She appeared to be strangling the asparagus as she washed it.

"I never noticed before how much these look like penises."

Gwen rolled her eyes and took the bundle away in one swift motion. She exchanged it for a red onion.

"Chop," she said and handed Racine a knife and a cutting board.

"Crap. Cutting onions always makes me cry. Isn't there something else you need done?"

"Cut the top off first and do it under running water. Cold. water."

Racine regarded her suspiciously, as if she were expecting a trick.

"Seriously, it works," Gwen told her as she turned back to deveining the shrimp.

Out of the corner of her eye she saw Racine glance at the shrimp and wrinkle her nose. She must have decided chopping the onion wasn't such a bad job. She went at the task without another complaint.

"I'm surprised not to see Harvey and Jake. Don't you usually take care of Maggie's dogs?"

"Ben has them. His backyard is much bigger."

"Ben? I thought they broke up?"

Gwen stopped herself from saying that you couldn't break up if you weren't in a relationship in the first place. Maggie and Ben hadn't even gotten there before they decided to "put the skids on," as Maggie called it. But the two of them were still friends, good friends, and Gwen hoped that it might eventually be more. Instead of telling Racine any of this, Gwen shot her a warning look.

Maggie and Racine had forged a friendship in spite of their differences and in spite of the fact that Racine had hit on Maggie shortly after they'd met. As far as Gwen knew, Racine lived with a partner now, a journalist for the *Washington Post*, and she was even helping raise the woman's daughter. Gwen didn't need a degree in psychology to see that Julia Racine still had a thing for Maggie.

Racine noticed the look and raised an eyebrow. "What? I'm just asking. I thought the baby thing ended it for them."

"I'm not gossiping about Maggie's life."

"I understand."

But she was hesitating. She had something more to say.

"I know you know," Racine said, one hand on her hip.

When Gwen met her eyes she noticed that Racine was biting her lower lip like this was a sort of confession. Oh, God, why did people always think they should be confessing to her? She was a psychologist, not a priest.

"I know Maggie probably told you about two years ago. It really was just one kiss."

"So how was it?"

"Excuse me?"

She'd thrown Racine completely off and tried not to smile at the expression on her face. That'll teach her, if she thought she was going to get absolution for her confession.

"The kiss. How was it?"

Racine smiled, definitely relieved, then said, "It actually was very nice."

"You know the most difficult affairs to get over are the ones that never happened." Gwen let it sink in before adding, "They remain forever perfect in our minds. No bad memories to get in the way."

"So what are you saying?"

"Enjoy it for what it was. Don't invest in what might have been," Gwen said.

"Is that the kind of crap you tell your clients?"

"Yes, and you're lucky I'm not charging you, because you're a pain in the ass and you can't afford me." Then Gwen pointed to the onion, indicating that Racine should get back to work.

Amazingly she did, but of course, she couldn't do it silently.

"So have you heard from Maggie or Tully?" Racine asked.

"Both of them have been checking in with me almost every night."

"Alonzo's been filling me in on the details. Pretty crazy stuff. There doesn't seem to be any rhyme or reason to the victims he chooses. Male, female, different ages, occupations, and backgrounds. I've been beating my brain trying to find some common denominator. There doesn't appear to be any connection in where they're taken or their destinations. I even had Alonzo do a vehicle comparison. You know, thinking maybe all of them drove Fords or SUVs."

"And?"

"Nothing. Alonzo can't come up with anything and that guy is like the king of data. Best guess is that he's a long-haul trucker who enjoys killing a smorgasbord of travelers."

"Can we please keep food references out?"

Gwen glanced up to see Racine had been chopping like a pro. She seemed to have no problem with kitchen prep as long as she kept her mind on work.

Gwen's cell phone started ringing and she did a quick hand wash before answering.

"This is Gwen Patterson."

"Gwen, it's Dr. Halston. I apologize for calling you at home."

"Oh, that's no problem," she said, but immediately realized that she'd never had a personal phone call from her doctor, after hours or otherwise. Someone from Dr. Halston's staff usually called to set up appointments or answer questions and her nurse always called to go over test results. *Results.* Something was wrong. She knew it before Dr. Halston continued.

"I got the results for your mammogram and there's . . . well, a questionable area on your left breast. I'd like to set up an appointment for a core biopsy."

"Biopsy? That sounds serious. Are you saying it could be cancer?"

"It might be nothing. But I'd rather we err on the side of caution."

"I guess I could make time late next week."

"Gwen, I think we should do it before next week. I'll have my nurse call you tomorrow and set something up."

Gwen wasn't quite sure what else Dr. Halston had said after that. When she ended the call she turned around and saw Racine staring at her. Then she did the strangest thing, something that Gwen would never have expected of the tough and often crass detective. Without a word, Julia Racine walked over to Gwen and hugged her.

CHAPTER 44

Maggie handed Creed a bottle of Mountain Dew and took her place beside him in the reception area. The waiting was excruciating. It was going on three hours since they had talked to the young surgeon, Dr. Towle. Her team of students and professors were still in surgery working on Grace.

Earlier the internal medicine chief resident, Dr. Smee, had examined Grace then ordered an assortment of tests, scans, and X-rays while the surgical staff prepped. Though they wouldn't know the full extent of Grace's injuries until she was under anesthesia, they were able to tell Creed that Grace's left hind leg had sustained the worst of the impact. It was broken in at least two places.

"I've heard good things about this place," Creed said, breaking the silence.

Maggie didn't tell him that he had already said that twice before.

"You sure I can't get you something to eat?"

He shook his head. Then he added, "You don't have to stay. I'm okay."

"I'm not here for you. I'm here for Grace."

She saw the corner of his mouth hitch up. It was the closest to a smile she'd seen since morning.

"She likes you," he said.

"I like her. She's not stubborn like her master."

That garnered a full smile. "Don't count on it. Hannah says all our dogs have a streak of my stubbornness."

"Is Hannah your wife?" Maggie asked without thinking. Thankfully Creed didn't seem to care.

"She's my business partner."

Maggie knew there was more to the relationship. She could tell by the way he had said Hannah's name. She waited. But Creed didn't offer anything else.

When she went in search of a vending machine she had checked in with Tully. He was still back at the ravine. Detective Lopez had called in a CSU team and the county medical examiner. According to Tully, they hadn't finished removing Ethan's body. Tully said that the teenager had not been decapitated. His body had, however, been partially dismembered. And there was more, he had told her. Chunks of flesh had been cut out.

For a killer who had directed them to one of his dumping grounds and left so much for them to find, Maggie couldn't figure out why he would leave Ethan's body down a ravine. He certainly wanted them to know about this murder or he wouldn't have left her cell phone number with the severed finger. But perhaps he didn't want them to actually find Ethan's body. She didn't want to think about it. Not until Grace was out of surgery.

Dr. Towle had warned them that the surgery might take three to four hours. The wait was bad enough, but Creed's silence was unbearable. They had watched two cats and more than a dozen dogs of various breeds come and go with their owners. Several were hard to watch. Maggie knew she wouldn't shake the image of the elderly couple with an old and worn-out border collie, so weak a student had to carry the dog to an examination room.

It was at the end of the day and the reception area, which had been bustling with activity, was quiet. They were the only two left.

"Tell me about Grace," she said, hoping to keep him talking.

"What about her?"

"She doesn't seem like the typical cadaver dog. I know you said it's not about the breed as much as the individual dog, but she just seems—"

"She's small but she's strong," he interrupted. "And she's a workaholic."

He sounded defensive. The last thing Maggie wanted.

"Almost all our dogs are rescue dogs, so none of them are typical." He opened the bottle of soda and took a sip. "By rescue, I mean we've found them literally on our doorstep or I've gotten them from the pound. Some of them have a lot of issues and it takes longer to work with them. And to be honest, we've had some we just couldn't train."

"What happens to them?" From his expression, she wasn't sure she wanted to know.

"Hannah finds them a good home. She gets dragged into doing a whole lot of things she never bargained for."

The mention of Hannah's name made him pull out his cell phone and check it. She had seen him send several text messages when they arrived and after Grace went in to surgery. Now she realized it must have been Hannah he was keeping posted. As usual, the gesture made her recognize that she didn't have anyone she felt such urgency to talk to that she needed to text and communicate in real time. Anything she had to say could wait.

It was always that way even when she was married. There was a time she believed Benjamin Platt would change that. She had even hoped he would. Ironic. Since her divorce, Maggie had felt it would be too encumbering to be held down in a relationship. She didn't want to be obligated to tell someone where she was, what she was doing, or when she would be home. She refused to live up to someone else's expectations in exchange for being loved. She had done that for too many years in a marriage that was more exhausting than rewarding.

But lately she found herself wanting there to be someone who couldn't wait to find out how she was doing. Someone she couldn't wait to talk to, who would be at the other end instantly answering her texts. Sitting next to Ryder Creed, she realized that being alone could sometimes feel terribly empty.

Creed interrupted her thoughts. "I shouldn't have let Grace do the search today."

Maggie glanced at him. He was sitting forward now, his elbows on his knees, his hands clasped together and anchored under his chin.

"You couldn't have possibly known about the ravine."

"No, but I did know that Grace wasn't used to rocky terrain. It was dangerous. It was foolish." He was staring straight ahead, looking down the hallway where they had watched the surgeon leave them.

Then he said, "Thanks for staying."

It caught Maggie off guard. Before she could respond, he added, "For Grace, that is."

CHAPTER 45

Maggie left Creed once Grace was out of surgery. Dr. Towle was
pleased with how well everything went.

"No surprises," she had told them. "Grace was a very lucky
little dog."

Then she explained the procedure she had gone through to
put Grace's left leg back together again. The cast would cover the
entire leg. They wanted to keep her overnight, maybe tomorrow
night, too. Creed wanted to see her immediately. Maggie took that
opportunity to leave.

She had the rented SUV, since Tully had stayed with Lopez and
his crew. Before checking in with Tully she found her way back
to Noah Waters's house. She parked along the curb opposite the
split-level house. She punched in the phone number and watched
through the Waterses' front bay window. Though the sheer cur-
tains were closed Maggie could see someone walk by to pick up
the landline phone that Maggie remembered seeing on a bookcase
in the corner.

"Hello?"

It was Noah's mother.

"Mrs. Waters, this is Agent Maggie O'Dell. I met you earlier
today."

Silence. Of course, the woman remembered. She had spent a good deal of time staring darts at Maggie. She had complained when Maggie wouldn't allow her to stay in the room while she interviewed her son.

"Mrs. Waters, I need to speak with Noah."

"He's not here," she said quickly.

"He's not allowed to leave your house, Mrs. Waters. If he's not there, I'll need to notify Detective Lopez and an arrest warrant will be issued." She said this while she watched Mrs. Waters through the window waving her hands at someone in the room in an attempt to get him to stay quiet or leave.

Maggie got out of the SUV, crossed the street, and started up the sidewalk.

"He's with his father. They'll be right back," she lied as Maggie rang the doorbell. "Oh, I have someone at the door, you'll need to call back." And she hung up.

When she answered the door the woman's expression quickly changed from a smile to surprise and then anger. "That wasn't very professional," she scolded Maggie.

"And lying to a federal officer is a felony," Maggie said as she saw Noah sitting on the edge of the sofa.

"You can't just come in here whenever you want."

"Would you rather I come back with an arrest warrant?"

"Don't be ridiculous. I won't let you—"

"You found him," Noah interrupted, but he didn't move from his seat.

"Oh, my God. You found Ethan? Is he okay?"

"He's dead. Just like your son told us."

"I'm calling your father, Noah." And the woman was already heading back to the phone. "You shouldn't talk to anyone without a lawyer."

"It's time you told me the truth, Noah," Maggie said.

He looked over his shoulder at his mother, now talking on the phone in a hysterical tone. Noah stood, grabbed a jacket, and said to Maggie, "Can we take a walk? I haven't been outside all day."

CHAPTER 46

Noah couldn't believe how calm he suddenly felt. Finding Ethan meant he hadn't imagined that horrible night. It shouldn't have made him feel better, and yet there was relief. He breathed in the crisp spring air. The sun had started to slip behind the ridge and the sky was already filled with streaks of pink and purple. With the sun went the warmth of the day and he shoved his hands deep into his jacket pockets as he walked alongside the FBI agent.

She was shorter than him. The jeans she wore were soiled at the knees and he noticed some raw scrapes on her forearms where she had her shirtsleeves shoved up above her elbows. Her short hair was tousled, though it wasn't windy. Despite the chill in the air, she didn't appear cold at all. And here, right now like this, she appeared younger. Not as intimidating. She certainly didn't look like an FBI agent.

He had questions for her but he wasn't sure he wanted the answers. He knew she was waiting for him to speak first. They had walked a block before he realized he'd have to tell her something.

"It wasn't us that was stranded," he finally started. "We thought he was. He said his car wouldn't start and his cell phone battery had died. He had his arm in a sling."

And stupid Ethan rolled down the car window. We were so close to home.

"What did he look like?"

"It was dark. He wore a ball cap low over his eyes." He knew he'd never forget those eyes, narrow set and black. They looked like they belonged to a wolf.

She was waiting for more. He'd never tell.

Can't tell. Promised I wouldn't tell.

"How tall was he?"

Noah shrugged like he couldn't remember.

"As tall as you?"

"Yeah, I guess."

He saw her push back a strand of her hair and let out a frustrated sigh.

"You've got to give me more than that, Noah."

The tightness returned to his chest. What if the madman was watching his house? What if he was watching them right now? Did he know this woman was an FBI agent? No, there was no way he would think she's anything more than a family friend.

"He had a knife hidden in the sling." Noah's eyes darted around and over his shoulder.

She glanced at him but didn't say anything. He could feel his breathing change. That fight or flight panic kicking him in his gut.

"I ran." He wiped his sleeve across his forehead. He was still chilly but sweating. "I left Ethan and I ran."

"That's it?"

That was it. That was all she was getting. Can't tell. Don't tell.

"I ran. I left him there with that madman."

He took a gulp of fresh air. Let it out slowly. Their pace had slowed but they continued walking. His pulse was still racing. He was two or three steps ahead when he realized she had stopped.

"So how did you end up with Ethan's blood on you?"

"I guess he must have cut Ethan." He shook his head, wanting the images to stay away. He did *not* want to see the knife plunge in again. The blade slicing flesh. The sound of joints snapping. "There's a lot that's still blurry," he lied and closed his eyes against the memories that came flooding back without control. There was nothing blurry about them, but with any luck, that's what Agent O'Dell might think.

When he opened his eyes she was staring at him. She didn't believe him and she didn't care if he knew that she didn't believe him. She waited for him to meet her eyes.

"I'm your best bet for catching this killer, Noah. And if I don't, you have to know he'll be back. He won't give you a chance to run a second time."

Then she turned and walked away from him. He watched her return to her SUV, never once glancing back at him.

CHAPTER 47

Maggie got back to the Holiday Inn just as twilight transformed the sky into a neon blue. When she walked into the hotel room she noticed the doors connecting hers and Tully's rooms were still open. She could see Tully's bathroom door was closed and the sound of the shower brought her overwhelming comfort. She left the doors open.

Earlier her nerves had been frayed. She had come close to grabbing Noah Waters by the jacket collar and shaking him until he told her the truth. Now exhaustion seeped in, replacing adrenaline. Her body ached from climbing down the ravine. At the veterinary hospital she had washed off the dirt and wiped her face with harsh brown paper towels. She knew she'd find cuts and bruises once she started removing her clothing. A long hot shower would help.

She was glad Tully was here. He'd listen and shrug and say something that would put everything back in perspective. Then he'd suggest they order room service, some beers, more of those sliders that he gobbled up last night.

She heard the shower turn off. She'd give him time to put some clothes on. She checked her cell phone. The battery was almost dead. There was only one voice message, from a number she didn't recognize. She dug her charger out of her laptop case and plugged it in. Checked again and noticed a text from Ben.

"YOUR BOYS R MISSING U."

A photo was attached and she opened it to find not just Jake and Harvey mugging for the camera, but Ben and his Westie, Digger, too.

"Your boys." She read the single line of text again. Did he mean Harvey and Jake or was he including Digger and himself?

She heard noise next door. Tully was out and it sounded like he was shoving around furniture.

She went to the adjoining doorway. "Hey, are you decent?" she asked as she walked in. Creed stood at the other side of the room wearing only a towel wrapped around his waist.

"Oh, my God, I'm sorry." Immediately she felt her face go hot. "I was expecting Tully." She took one step back and dipped her head but her eyes darted back to his chest, his torso, his legs.

"No, it's okay. Come on in. I don't mind if you don't mind."

To leave now would be an admission that she actually did mind. And he honestly didn't seem to care. He went back to what she had interrupted, spreading out a folded map over the bed closest to the window. Her eyes took the opportunity to scan the length of him. But then she felt the heat flush more than her face. What the hell was wrong with her?

"Is Tully here?"

"He should be back pretty soon. He took my Jeep. Had an errand or something."

He kept opening the rest of the accordion map, fold by fold, and smoothing the creases. He seemed completely unaware of how low the towel hung on him, exposing the indent of lean hip muscles.

When she didn't say anything, he continued, without looking up, "Lopez dropped him off at the vet hospital. The Holiday Inn doesn't have any more rooms. Tully said I could crash with him." He was intent on the map, bending at the waist now and running an index finger over it in search of something. Then suddenly Creed glanced up at her. "I'm sorry. We should have cleared it with you."

"No, don't be silly. It's fine. And there's plenty of room. Two double beds in both rooms." Now she was babbling and she wasn't a woman who babbled. Why did she just tell him how many beds there were?

"How's Grace?" she asked, wanting to take her mind off his long legs and broad shoulders. He could be the poster model for six-pack abs.

"She's good." He stood up straight, his thoughts back to Grace instead of the map. His hair was still damp and tousled from the shower. His jaw, dark and unshaven. He rubbed a hand over his face. "I waited until she woke up before I left. I wanted to stay long enough to make sure she understood I was there. That she was okay. Not scared. Well, you know, you've got dogs. You reassure them as best as you can."

She kept her eyes on his as she listened and witnessed yet another transformation of this man. Over the course of two days she had watched him go from quiet, proficient professional to frantic, macho protector to sullen, contemplative rescuer to this: a concerned, gentle—totally hot—caretaker.

She didn't realize that they were staring at other each for a beat too long until he smiled.

"So what exactly are you doing?" She dropped her eyes to the map but she could feel his still on her.

"I bought this map downstairs." Thankfully, his mind was

back to his search. "It has South Dakota and Iowa, Nebraska and Kansas. I thought there might be some connection, some pattern, to the highway sections he's chosen. Interstate 70 goes all the way to Washington, D.C. Take a look." And he gestured for her to come around to his side of the bed.

"I don't mind waiting if you want to throw some clothes on."

"I don't have any. My duffel bag's still in the Jeep." He looked up at her, again. She hadn't moved. "If you're uncomfortable—"

"No, of course, not." She made herself take one step, then another, until she was at the end of the bed, hitching her neck to the side so she could see the map without coming around the bed and standing right beside him.

"Okay, so show me what you've got," she said and immediately blushed at her poor choice of words.

Creed didn't seem to notice, or if he did, he was giving her a pass. She pushed a strand of hair back behind one ear. Then planted her hands on her hips and stared at the map.

Focus, O'Dell, she told herself.

This close she could smell his freshly scrubbed skin, the hotel's shampoo. A quick glance and she noticed a scar on his jawline, a half inch of white more pronounced in the unshaven bristles. Her body was still too conscious of his. She was exhausted, that's all. It was more difficult to shut down basic physical responses when the body was fatigued. This time when he glanced up at her, he did notice. And his eyes locked on hers.

She wasn't sure how it happened. But she knew she had done nothing to stop it. It started with a kiss, gentle and tentative, almost as a test. When he pulled her against him, Creed lost his balance and fell backward onto the bed. An accident? Intentional? At that point it didn't matter. He fell and didn't let go, bringing her down on top of him.

She had one chance to call it all an accident. In an attempt to catch her balance, she ended up with one outstretched arm on each side of him, holding herself up, mere inches keeping their chests apart. But the rest of her body was already pressed against his. He could have pulled her down the rest of the way, but he left the decision to her. Left her on her own to fight the magnetic field. Eyes serious. No hint of humor. Locked on each other again. Creed arched his back and lifted his head, eyes still not leaving hers. His lips teased her chin, then her jaw, her neck, and moved down to her collarbone.

The knock on the door sounded like a warning gunshot.

"Hey, Creed, it's Tully. I forgot, I gave you my key card."

In an instant, Maggie felt like a busted teenager getting caught. She scrambled awkwardly off Creed and off the bed. The map beneath them crackled in an explosion of noise and her feet hit the floor with a thump. She was embarrassed and flushed—even more flushed when she saw that Creed's towel had come loose.

"Creed, you there?"

She tiptoed toward Tully's voice.

"Hold on. I just got out of the shower," Creed called out to Tully.

Maggie was across the room and almost out the adjoining room's doorway when she stopped and glanced back at him. He met her eyes and gestured for her to continue. But there was no playful smile. No signal of regret or cocky swagger. Just an intensity. She could still feel it between them, so much so that when she stepped into her room, she closed the door that connected the two rooms and locked it.

CHAPTER 48

WASHINGTON, D.C.

Maybe it wasn't such a good idea for Gwen to host a meeting about a serial killer in her home. Agent Alonzo had managed to turn her warm and friendly dinner into a grotesque slide show. Her mind still reeled from her doctor's phone call, making it difficult to concentrate. Several times when she looked across her huge mahogany dining room table she caught Julia Racine watching her. Thankfully the detective had the good sense to look away, even appearing a bit embarrassed at getting caught.

Once again, despite the wireless electronic gadgetry that Agent Alonzo had brought, he now focused on the paper map of the United States attached to a poster board. He had set it up at the end of the room on a very thin and sleek easel. It had reminded Gwen of a magician's wand when Agent Alonzo unfolded it from a small bundle of foot-long rods that he had pulled out of a cute satchel. When she first saw that satchel she had smiled, thinking it looked like the agent had brought a toiletry kit for an overnight stay. That's the way her mind was working tonight, ever since the phone call. She could take the simplest of things and turn them into the absurd. Perhaps that's what cancer did to one's mind.

When he took out pins and stuck them into the map, she wondered if it wouldn't have been easier to keep track on a computer? And almost as soon as the thought came to her, she noticed a look exchanged between Assistant Director Kunze and Agent Alonzo, and she realized it was Kunze who insisted on the dinosaur equipment. And for a brief moment she found herself liking Kunze a little more.

We dinosaurs need to stick together.

Alonzo wore another purple button-down with khakis and Sperry Top-Siders. He had traded his wireless glasses for thick black-framed ones.

When had glasses become a revolving fashion accessory?

Her mind was all over the place. The others were discussing trace evidence and motives of murder while Gwen was evaluating the psychology of everyone's fashion statements.

She didn't think she had ever seen Keith Ganza without a white lab coat. His long gray ponytail actually went better with the T-shirt and suede vest he was wearing now, making him look hip instead of lab-coat nerd. Even Kunze had relaxed a little and wore a long-sleeved polo shirt, light blue, tucked neatly into the waistband of charcoal-colored trousers and nicely finished off with tasseled leather loafers.

Murder didn't much interest Gwen at the moment. But shoes did and she knew shoes, men's or women's. It didn't matter. Maggie teased her constantly about her shoe fetish. She'd never been able to get Tully to appreciate fine leather shoes, though she had bought him some sexy Italian leather loafers. And suddenly she missed them both terribly.

In the middle of her home, in the middle of this group of colleagues, she felt completely alone. The two people she loved and trusted and confided in were twelve hundred miles away. She felt like she was losing her mind, and it didn't seem like a topic to cover sufficiently over the phone.

That's when she noticed everyone in the room had stopped talking. What was worse, they were staring at her. Waiting. Had she missed something?

"I'm sorry, what was that?"

"Are you okay, Dr. Patterson?" Agent Alonzo asked.

"I'm fine. Just fine."

"Before we get to Otis P. Dodd," Kunze interrupted and she realized he was giving her a pass, "let's go over the victims, the chronology, and what we know."

"Sure," Alonzo said, still eyeing Gwen with concern.

He replaced the poster-board map with a three-by-five white-board. Definitely Kunze's idea, Gwen thought again. Agent Alonzo probably had a PowerPoint presentation ready to go.

Alonzo divided the board into six sections, then listed the name of each victim in order of their discovery at the top, left to right. He talked as he jotted down keywords, the data technician becoming professor.

"First is Orange Socks number one. Selena Thurber on her way home to Jacksonville, Florida. Her vehicle was found at a rest area off I-95 south of Richmond, Virginia. Her body was found in a culvert under a remote gravel road about a mile away. But only after Otis told a reporter where to look. It was recovered intact, though in very late stages of decomp. She had been missing for over a year. Identification was made from dental records. Coroner's estimation is that she was killed shortly after being taken from the rest area.

"Victims number two and number three are Gloria Dobson and Zach Lester. Business colleagues from Concordia, Missouri. They were almost to their destination, a conference in Baltimore, when they were killed. Dobson was found in an alley beside a burning warehouse. Lester and their vehicle were recovered from a rest area off I-64 east of Covington, Virginia. Dobson's face and teeth were bashed in, leaving her unrecognizable. She was ID'd by the serial number on her breast implants."

Gwen refused to look at Racine, who would be watching her again. Gwen already knew this about Dobson. She also knew she had been a wife and mother of three, a breast cancer survivor. None of these victims was ordinary or an easy target.

Breast implants—good Lord, she hadn't even thought about that.

She had missed the rest of Agent Alonzo's rundown on Lester. Didn't matter. She knew the poor man had been decapitated and his body eviscerated. "Left for the crows," was how Tully had worded it.

Life was so fragile. In the end did it really matter whether it was cancer metastasizing through your body or a serial killer slicing out your guts or a bus plowing into you at an intersection? A quick glance and yes, Racine was watching her.

"Victim number four has been identified as Wendi Conroy from Philadelphia," Agent Alonzo was saying. "She was on her way to Greensboro, North Carolina, to visit her sister. Her vehicle was discovered last month at a rest area off I-95 just south of Dale City, Virginia. Her body was found two days ago in a garbage bag buried at an Iowa farmstead. That property borders a rest area off I-29 just outside of Sioux City, Iowa. Her body was decapitated. She, too, was found wearing orange socks, but we believe they were put there by the killer postmortem. He left the receipt for the socks in the same bag he stuffed Ms. Conroy's head into. He did us a favor and left her driver's license with the body.

"At that same farmstead, inside the barn, was victim number five, a male. We're still waiting for more information on him as well as an ID. Agents O'Dell and Tully did examine a tattoo that leads us to suspect the man may have been a motorcycle enthusiast."

"Oh for Christ's sake," Kunze interrupted again. "He was a biker with a Sturgis tattoo."

"Yes, that's correct." Agent Alonzo didn't take offense and continued. "The local coroner hasn't performed an autopsy or given any assessment for time of death.

"Victim number six was discovered today. I heard from Agent Tully earlier. They believe the remains found in a ravine outside Manhattan, Kansas, are those of a missing teenager named Ethan Ames. He's been missing for two days. His vehicle was left at a rest area off I-70. Also just outside of Manhattan. His body, according to Agent Tully's early assessment, was partially dismembered. Oddly, however, the boy's friend survived the attack but has provided no information on the attacker."

"That doesn't sound right," Keith Ganza said. "How do we know this is the same killer?"

"Agent O'Dell's phone number was left at the scene," Alonzo said.

"In a plastic bag with the kid's severed finger," Kunze added. "It's him. And he's playing some jackass game."

"What I don't understand," Racine spoke for the first time, "is why he was willing to give up such a primo dumping ground. That farmstead sounded perfect. Vacant for years with nobody around. He even had a house to stay in. He could come and go as he pleased."

"Actually, I checked on that," Alonzo said. "When the owner passed away she left instructions in her will for her executor to donate the farmstead for a wildlife preserve within ten years of her death. The deadline was coming up. The executor's in the process of handing over the land to the federal government."

"Which makes me wonder if this killer has another place like this," Kunze said. "Otis told Dr. Patterson that Jack has other dumping grounds. Otis claims to know exactly where another one is. If it's like the Iowa farm and he feels comfortable enough to come and go, we might be able to take him by surprise. Or at least find something that could incriminate him, reveal who he is."

"You're actually thinking of taking Otis up on his offer?" Gwen asked.

"They're digging up remains of possibly five more people on that Iowa farm. We already know of six victims. Four of them were murdered in the last month. Maybe that's a fluke or maybe that's his monthly kill number. Heaven forbid. Both Tully and O'Dell seem to think he's accelerating. Could be he wants more bodies just for this crazy game he's playing with us. I don't know. What I do know is that we may not get this close again. If he gets bored with us, he could slip away to one of his hiding places. He's a smart guy. He goes quiet for a while. Doesn't mean he stops killing."

Kunze looked around the table at each of them. No one disagreed.

"Otis was on target about the first woman with the orange socks." Kunze looked at the whiteboard then added her name. "Selena Thurber. The Iowa farm is all over the national news now, but two days ago it hadn't made the local news and yet Otis knew exactly where this dumping ground was. And he knew about the tattooed biker in the barn. Not just that there was a body in the barn, but a tattooed biker."

Kunze looked to Gwen. "What do you think, Dr. Patterson? Should we take Otis P. Dodd up on his offer?"

All eyes were on Gwen. The director had given her a pass earlier. She may have been brought onto this task force for political cover, maybe even as a scapegoat, but Kunze was now sincere in eliciting her advice. Advice, not just her opinion.

"When I met Otis he was quick to point out that he was a 'powermaniac,' not a 'pyromaniac.'" Gwen tried to focus. Her mind had been scattered all evening. "I've studied a good deal of his arsons. They were big fires. They were dangerous ones. But for all his talk about power, his fires have amazingly had no casualties. That would indicate that he enjoys and craves the excitement and the attention. He's been in prison for about a year now. He knows he has valuable information and he wants something in return."

"Actually he's added a caveat to his original request," Kunze said.

"I won't go along," Gwen said quickly. "I'm not trained."

"No, no, it's not you he wants to tag along. All the recent media coverage of the Iowa farm got his attention. He wants that pretty FBI agent to come along."

"Maggie?" But Gwen wasn't surprised. She remembered how charming Otis had been when she suggested she was too old for him. Like a teenage boy with a crush.

"He knows the two of you are friends."

"The CNN profile?"

A reporter had done a profile on Maggie last month during the arson investigations in the District. He had been very thorough.

"They've played the piece a couple of times already. It doesn't matter. This trip would be part of O'Dell and Tully's scavenger hunt. Of course, I would want them along. But does it affect your decision about Otis?"

Gwen glanced at Racine, Ganza, and Alonzo. If she said no, there could be another dozen bodies that would never be found. And they wouldn't be any closer to finding Jack.

"Let Otis have his trip."

CHAPTER 49

When Tully suggested the three of them go out for a late dinner, Maggie welcomed the escape despite her exhaustion. Had they stayed in their adjoining rooms she knew the space would be too confining—two's company, three's a crowd, especially when two of the three were sending sparks off each other.

Not far from the hotel and not far from the university's campus was a section of the city called Aggieville that included shops, eateries, nightclubs, and bars and grills. They decided on New York style pizza, appropriate for a city nicknamed the Little Apple. Tully took the liberty of ordering them a large pizza called the 18th and 8th, one of the restaurant's specialties that included pepperoni, ground beef, Italian sausage, pork sausage, and Canadian bacon. Maggie added a salad. Creed was pleased to see sweet tea on the menu. Tully ordered draft beer. Maggie asked for a Diet Pepsi, not trusting herself, not wanting to let her guard down.

Tully filled them in on the recovery effort of Ethan's body. The pizza arrived when Tully was pulling up the photo gallery on his smartphone. He slid the phone across the table to Maggie and Creed. It was a round bistro table that allowed the three of them their own space quite comfortably, but in order to see the smartphone's screen Creed scooted his chair closer to Maggie. While

Tully served up the pizza, Maggie slid her finger over the screen, going from one photo to the next, taking in each gruesome discovery, just as Tully and Detective Lopez's crew had.

The body was a mess and at some point Maggie realized Creed had moved his chair back away to his original place. She remembered him telling her and Tully, when Grace alerted in the barn, that he didn't help with the digging. But certainly he must have seen plenty of dead bodies, many of them brutalized.

"You okay?" she asked.

"Not my favorite part of the job."

He chugged down the rest of his iced tea and started looking for the waiter to order another. Maggie wondered if he wished the tea were something stronger.

"Oh, hold on," Tully said and took the smartphone back. "I have a picture of the boots they found in the garbage from the rest area. I showed the boots to Creed earlier," he told Maggie as he searched for the photo. His finger swiped across the screen several times. "Lopez agreed to let me overnight them to Alonzo. So that's what I did after I dropped Creed at the hotel."

Finally, he found the one he wanted and handed the phone to Maggie.

They looked like ordinary, lace-up hiking boots, but on the toes she could see rust-colored splatters.

"Blood?"

"Won't know till the lab tests it but it sure looks like it. Notice the white stain?"

The bottom quarter of the leather was covered in a zigzag white powdery stain.

"What is it?"

"Creed said it looked like—well, you go ahead and tell her."

"My boots get that way after I've spent some time walking in brackish water." He scooped up a slice of pizza in one hand and took a bite. Whatever squeamishness he'd had was thankfully gone.

"Brackish?" she asked.

"Mix of salt water and fresh water. Usually a bay where a river meets the ocean or the gulf."

"If the boots are Jack's," Tully said, "it could mean he lives someplace close to the ocean or the gulf."

"Are we sure they're not Ethan's?"

"They're not Ethan's," Tully assured her. "His feet are still in his sneakers. They're just not attached to his legs."

"So Jack spends a good deal of his time in a coastal area. That doesn't narrow it down much."

"Creed showed me the map you two were looking over."

Maggie almost choked on a bite of pizza. Her eyes darted to Creed and she hated that a flush was already spreading to her face. Tully, however, didn't notice any of this. He was busy searching his pockets for a piece of paper and finally settled on a napkin, his second favorite thing to write on. He pulled out a pen, and Maggie, searching to get her mind on anything other than Creed and what had happened back at the hotel, pointed at Tully's pen. This thing was fancy. Nothing like the cheap throwaway pens Tully usually had in his pocket.

"Whoa, where did you get that?"

"Gwen gave it to me for our anniversary."

"You guys have anniversaries that you celebrate?"

He ignored her jab, pointed the pen in her direction, and smiled as a blue light-beam shot her in the face.

"That's not all," he said and twisted the pen until it came

apart. He spilled out the contents hidden in the top section of the pen. Two X-Acto blades and a two-inch-long serrated blade. He turned the other section to show the now exposed stainless-steel screwdriver.

"Wow! Just like James Bond," Creed said.

"So Gwen thinks you're James Bond?"

"As Emma would say, Bond is so yesterday. More like Jason Bourne."

"Oh right." Maggie laughed. "That's exactly who I see when I think of you."

"Wait, there's more," he told them as he put the pen back together again. He screwed off the very top of the pen and showed them the display.

"A compass?"

"Not a compass," Creed said. "Is that a GPS?"

"Yup." Tully snapped the top back in place and started making marks on the napkin. "And it writes, too. Does my woman love me or what?"

And that's the moment that Creed found Maggie's eyes. Something passed between them, strong enough that Creed looked away. Not just looked away but took a deep breath.

"How about another drink?" he asked them, and he was already waving over the waiter.

Maggie's cell phone started ringing. She glanced at it. No caller ID but she recognized the number. It was the same one that had called earlier and didn't leave a voice message.

"This is Maggie O'Dell."

"That bastard tried to kill me."

"Excuse me. Who is this?"

"It's Lily. Your new best friend from Iowa. You already forgot who the hell I am?"

"Slow down. No, of course I haven't forgotten."

"The damned bastard bashed me in the head."

"Lily, what are you talking about? Who tried to kill you?"

"The son of a bitch who's been burying all those bodies. That bastard in the stupid *Booty Hunter* cap . . . he tried to kill me."

CHAPTER 50

It was almost midnight when Maggie called Sheriff Uniss in Sioux City, Iowa. She was ready to apologize but the sheriff beat her to it.

"I don't know how it happened." He was immediately defensive. "Nobody got your name from me."

"What exactly are you talking about?"

"The media. They swarmed the place like locusts almost as soon as you two left. We've got them all out there: CNN, ABC, FOX, even frickin' *Entertainment Tonight*. I didn't give them your name."

She hadn't turned on a television or listened to a radio since her and Tully's drive down. While she listened to Sheriff Uniss, she walked across her hotel room and turned on the TV, found CNN, and within seconds saw why the sheriff was frazzled by her call. Her photo was set in the upper right corner of the screen while a reporter spoke from the scene. She recognized the long driveway of the Iowa farm in the background. She left the Mute button on. Sat on the edge of the bed and ran her fingers through her hair.

This is not a big deal, she told herself.

"That's not why I'm calling, Sheriff," she said.

"One of the men said they've been running some kind of profile piece on you. I swear to you, they didn't get a single thing from me or my men."

Maggie switched the channel to FOX and saw that her photo was a part of their "breaking news" alert, too. Must be a slow news cycle and again, she brushed it off.

"Sheriff, listen to me for a minute, please. The construction crew that was helping, are they still there?"

"Construction crew?"

"Yes, the foreman, Buzz, and his crew." She shook her head in frustration. Why hadn't they gotten more than the men's first names?

"No, those guys have moved on. We've got this place marked off as a crime scene indefinitely. Those guys won't be back any time soon."

"They've already loaded up their equipment?"

"Early yesterday."

Damn it!

She heard a knock at the adjoining doorway, which was open, and Creed peeked around the doorjamb. He held up two cans of Diet Pepsi. She waved him into the room.

"We need to bring in Buzz for questioning. Is that something that your department can handle?"

"Of course we can handle that, but you'll need to tell me what the hell we're questioning him about."

Creed was watching the television screen and she wished she'd shut the damned thing off.

"I got a call from Lily."

"Lily?"

"The woman we found in the house."

"That lot lizard?"

"Yes. She said Buzz tried to kill her."

"Oh, for heaven's sake. And you believed her? She's probably strung out again on high-speed chicken feed."

"High-speed chicken feed?"

"Meth. That's what the truckers call it."

"Look, Sheriff, you need to find Buzz and, if possible, Lily."

"She called you but she didn't tell you where she was? I hate to say this, Agent O'Dell, but sometimes people on meth hallucinate the wildest things."

Maggie knew that. She remembered Lily trying to pick imaginary bugs off herself. But the woman had sounded genuinely in distress. And Buzz fit their general profile. A man who traveled from worksite to worksite across the country. Mid to late thirties, lean, and in good shape. Used to hard, physical labor but smart and able to manage people. He could overpower a victim easily, and yet he was friendly enough to win over those same victims. She remembered him giving her the cap and making her feel like a part of his team.

"If you don't have the manpower to find Lily and Buzz, just tell me now," Maggie told him.

There was silence and she waited it out. He was probably thinking of the media fallout if he said no. Or worse, if it leaked that he hadn't acted on an FBI agent's request.

"Are you going to want to question him when we bring him in?" he finally asked.

"Yes. As soon as you find out his name, text it to me."

"Sure enough."

"And, Sheriff, please let me know the minute you find Lily. You might check the house at the farm."

"There're people crawling all over the place. I doubt that she's there at the house."

"Check the house."

He didn't bother to muffle his heavy sigh. Then he added a second "Sure enough."

Creed sat on the corner of the other bed and when she looked over at him he held out a can of Diet Pepsi.

"Turns out they have your brand in the vending machine."

"Thanks." She tried not to be impressed that he remembered her favorite soda.

He'd already popped the tab on both cans. She took a sip. Felt his eyes watching her. She turned around and shut off the TV. She could hear Tully's voice in the next room. She knew he had the more difficult phone call—their boss.

This was the first time she and Creed were alone together since they had kissed and . . . whatever that incident was on the bed. She wasn't sure what she was supposed to say. Maybe that sort of thing was a common occurrence for him. It certainly was not for her.

"About before," she said and immediately his eyes told her he knew exactly what "before" she was referring to and that she didn't need to finish the sentence.

"Don't worry about it."

"It's no big deal?" she asked too quickly, surprised at the slight sting. Isn't that what she wanted? That it not be a big deal.

But his face was serious. There was no trademark hitch of a smile at the corner of his mouth when he said, "Only if you want it to be."

And there it was. She could feel it all over again. Electricity. Too strong for comfort.

He stood up but his eyes stayed on hers even as he took two steps back, away from the bed, away from her. His attempt to break the circuit?

"You should try to get some sleep," he said.

She nodded. Smiled. "I haven't been sleeping much lately."

"Insomnia?"

"Guess it comes with the territory."

"I've found that Scotch or bourbon usually works."

"You, too, huh?"

"There's a legend that says when you can't sleep it's because you're awake in someone else's dream."

She thought about that. Took a few more sips of the soda, then said, "Someone else's dream? Or someone else's nightmare?"

That's when Tully came into the room. His hair stood up where he'd raked his fingers through it too many times. Maggie noticed a fresh stain on his shirt—pizza sauce. He looked exhausted. He leaned a shoulder against the wall as if he needed it to prop him up.

His eyes found and held Maggie's. "Sounds like you and me are going to Florida."

CHAPTER 51

Before Agent Tully could finish explaining why they were being sent to Florida, Creed's phone began to ring. It was Hannah. He left the two agents and retreated to the other room as he checked his watch. His jaw clamped tight. Only bad news came at this time of night.

"Is everything okay?" he asked in place of a greeting.

"Everything's fine. Don't get your Jockeys in a twist. I knew you'd spazz out but I also knew you'd be awake."

"Dogs are okay?"

"Everybody is fine. How's Grace?"

"I can pick her up at seven tomorrow morning. Actually, this morning. I called and checked on her two hours ago and they said she was resting. Doing good."

"She's a tough girl, but I won't lie, I'll be glad to have her back home where I can fuss over her."

That made him smile. Hannah probably already had a place set up for Grace in their office where she'd be able to watch her.

"I just got a phone call from Agent Alonzo," she said. "He wants to know if we can provide a cadaver dog and handler on Saturday here in our neck of the woods."

So that's where Maggie and Tully were headed. Creed hated that his first response was a twinge of excitement.

"Felix isn't back until next week. Andy is still on the West Coast," Hannah continued.

"It's an extension of this case," he told her. "I can do it."

"Rye, seriously? You're going to be on the road all day tomorrow."

"If I leave here by seven, I'll be home late evening. I can meet them at the site on Saturday."

"What's up with you? Something's going on."

"This killer's taking his victims from rest areas, Hannah. That farm up in Iowa—they think he's had access to it for about ten years. If they've found another site, who knows how long he's been using it."

She was quiet for so long Creed thought he might have lost the connection.

"Rye, this has already been a long stretch for you."

Her voice was soft and gentle, that nurturing tone that set him on edge.

"I told you I'd let you know when it was time to worry about me."

"That you did," she admitted, and he could hear her let up. He supposed it was a bit like saying if a crazy man knows he's crazy, then maybe he hasn't quite fallen off the ledge . . . yet.

"I know I might never find her, Hannah. But I can't just stop looking."

More silence.

"Okay, but I'm charging the FBI extra for this one," she finally said.

He smiled, but realized it was more out of relief than humor.

FRIDAY, MARCH 22

CHAPTER 52

Maggie didn't realize she was gritting her teeth.

"No rain in the forecast until tomorrow," Tully said, glancing at her grip on the armrest of her seat. "No thunderstorm turbulence."

Maggie didn't let up.

They had been greeted by roller-coaster turbulence at the beginning of the week when they flew into Omaha. No threat of turbulence was good. But it really didn't matter. The plane was still climbing, that awful tilt, the pressure pressing her back against the seat cushion. She hated flying. Hated being thirty-eight thousand feet above control.

But Tully? He was actually excited. Kunze had booked them in first class.

"We get lunch on this flight." Tully said it like a little boy awaiting a surprise. Maggie even noticed him leaning into the aisle, head tilting as he tried to catch a glimpse of what lunch might be. "First class is real plates, cloth napkins, real food."

She shot him a look. Like "real" mattered to him. Maggie had seen the man eat Pop-Tarts from a vending machine that were three months past their expiration date. Sometimes she wondered if food was all he thought about. The man could put away a pile and was amazingly indiscriminate about it. Good thing he was with Gwen, a gourmet cook, who loved to cook as much as Tully loved to eat. Tall and lanky, his knees still didn't seem to have enough room between his seat and the one in front of him—even in first class.

"Aren't you hungry?" he asked. "You didn't have any breakfast."

"I can't believe you didn't wake me. Or that I slept, for that matter."

"You obviously needed it."

What she'd wanted to say all morning was that she couldn't believe Creed had left without saying good-bye. He was gone before she got up. Tully said that Creed had knocked and glanced into her room before he left but saw her sleeping and knew how much of a commodity sleep was for her.

"He was anxious to pick up Grace and get her home," Tully had explained. "Besides, we'll see him tomorrow. Alonzo hired him to bring another dog and help track at the new dump site."

The new "dump site." All they knew about the site was that it existed somewhere east of Milton, Florida, off Interstate 10 in a heavily wooded area close to some rivers and creeks. That's all Otis would divulge. He took his job as guide seriously, as well as his ability to manipulate and milk the situation for all it was worth.

Kunze and Alonzo were convinced that Jack had another hiding place close to this new dump site, just like the Iowa farm, complete with privacy and a vacant dwelling. Someplace for him to stay while he took his time with the victims' bodies. Jack had led them to Iowa. He wanted to share his handiwork. Since the federal government had started building the wildlife preserve, they would have started finding the bodies anyway and Jack would never get credit.

But Kunze hoped to catch the killer off guard by invading this site without his invitation. Jack had no reason to believe Otis P. Dodd would suddenly share his stories after a year had gone by. Kunze believed that Jack had probably forgotten about the odd, soft-spoken giant who appeared a little slow and awkward.

Jack—but that wasn't his real name. Not the one he went by anyway. After Lily's frantic phone call, Maggie and Tully believed their highway killer's name was Buzz. Thanks to Sheriff Uniss and Agent Alonzo, they now knew that the foreman, Buzz, was Stanley Johnson. However, he had disappeared from Iowa and apparently so had Lily.

"We thought he was watching us," Maggie said, trying to relax into her seat. "We just didn't know from how close."

"It was strange how he gave you that cap and then it just disappeared from our table at the truck stop."

Maggie pulled out her laptop from the case she'd stuffed under the seat in front of her. She'd downloaded a file Alonzo had e-mailed them just before they boarded. Now she was anxious to open it and get her mind off being locked in a metal tube miles above the earth even if it meant digging into the psyche of a serial killer.

"He doesn't exactly fit the profile," Tully said. "And Buzz was managing that construction crew before we got there."

"According to Alonzo's information, thirty-six-year-old Stanley 'Buzz' Johnson is an independent contractor. He travels across the country doing mainly federal government projects. He lists his permanent residence as Dothan, Alabama. No criminal record. No traffic citations. No fingerprints on record. Alonzo found a Ford F-150 truck registered to him in the state of Alabama. No other property listed under his name."

"Wait a minute." Tully grabbed his messenger bag and pulled

out the map Alonzo had faxed earlier. It showed the general area in Florida where Otis was taking them tomorrow. Tully pushed up his glasses and took a closer look. "Check this out."

He yanked his tray down in front of him and laid out the map. With his index finger he found and pointed to Dothan, Alabama, then traced down to I-10 directly below. Maggie's eyes found Milton, Florida, on the map before Tully's finger did. Buzz Johnson's permanent residence was less than a hundred miles away from the new dump site.

SATURDAY, MARCH 23

CHAPTER 53

Kunze had reserved two rooms for Maggie and Tully at a Red Roof Inn. Just off Interstate 10, the area was tucked up against a forest of pine trees. Clean and comfortable, but Maggie actually missed their adjoining rooms at the Holiday Inn. And surprisingly, she missed Creed. Silly, really. She barely knew the man. Probably missed having the extra company. That was all. She and Tully had been on the road together for too long.

Tully, however, was happy. There was a Waffle House right next door.

Maggie wanted to go home and spend time with her dogs. This stretch had been too long. Though she had to remind herself that she didn't have a home right now. Hers had been gutted by fire. Cleanup had been heart-wrenching. She had left in the middle of rebuilding as electricians, plumbers, and drywallers tramped in and out, removing, restoring, and replacing. Maybe staying on the road wasn't such a bad idea.

There had been no word on Stanley "Buzz" Johnson. Agent Alonzo had gotten a photo from the man's driver's license and was now working with Detective Lopez in Kansas to see if Noah Waters might identify Buzz as the man who attacked him and his friend Ethan. Maggie didn't believe that would happen. Noah was still too frightened.

Thunderstorms had rumbled through Florida earlier in the morning, leaving the air thick with humidity and making sixty-three degrees feel damp and chilly even as the sun broke free of the clouds. More thunderstorms were predicted for later in the afternoon.

Both Maggie and Tully had their FBI windbreakers with them. Before they left Kansas they had bought ankle-high hiking boots. Maggie wore jeans and a T-shirt with the long sleeves pushed up to her elbows. Tully chose to look more official in khakis and a polo shirt. Both also wore their shoulder holsters and weapons.

Tully had already spoken to Creed. He was running late and said he'd meet them at the site. This area was Creed's backyard. His training facility was less than half an hour away. Tully agreed to text GPS coordinates as soon as they arrived wherever Otis was taking them.

At exactly noon—right on time—two black Chevy Tahoes with Florida Highway Patrol insignias pulled into the empty back parking lot of the hotel. They stopped in the farthest corner, where the pine trees bordered them on two sides. Maggie and Tully had been waiting in the lobby and came out to greet them.

Both of the Florida state troopers were dressed in gray uniforms and wide-brimmed black hats. They introduced themselves as Wiley and Campos. A man emerged from the front passenger side of the lead SUV. Maggie knew he had to be Warden Demarcus. Kunze had told them the man insisted on accompanying his prisoner.

Demarcus looked like a politician—a shot of gray at the temples, square shoulders, confident gait, freshly creased trousers, white oxford with a silk tie, and expensive leather shoes that she immediately noticed were polished and shiny. It was the perfect outfit for a hike in search of dead bodies. Maggie wondered if he expected a TV news crew to meet them at the site. Instead of a warden taking responsibility for his prisoner, he looked like a man wanting to capitalize on a celebrity moment.

Left in the backseat of the first SUV was Otis P. Dodd. Maggie was close enough that she could see him behind the tinted glass. He was watching them, smiling and eating a chicken drumstick.

"He insisted we stop for fried chicken," Demarcus told Maggie. "We barely get off the plane and he wants KFC."

"I guess he gets whatever he wants today," Tully said.

"Within reason," Demarcus shot back.

Gwen had described Otis as being a giant of a man, and just the glimpse through the window told Maggie that was true. Despite his receding hairline and droopy eyes with crow's-feet at the corners, when he gave her a lopsided grin—one that looked quite content but with almost an innocent quality—he did remind her of a teenager.

Maggie and Tully went to the second SUV with Trooper Wiley. Tully conceded the front passenger side to her. Campos and Demarcus got back inside the lead SUV with Otis. Before Wiley could put the vehicle in gear and follow, Demarcus was back out in the parking lot, trying to manage the fury that was taking over his face. He stomped to their vehicle and stood in front of Maggie's door. Both she and Tully, who was sitting behind her, opened their windows.

"Is there a problem?"

"He wants *you* to ride in his vehicle," Demarcus said through gritted teeth, not only with anger but with accusation. "I told them it was a bad idea to have a woman along."

His fingers reached for Maggie's door but she opened it before he made contact. She let the heavy door swing open a bit too fast, knocking Demarcus smack in the chest.

"Oops, sorry," she said. "Sometimes we women can be a little clumsy and we just don't know our strength."

She heard both Wiley and Tully laughing as she exited the vehicle.

CHAPTER 54

Maggie sat at an angle in the Tahoe's leather captain seat, so she could see Otis. He was shackled to the floor of the SUV, sitting in the seat directly behind Trooper Campos. A metal grill separated the front from the back of the vehicle.

The interior smelled of fried chicken. Otis's chin was still shiny where he hadn't wiped it. He was excited to have her in his SUV.

"You're Miss Gwen's friend, ain't that right?"

And Maggie immediately understood what Gwen had meant when she said the man had a simple-minded charm about him.

Now his face was turned toward the window and his gaze was intense. The nervous lopsided grin, which was as much a part of his features as his nose, was subdued. He appeared to know exactly where he was taking them. Yet it wouldn't surprise Maggie if he had lied about a second dump site just to get a day outside the prison walls. He'd be able to take a plane ride and go for a drive. Get some fresh air and some fried chicken. When he let them pass the exit for the interstate rest area, Maggie suspected that was exactly what Otis had done.

However, he directed Trooper Campos to the next exit and instructed him turn by turn. Ten minutes later they entered Blackwater River State Forest and Maggie thought to herself, "We're not in Kansas anymore."

The narrow road was flanked on both sides by tall, thin pine trees so close together daylight had to fight to get through. They passed by the entrances to a couple of dirt roads, two tracks in red clay that twisted and disappeared into the trees. Trooper Campos continued farther into the forest. He drove over a bridge and Maggie noticed that the water beneath was tea-colored but clear and shallow enough to see the bottom. A sandbar with pristine white sand appeared in the river. Surrounded by the pine trees, the beach looked out of place. In season, it would be a perfect retreat, but in March it was empty.

"If you had mentioned the forest," Campos said in his rearview mirror to Otis, "I would have called one of the rangers."

"Wouldn't be no need for that," Otis told him.

"You been here before?" Campos asked.

"No, sir. Never been to Florida before." He was polite and soft-spoken with a pronounced Southern drawl.

"Then how do you know where to go?"

Otis gently tapped two fingers to his temple and grinned but didn't take his eyes away from his side window.

"When people tell me stuff, I remember. I don't know why it is, but I get a real good picture in my mind."

Campos shot Maggie a look but thankfully he didn't roll his eyes. The trooper looked about forty. Old enough to have heard all kinds of stories, and Maggie could see he was also beginning to wonder about the validity of Otis's claim.

"There's nobody around out here," Campos said to Maggie. "Not this time of year. Milton is canoe capital of Florida. Blackwater River runs through the forest. A bunch of other creeks and tributaries flow into it. Coldwater Creek, Juniper, Sweetwater."

"How big is the forest?" Maggie asked.

"Over two hundred thousand acres. Stretches all the way north to the Alabama state border."

Maggie glanced back at Otis. She had a feeling of dread. How deep into the forest would he take them? How long would he have them walking in circles before he admitted there was no dump site?

To the west through a clearing in the thick forest, she could see storm clouds gathering. It wasn't even six months since she had spent an evening in a forest in Nebraska. She had never experienced such a sense of isolation before. She wasn't looking forward to repeating it. Instinctively she pulled out her cell phone and checked how many bars she had. It blinked between one and two, then none.

Trooper Campos noticed. "Should be able to get reception," he said, then quickly added, "in most spots." He didn't sound convincing.

"After that big-ass tree up there," Otis said, pointing up ahead to a huge dead oak, "there's a little narrow road afterward to the right."

It was a landmark anyone would remember. Was that exactly what he was thinking?

Campos slowed down but still almost missed the road. It was more of a path than a road. The overgrowth hid the tire tracks and the entrance. He stopped the SUV. Made sure the one behind him had stopped and given him enough room to back up. Then he yanked the steering wheel hard to the right and drove into the forest.

The road curved, sometimes sharply. They bounced and jerked over the ruts. The road never widened. In several places branches scraped the sides of the SUV and Campos grimaced. The overhanging ones threatened to do the same. Every once in while Maggie saw splotches of color, spring blooms. As the sky continued to darken with clouds, so too did their path.

"How far are we going, buddy?" Trooper Campos asked, and Maggie thought she saw Otis grimace for the first time at the term "buddy." "You sure this is the right way?"

"Just a little bit more," he said.

A few seconds later, the SUV came around a curve and into a small clearing.

"Here we go," he said.

Maggie had to admit it was the perfect isolated spot to dump bodies. Remote but with vehicle access. The only problem—there didn't appear to be anything else. No cabin, no lean-to.

But when they got out of the SUVs, Otis told them they'd have to walk to the actual site and he pointed to a footpath.

"It's just up the way through them trees."

"Are you jerking us around?" It was Demarcus.

"Should be about a hundred to a hundred fifty yards up that way."

Otis went on to ask about getting the shackles from his feet removed.

Troopers Campos and Wiley looked to Demarcus for instruction. Demarcus looked to Tully.

"We've already come this far. Let's at least check it out before the thunder and lightning get here."

Otis was right. About 100 to 150 yards through the trees they came to another clearing. This one was much bigger, wider and with tall grass and yellow wildflowers, a meadow in the middle of the forest. Trooper Wiley walked beside Otis as the prisoner, with his hands still shackled, led them to the center and stopped.

Demarcus was close behind them, and Tully, Maggie, and Trooper Campos were about twenty feet back, bringing up the rear.

Again, Maggie noticed there was nothing else but thick forest surrounding the area. No shelters in sight. Although she couldn't see beyond the dark shadows inside the forest. Somewhere in the distance she could hear the beginning rumble of the brewing storm.

In fact, the first crack Maggie heard, she thought it was thunder until she saw Trooper Wiley fall to his knees, holding his throat. In a gulp of a breath, a second gunshot followed. Right next to her, Trooper Campos's head exploded, splattering Maggie in the face.

She ripped at her windbreaker as Campos fell against her, taking her with him to the ground. Her fingers yanked at her holster.

Then a third shot. This one hit Tully.

CHAPTER 55

Maggie belly-crawled to where Tully lay. The tall grass offered little camouflage. But Campos's body provided a barrier. Weapon drawn, she couldn't see the shooter. Could he still see her? All she knew was that the shots came from the trees and they came within seconds, easy targets.

A fourth shot and she heard Demarcus scream.

She ducked her head, her cheek against the cold, damp earth. Everything had gone quiet except for her heartbeat thumping in her ears. Her body was drenched in sweat.

She twisted her neck till she could see Tully.

Blood stained his windbreaker. An entrance wound. *Oh dear God.* Right over his heart.

"Damn it, Tully. No!"

She said it under her breath. Angry tears threatened.

She blinked hard. Pushed up on her elbows. Her pulse raced. She tried to sneak a glimpse over Campos's body.

No orange jumpsuit. Where the hell was Otis?

And where was his buddy Jack? Or Buzz, or whatever the hell his name was.

It was quiet now. Too quiet.

And then there was one.

The thought sent a fresh panic through her body. Tully had warned her that this guy was obsessed with her. It was *her*, not the scavenger hunt, that he was after. And now she was the only one left because Jack wanted it that way. He wanted her alive.

She gripped her revolver, trigger finger ready. She pulled herself up against Campos's body. With her free hand, she rummaged through the cases attached to his three-inch gun belt. She tucked his ASR (aerosol subject restraint) spray canister into the cuff of her left sock. His Taser went into her waistband, under her jacket at the small of her back. He was lying on his holstered service revolver. She couldn't get to it without rolling him over.

Something behind her moved. She turned around, ready to take aim.

A groan from Tully. His eyelids fluttered. He blinked, trying to focus. He looked to be in shock. And in pain.

A flicker of relief washed over her. It was quickly replaced by urgency. She needed to see how badly he was hit. She needed to stop the bleeding. But there was something else she needed to do and quickly.

She clawed at the case on Trooper Campos's belt, yanked it open, and removed two items. One she slid into her other sock, shoving it all the way down. Then she crawled, using her elbows to pull her so she could stay down as low as possible to the ground. Just a few more inches.

She heard the crunch of footsteps. Close. Too close.

She reached out and touched Tully. She had to put her revolver down for three seconds. One second—she grabbed his wrist. Two—snapped a handcuff on. Three—snapped the other onto her wrist. Then she reached for her revolver just as a shadow came over her.

"Leave it, Magpie," a voice said from above and behind her.

The use of her nickname made her catch her breath. It was a term of endearment that only her father and mother had used.

CHAPTER 56

- - - - - - - - - - - - - - - - - -

Gwen hated hospital gowns. They were always three times too large. Her feet were freezing cold. Why hadn't she thought to bring socks? She was filling her mind with trivial things to keep it from remembering the biopsy needle sinking into her flesh. She had had the procedure explained to her three or four times now. They gave her a local anesthesia and used an ultrasound-guided needle instead of a freehand needle biopsy because the mass couldn't be easily felt. There'd be no scars or bruising. It was much less invasive than an open surgical biopsy. She'd be able to return to work or go home right away.

She had been assured that it had "gone very well." But they wanted her to "lie here for a short time." All simple and fine, and yet the nurse seemed surprised that she was alone, that no one would be picking her up. But Gwen hadn't told anyone. Only Julia Racine knew and Gwen had made her promise not to tell.

Her clothes, jewelry, cell phone, and shoes were placed neatly on the side table beside her bed. Her cell phone—which she had set to Vibrate—now rattled against the table surface. No one had told her she could not use her phone. She reached for it and felt an ache and tenderness where the needle had gone in three times, taking three tissue samples.

"This is Gwen."

"Dr. Patterson, it's Agent Alonzo. Do you have a minute to talk?"

"Of course," she said as her eyes darted toward the door.

"I'm going over some information and I'm wondering if you can tell me about something Otis Dodd said."

"Okay."

"Do you remember if he told you how he knew about the body in the Iowa barn? The biker with the tattoo?"

"I'm sure he said Jack told him."

"Do you remember if he said *when* Jack told him this?"

Gwen stopped to think. Otis had thrown the information out at her, right before he left. He'd done it in anger when he thought she didn't believe him. Almost out of spite; perhaps he had not intended to tell her at all.

"I don't think he said when exactly. He and Jack spent an evening at a bar, drinking." Alonzo was quiet and before he responded she asked, "Do you finally know the man's identity?"

"Yes, I believe so."

She heard computer keys tapping.

"He's Michael James Earling of St. Paul, Minnesota. Did Otis ever say if he talked to Jack after that evening of drinking?"

"No, he always referred to it as one evening, sort of a chance encounter with a stranger." She tried to remember how Otis had worded it. "There was something he said about him and Jack being messed up. That they weren't normal. He seemed pleased that they had that in common."

Again, she waited and Agent Alonzo was silent.

"Why do you ask? What's going on?"

"Otis has been in prison for almost a year. Michael James Earling disappeared only three weeks ago. The medical examiner says that's a fair estimation of how long the body has been in the barn."

The realization came over Gwen in a cold sweat.

"Otis couldn't possibly know about a tattooed biker in the barn," Alonzo said. "Not unless he was still in touch with Jack."

CHAPTER 57

"Just slow and gentle like," the man told her.

Maggie pulled and eased her body in front of Tully before she looked up at him. He was pointing what looked like a Glock, aiming it at her head. He still had the *Booty Hunter* cap on. But Jack wasn't Buzz.

It took her a moment to recognize him.

"You had me in Iowa. Why bring me all the way down here?" she asked Howard Elliott.

She felt Tully stirring. Heard him groan.

"What would be the fun in that?"

"He's still alive," Otis said.

Maggie's stomach clenched. She thought he meant Tully, but she could see Otis standing over Trooper Wiley's and Warden Demarcus's bodies. He had Wiley's service revolver in his hand and it looked like a toy swallowed up by Otis's huge fingers.

"The executor from the farm is Jack?" Tully mumbled. "Son of a bitch."

"Looks like this one's still alive, too."

"So do I call you Howard?" Maggie asked, surprised at how

calm and steady she was able to make her voice sound when the panic continued to crawl like ice through her veins.

"It's John Howard," Otis said, coming up beside his friend. "But he likes to be called Jack." Otis's grin hadn't disappeared. His tongue poked out and licked his lips as he shot a glance over his shoulder. "He's still alive."

It was Demarcus Otis seemed concerned about. The warden was squirming on the ground. Maggie could see his arms wrapped around himself.

"It's a stomach wound," Jack told him without taking his eyes off Maggie. "He'll die. It'll just take a while, I thought you might want him to suffer a bit. But we have a problem here. I might have just winged this one."

Tully shifted and Jack raised his Glock.

"I'm not going anywhere without him," Maggie said, lifting her left hand and showing him the handcuffs.

"Now, why'd you want to go and do a thing like that?"

Otis laughed but it was a nervous, forced sound followed by his tongue darting out again and wetting his lips.

"You realize I can shoot that off."

"Jack hates guns," Otis said. "Ain't that right?"

Otis stood a head taller than Jack and was about two times his size. He could easily pick up Jack and snap him in two, yet the giant fidgeted around him like a boy, looking to please a mentor.

"What's that you're always saying?" Otis continued. "Bullets ruin the meat."

She noticed the hunting knife in a sheath attached to Jack's belt and Maggie's pulse started to race. Meat? Then she remembered that the bodies had been cut. Several decapitated. Ethan's dismembered. Zach Lester's intestines pulled out and strung across the branches of the tree above him.

"He better be able to walk," Jack said, gesturing to Tully. Then to Otis, he said, "Get his gun out of his jacket."

Jack's eyes met Maggie's and this time he was smiling like he suddenly found the situation amusing.

"Actually doubles are much more interesting," he told her. "Maybe I'll just cut him off of you, piece by piece."

CHAPTER 58

Maggie could hear the storm growing closer. Back inside the forest the tall pines provided her only a sliver of a view. The sun had been playing hide and seek all afternoon. Now it was gone, replaced by a bruise-colored sky.

She had struggled to get Tully up on his feet. Jack wouldn't allow her to check his wound. Although Tully stayed conscious he seemed to slide in and out at different levels. She had handcuffed her left wrist to his right. In order to help him walk she had to loop his right arm up over her shoulder and neck, then keep her left wrist held up to his at her right shoulder.

It was awkward. Maggie had to walk with her left arm stretched across her body. Since Tully was about six inches taller he had to lean down onto her. It felt like walking with a straitjacket and a backpack on at the same time. Every time Tully lifted or jerked his arm, he also wrenched hers. The handcuff bit into her flesh and her arm felt like it'd be yanked out of its socket.

And Jack, of course, found all of this amusing.

They hadn't walked far when the river appeared. A fog hung over it like a displaced cloud had fallen out of the storm-brewing sky. A rowboat had been dragged halfway up the beach. Tall reeds made up the rest of the bank and they waved in the breeze, further indication of the change in weather.

Maggie knew if she got in the boat it would mean leaving behind anything and everything that was familiar. She remembered Trooper Campos saying this forest was over two hundred thousand acres, most of it isolated this time of year. And Jack looked like he knew the terrain quite well. She wondered if there was even a dumping ground. Or had Otis simply made it up as part of the game to deliver her to Jack.

Earlier he'd had Otis pat her down after he finished with Tully, and immediately he found the Taser. Jack made a *tsk-tsk* sound and gave a slow shake of his head to scold her, but again he smiled, and this time he actually looked pleased.

He'd also taken both hers and Tully's cell phones. But neither of them had thought to feel around her ankles. Not like the ASR spray would do much good. She couldn't act quickly enough with Tully shackled to her. And she would have seconds, not minutes, to take down both men while trying to strong-arm one of their weapons away. But Otis had stayed back after Jack had told him "to take care of business." This might be her only opportunity with only one of them.

"Get in," Jack told her, throwing one of his legs over the side of the rowboat and holding it steady.

"And if I refuse?"

"Have you ever cut into human flesh? I mean really cut. Deep down. Maybe right at a joint? Snaps just like butchering a hog."

She didn't flinch. Didn't look away. She'd seen plenty.

"So why not cut me here instead of taking me somewhere?"

"Oh, I'm not talking about you."

He pointed to Tully and the implication felt like a punch.

"He's an asshole," Tully mumbled.

"Get in the boat."

She could shove Jack while she pretended to help Tully in. But what if it didn't work? She was playing with Tully's life, too, not just her own. Maybe if she got into the boat, then sprayed Jack with the ASR canister and shoved him out. Could she row far enough down the river that Otis couldn't come running after them?

She eased Tully up and over into the rowboat. It started rocking and nearly yanked her off balance and into the river. The handcuff sliced into her wrist and Tully let out a groan, but he caught her. He conjured up enough strength to hold her up.

Jack just stared back at them. He shook his head again, and Maggie knew the opportunity was lost.

A scream made all three of them jolt. It was blood-curdling, wild and pained and definitely human. Maggie felt it all the way down her spine. Birds fluttered up in response. Even the breeze seemed to pause.

Demarcus.

Then Otis came thrashing through the trees, a mountain of a man pounding up the same path they had just followed. He was drenched in sweat, his orange jumpsuit splattered with blood all over the front where there had not been a splatter before. He was grinning like a madman and holding up something in his right hand like it was a trophy.

"You're right. Ain't nothing to it," he said to Jack.

Now at the side of the boat, he was breathing hard and Maggie noticed he had Jack's knife in his left hand. In the other he held up what had to be one of Demarcus's fingers.

CHAPTER 59

BLACKWATER RIVER STATE FOREST

Creed had gotten Tully's text message. But the GPS readings he sent were surprising. He would have never guessed the killer's dumping ground to be in the middle of a state forest. But as Creed drove along the winding road he thought, What better place?

Bolo sat in the back, mouth open, tongue out, anxious and panting. Creed had gotten Grace home safe and sound and into Hannah's protective hands. Unlike Grace's, Bolo's body filled the back half of the Jeep.

As far as Creed could tell, the dog was part Labrador, part Rhodesian ridgeback. He got the happy, tongue-lobbing attitude from the Lab part of him along with webbed paws, which made him an excellent swimmer. From his ridgeback ancestry, Bolo had acquired an unshakable bravery. He was hands down the best multitask air-scent dog Creed had, but he was careful about when and where he used Bolo. The dog was overly protective of Creed, almost to the point of being fanatical. The last time he used the big dog, a sheriff's deputy had yelled at Creed and seconds later the man was flat on the ground, pinned there by ninety pounds of muscle and bared fangs.

In police slang, BOLO was an acronym for Be On the Look Out. Seemed totally appropriate.

From Tully's text messages, Creed knew that he and Maggie were accompanied by two state troopers, a Virginia prison warden, and Otis P. Dodd. Though the prisoner would be shackled, Creed was glad to have Bolo along this time. As well as his Ruger .38 Special +P placed under the driver's seat.

Creed found the two black Chevy Tahoes and sent a text to Tully that he'd arrived. As Creed gathered his gear from the back of the Jeep he scanned the trees that surrounded this small clearing. He had one last GPS coordinate from Tully. He glanced at the gadget's screen and it looked like they were close by, yet he couldn't see them inside the thick forest.

They were losing light and soon the rain and thunder would arrive. Right now the storm was a rumble on the other side of the west tree line. He had warned Tully that it would be too dangerous during the storm. He wouldn't allow his dogs to be out in lightning. Tully had assured him if they didn't locate the site before all that happened, they would resume tomorrow.

Bolo whined, excited and filling the liftgate opening. He nosed Creed's hand as Creed loaded his backpack. Then he head-butted Creed's shoulder.

"Bolo, take it easy."

He glanced at the dog and stopped what he was doing. Something was wrong.

Bolo's eyes were wild. The hair on the back of his neck stood up straight. His nose was working the air and he was already breathing hard and fast.

Creed stood completely still and tried to listen. Bolo looked as if he heard something. But to Creed's ears, it was quiet. Almost too quiet.

He checked his phone. No return text message from Tully, but reception would be spotty in the middle of the forest. He told Bolo to stay still while he put on and buckled the dog's vest and harness. He could smell the dog's sweat and feel the tension in his body.

Dogs didn't associate different scents with different emotions. But some large scents would elicit a reaction. A large scent could mean a cadaver exposed and in the early stages of decomposition.

Creed felt a knot start to twist in his gut. The other possibility for a large scent would be blood—fresh blood and lots of it.

CHAPTER 60

Jack had chained Maggie's right ankle to an iron ring in the floor at the back of the boat. Not like she'd be able to fall over the side and disappear under water and out of sight. The river was too shallow.

Otis rowed while Jack directed him around the fallen branches and tree stumps that appeared in the middle of the river. A snarl of tree roots appeared out of the fog like a sea creature with tentacles. It even startled Otis. Maggie tried to commit landmarks on the banks to memory, discouraged each time Jack directed Otis into another outlet from the main river.

There seemed to be dozens of creeks and streams that forked off. Each one snaked and curved. Sometimes it looped around what appeared to be a dead end with a sandbar of sugar-white sand or a bank of red clay. Then Jack would point out yet another channel for Otis to take, one that was hardly visible beneath the overhanging branches and the tall reeds.

The forest towered over them on both sides with very few clearings. Water lilies covered the surface of the water in some areas. Birds had quieted, either because of the approaching storm or the approaching madman. The sounds of the water swooshing under the oars would normally be soothing. Now it reminded

Maggie that the farther they went, the farther away he was taking her from civilization.

Otis asked questions, even more soft-spoken out here, as if paying reverence to nature or to Jack.

"Why is the water so clear but it looks dirty, almost like weak tea?"

"The water's clean. It's stained from the tannin in the tree bark." Jack gestured to the bank, where huge trees grew halfway in the water, their roots sticking up like gnarled fingers.

"The color'll change depending on the depth of the water. Shallow is tea colored. A bit deeper, caramel. Deeper still, almost a cola. The deepest is black."

Otis nodded like he finally understood. "I get it—that's why it's called Blackwater River."

"Lots of creeks flow into Blackwater. We're traveling several of them. Juniper, Coldwater. The first time my daddy brought me out here I knew it was the most fascinating and beautiful place I'd seen. I didn't even mind when he started bringing me out and leaving me. Thought he was teaching me something."

Otis was nodding. He had his back to Maggie and Tully as he rowed. Jack sat at the bow of the boat with his body turned sideways so he could glance back at his prisoners but also up ahead so he could direct Otis.

"This where he left you out all night?" Otis asked, gently, like he was coaxing a child.

"A couple miles back. Tied me to a tree. Left me for the night. Middle of summer. Mosquitoes were a bitch. There was a thunderstorm, too. Magnificent display of Florida lightning. I told you about Florida being famous for its lightning, haven't I?"

"Most lightning strikes per year than anyplace else."

Maggie watched the two men. It was as though Otis had heard this story many times and his nods and questions were just another part of the telling.

"But you weren't scared," Otis said.

Jack stared off into the fog and continued, "My daddy told me it'd make a man of me. Staying out there like that. Finding my own way home. Guess he was right because two days later I slit his throat. Cut him into pieces in his own shed using his tools."

Maggie could only see Otis's head bob again. With his hunched back to her, she couldn't see his face. Jack's expression remained unchanged. He didn't flinch, didn't break his gaze. And her panic started to claw around inside her.

Tully stirred. Had he been listening? He sat slumped against her, eyes closed. He was conscious but his breathing was labored. Once in a while he winced when the boat bumped against something.

Maggie had found a roll of paper towels on the floor of the boat, partially damp and water-stained. Surprisingly, Jack let her have the roll to stop Tully's wound from bleeding, though she had no intention of pressing the musty-smelling paper against him. Instead, she pretended she was cleaning, her hand still smeared with Tully's blood. It nagged at her that she couldn't rip open his jacket and see how bad the wound was. She did know that if a major artery had been severed there would be much more blood. That was good news. Bad news was the longer it went unattended the more likely it would get infected.

But there was another reason Maggie wanted the paper towels. She had been drenching them with as much blood as she could from her hand and from Tully's windbreaker. She wiped Trooper Campos's blood and brain matter from her face and out of her hair. Jack didn't seem to mind that she was preoccupied with cleaning herself and so he didn't even notice that every time she stained a paper towel, she wadded it tightly in her fist and then dropped it into the water behind them. She only hoped that Creed might have a way to track them if she left a bloody trail.

CHAPTER 61

QUANTICO, VIRGINIA

The others were already gathered in the conference room by the time Gwen came rushing in. She was breathless and her pulse had been racing since she got off the phone with Agent Alonzo.

"Aren't you supposed to be—" But Julia Racine stopped herself, then continued, "Somewhere else?"

"What do we know?" Gwen asked, ignoring the question.

Racine was the only one who knew about the biopsy but that was by default. The entire hour drive out to Quantico, Gwen had been frantic. She had thrown her clothes on and rushed out of the surgical suite before any of the nurses had noticed. Now, as she sat down and rolled her chair to the table edge, she saw that she had not paid close enough attention while getting dressed. Under her suit jacket she could see from the cuff of her blouse that she had put it on inside out. She pulled her jacket lapels together and scooted closer to the table.

"We haven't heard from anyone," Kunze told her. "That might mean only that the cell phone reception is not sufficient."

Gwen tried to make eye contact with the director but he looked away, and she knew instantly that he didn't believe a word he had just told her. He was worried, too.

"Tully sent a text message about two hours ago saying they had entered someplace called Blackwater River State Forest," Agent Alonzo told her.

"The forest must have an office. Has anyone called? They could send someone to check."

"There is an office, but it's after hours."

"What about emergencies?" Was she the only one frantic? How could they all be so calm? Otis had lied to her. He knew Jack. Was still in touch with him. Not only had Otis lied, he'd tricked her. He had tricked them all.

"I've called the Florida Highway Patrol. Two of their troopers are with Maggie and Tully," Agent Alonzo said. But when he didn't continue, Gwen knew why.

"And the Florida Highway Patrol hasn't been able to get in touch with them either," she said.

No one responded. Keith Ganza stared at a spot on the table. Kunze still wouldn't look at her. Only Racine dared and there was a mixture of anger and sadness in her eyes, something Gwen did *not* want to see.

Alonzo's phone rang and all of them startled. He checked the caller ID and immediately answered.

"Hello, Mr. Creed. This is Antonio Alonzo. You got my voice message."

All of them leaned in, anxious but unable to hear the other side of the conversation. Gwen watched Alonzo's face and watched his eyes dart then go wide. His jaw clamped tight. Kunze stood over him as Alonzo grabbed a notepad and started scribbling a list that Ryder Creed must have been dictating to him. Before the agent ended the call he said, "Give me a few minutes to arrange this and I'll call you right back."

He pushed his chair back and looked up at Kunze.

"Both troopers are dead at the scene," Alonzo said.

Gwen heard a gasp and realized it had come from her.

"Demarcus is alive, with a bullet wound in his stomach. Maggie, Tully, and Otis—all three of them are gone. Mr. Creed gave me a list of things he needs. And he asked me to call the Coast Guard."

"Does he know if Tully and Maggie are okay?" Racine asked the question when Gwen couldn't find her voice.

Alonzo's eyes dropped to the floor and she could see he was hoping no one would ask that question.

"Mr. Creed says it looks like at least one of them is bleeding."

CHAPTER 62

When the rain came it did so in angry and relentless torrents. It pounded on the tin roof of the fishing cabin. Maggie could feel the vibration of the thunder through the floorboards and thin walls. The place smelled damp and moldy, but after being in the boat and watching the storm approach in flashes of lightning, the wooden structure felt solid against her back.

With the storm came darkness. Jack had instructed her and Tully to stay on an old, worn sofa in the corner farthest from the door. Streaks of lightning exploded outside the single-paned windows while thunder sent the glass rattling.

Jack lit a kerosene lamp and opened a drawer to take out two flashlights. Otis walked the length of the cabin, hands on his hips, tongue darting out to wet his lips.

"This is real nice," Otis told Jack. "It's just as nice as you said."

"No electricity, but you don't need any." Jack pulled open the hatch on a cast-iron potbelly stove and started filling it with the firewood stacked alongside it. "Got a chemical toilet through that door," he pointed.

He opened another door beside it, and through the fading light Maggie could see a bed. Despite the musty smell the place looked well taken care of, stocked and recently used.

"Got everything you need right here," Jack said.

"How about some water, a towel, and some alcohol?" Maggie asked.

Both men looked at her as though they had forgotten her presence.

She didn't care. She no longer had anything to lose.

Her heart had been pounding with the rhythm of the rain, both filling her ears. Her panic had settled into a heavy weight that crushed against her chest and left her nerves raw. She had spent the last of her adrenaline. She was exhausted, damp with sweat, and cold. In her hurry she had shoved and snapped her handcuff too tight and the metal had been chewing into her flesh every time Tully jerked his hand. And Tully had not said anything more than what sounded like the mutterings of a man in pain. His skin was hot to the touch. His body was drenched with sweat. The bleeding had slowed but she had no idea how much blood he had lost.

Without a word, Jack went to one of the cabinets and, to Maggie's surprise, pulled out a small towel. From another cabinet he grabbed a bottle of water, and from a lower shelf he pulled out a brown bottle with a black seal. Whiskey, no doubt.

He brought the three items to Maggie and set them on the floor in front of her.

"You've seen what I'm capable of doing," he told her. "Are you sure it's worth cleaning him up?"

She ignored him and grabbed the water, hoping in the dim light he couldn't see how badly her hand was shaking.

"That's what I like about you," he said. "You take on a challenge even when it's thrown at you. We're a lot alike, Magpie."

She wanted to tell him to stop calling her that, but it would probably only please him to know it bothered her.

"So that's what this is about," she said, but wouldn't meet his eyes.

Instead she went to work on Tully, immediately finding it awkward to use one hand while the other was tethered. She pretended it wasn't a problem and continued with her attempt to sound brave.

"You send me running halfway across the country," she said, "just to get a good look at your handiwork. Then you drag me to the middle of nowhere to show me how much you and I are alike? Am I supposed to be flattered?"

"You want to know what it's about? I'll tell you." He squatted down in front of her, a safe distance away but so that they were eye level. "I knew the first time I saw you that you'd be a challenge like no other."

She hadn't noticed how wolflike his eyes were. Narrow set, black, and piercing in an otherwise handsome and amicable face.

"As soon as the rain lets up I'm going to let you go." He paused, and she knew he was looking for some sign of relief—a false relief. "I'll let you and your buddy have a chance to run. I'll even give you a head start. Just like I gave Noah."

It felt like a jolt of ice shot through her veins.

"But if I catch you, the two of you'll have to decide who I kill first." He smiled and sat back on his haunches. "You have a background in psychology. I think you'd appreciate my little . . ." He searched for the right word. "My study of human nature. It's quite interesting what a person will actually do or say to get me to kill their best friend first. I've heard all kinds of pleas and begging. Even bribes."

Then his face got serious again and his eyes bore into hers as he said, "What are you willing to do, Maggie O'Dell, to save yourself? What are you willing to sacrifice? *Who* are you willing to sacrifice?"

CHAPTER 63

Creed had heard the Coast Guard helicopter land in the field at the other side of the forest's entrance. It took them another fifteen minutes to find him. By then, Bolo had led him to where Maggie and Tully had left the bank and gone into the river. Bolo had even found what looked like a wadded paper towel, rust-stained with what Creed feared was blood.

Two of the Coast Guard crew had already taken the warden to the hospital. Two others stayed behind. They had an inflatable Sea Eagle SE 370 in the water ready to go, but then the clouds burst open. The downpour hadn't let up yet. Lightning streaked the sky, long flashes and flickers accompanied by claps and crashes of thunder. They waited in their vehicles, parked single file behind the two Chevy Tahoes.

An hour passed with the storm only growing stronger. There were no signs of it letting up anytime soon. Creed sat behind the steering wheel. From the backseat, Bolo laid his head on the console next to him, his nose nudging Creed's hand until Creed petted him.

One of the Coast Guard crew knocked on Creed's window.

"We've got to leave. If it lets up, we'll be back."

"I understand. Thanks."

He watched them in his rearview mirror. Their SUV had to back up and turn in the narrow space. Rainwater ran across the red-clay dirt path. It wouldn't take much more and the road would be a mess. But Creed made no attempt to follow. How could he leave when he knew Maggie and Tully were somewhere out there, one of them bleeding? That it could be Maggie gnawed at him.

There had to be a way. But night came quickly in the forest. The lightning only grew more intense, rippling clear across the sky with the crackle of thunder making it truly sound and feel as though the heavens were ripping apart and breaking into pieces.

Creed had gone through two thermoses of coffee. His eyes felt like sandpaper every time he blinked. Too little sleep. And too little to eat, but his stomach was churning acid. He couldn't even look at the sandwiches Hannah had prepared for him. He tried to feed Bolo, but the dog was as miserable as Creed.

Although dogs didn't associate scents or sights with emotions, they did read their owners' and handlers' emotions very well and could easily become depressed, upset, or subdued. It was one of the reasons Creed tried to keep his emotions in check when he was with his dogs, and the habit rubbed off into his personal life. Probably why he had no personal life.

His cell phone startled him and his pulse quickened. He saw the caller ID, hoping it was Tully. Then he recognized the number and his heart settled back down.

"Have you found anything?" he asked in place of a greeting.

"I checked the property taxes and federal land sales as well as leases like you suggested but nothing came up for Otis P. Dodd or any family members," Agent Alonzo told him.

"Did you check Santa Rosa and Okaloosa Counties?"

"Yes."

Damn it! There was a small portion of private property that bordered the forest. Creed knew there were some old fishing cabins on the river that had been battered by the hurricanes but were still used. It was a long shot, but he was so hoping it would pan out.

"Blackwater River goes up into Alabama," Creed said. "Starts in the Conecuh National Forest, right at the border. You might check Escambia and Convington Counties up in Alabama." But that was an even longer shot.

"I'll take a look," Alonzo promised. "I did find something interesting, though, when I started looking into Otis's family background. He left home when he was fourteen. Ended up at Boys Town in Omaha, Nebraska, then was sent to a foster care home. A couple in Iowa who couldn't have children of their own took in troubled boys. I could kick myself that I didn't check out Otis's childhood."

"What are you talking about?"

"Otis spent several years of his childhood with Helen and William Paxton at their farm. The same farm where you guys just found a half dozen bodies."

CHAPTER 64

A crash of thunder shook the entire cabin. It was enough to rattle everyone's nerves. Except Jack's. He looked calm and unfazed by the weather, even when Otis began pacing. Otis had changed from the bloody orange prison jumpsuit into clothes Jack had brought for him. The trousers were several inches too short, as were the sleeves of the shirt, but he didn't seem to mind. He hung on Jack's every word and did whatever Jack asked.

Jack pulled up two straight-backed chairs to the potbelly stove. He sat down in one and patted the other.

"Stop pacing," he told Otis.

"You know I hate storms." But he still had the grin, though it looked like he was clenching his teeth. He sat down, shoulders slumped and feet set and ready to go again.

"You know what a magpie is?" Jack asked Otis, and the big man shook his head.

"It's a bird. Colorful, unpredictable, high-spirited with high intellect and reasoning that it uses for deceptive schemes. The bird is a scavenger. They say it'll take down smaller birds and even rodents though it's not classified as a bird of prey."

"You sure do know a lot about them," Otis said, but his smile looked forced, as if he were trying to ignore a foul smell, and his eyes darted over to Maggie.

"My mother knew all kinds of superstitious nonsense. I remember her telling me about the magpie and all the legends connected to it. If you dare to kill one, misfortune will strike you down. It's best to treat a magpie with respect. It's believed that they carry a drop of the devil's blood under their tongue. Mother had a silly rhyme she used to say:

"One magpie for Sorrow
Two for Joy
Three for Silver
Four for Gold
Five for a tale never to be told
Six for one that'll make you cry
Seven you Live
Eight you Die."

Maggie's fingers struggled with the zipper of Tully's windbreaker. She glanced up and saw Otis look over at her again, but he didn't look amused or pleased. He didn't like that Jack was giving her so much attention. This was obviously a reunion of sorts for them. If Maggie remembered correctly, Otis had been in prison for almost a year. Did he not approve of Jack's game?

"You don't talk much about your mother," Otis said.

"She died when I was pretty young. Left me with that bastard I was supposed to call Daddy."

Otis's head wagged. "Remember, Miss Helen always told us we're better than who we came from. She was a real special lady, Miss Helen."

Both men went silent. Heads down, leaning forward, and Maggie was struck by what looked to be a show of reverence.

"Some days I still can't believe she made me executor of her will," Jack said, and Maggie realized they were talking about the woman who had owned the Iowa farm.

"She always said you were real smart. She sure was proud of the business you built all by yourself like that."

Silence again.

"You know she sent me a letter almost every week no matter where I was," Otis said.

"She did that?"

"Yep. Told me what all you were up to and what have you. She had a way of keeping me calm, you know what I mean? Keeping me from feeling so messed up in my head. Like as long as I knew she loved me . . ." Otis actually sounded choked up. He wiped a hand over his face. "I don't know much, but I do know I wasn't starting no fires until after she passed."

Jack stayed quiet. Up until now, he had been the one talking, telling, bossing, but the subject of Miss Helen subdued him. And Otis seemed to know it was a subject he could use.

"My little hobby keeps me in check," Jack said, raising his head and smiling at Otis. "It's a powerful thing. I can't even describe it."

"I like power." Otis nodded his head again, excited now. "I told Miss Gwen I was a powermaniac, not a pyromaniac." He laughed, what sounded like a nervous cackle.

"Miss Gwen?"

"The woman who came to see me in prison. She's a friend of your Magpie's."

Jack gave him a hard, quick nod. He didn't want to hear any more. "You liked taking that finger?"

Otis's tongue darted out to wet his lips. "The Demon was an

asshole but he was sure crying." The lopsided grin spread wide across his face.

"When you cut open a person there's like a steam that rises up out of the body," Jack explained, resuming his role of mentor. "But it's not just the cutting that gives you power. You know ancient warriors ate parts of their enemies. Did you know that?"

Otis shook his head. Stayed quiet.

"Just think of the power you'd get from a magpie."

And Jack settled back and smiled.

There was something terrifying about that smile, and despite the warmth of the room, Maggie felt a chill.

By now, Maggie had realized that she and Tully might never leave this forest alive. But she didn't want to think about what they might have to endure. Death might be preferable, and she wondered if she should have left Tully.

Her one hope was that Tully had actually sent off a text to Ryder Creed with their location. But that hope was fading fast. Too many "ifs." Even if Creed found the dead troopers, even if the dog he brought led him to the water's edge, even if his dog was able to follow the trail of bloody paper towels, he'd never be able to do it in this storm. And Jack giving them a chance to run? There was no way she could find her way through the forest with Tully barely able to walk.

Suddenly she felt Tully yank at his own zipper, helping her, not wanting her to stop. His head lolled with his chin to his chest. No words. A slight groan as she lifted and peeled the jacket off. She was able to tear away his polo shirt. And then she got a good look at the damage and she fought a wave of nausea. She had seen plenty of bullet wounds but usually on dead bodies that no longer required her help.

The hole still oozed dark blood that had the thickness of motor oil. The tissue around the rim of the wound was red and angry. Though she initially thought he had been shot in the heart, the bullet had hit much higher. It looked like it had gone all the way through his shoulder. She reached behind him and fingered the exit wound. He winced and stiffened.

Was it good or bad that the bullet had exited?

She started cleaning it, first with the water.

"You need to leave me," Tully said, so softly she barely heard him.

Maggie glanced back and was glad to see Otis and Jack busy opening cans and packages, hungry and not interested. The thunder was a constant rumble. If she had a hard time hearing him, then so would Jack and Otis. Still, she leaned close.

"I'm not going anywhere without you."

"Leave me," he said through clenched teeth. "I'll be damned if I'm gonna let him kill us both."

"It wouldn't matter because if I left you behind, *Gwen* would kill me."

She thought she saw a hint of a smile.

She held up the whiskey bottle for him to see. Then she ran a thumbnail through the seal and leaned close to him again. "This is going to hurt like hell."

He surprised her by putting out his hand for the bottle and she gave it to him. He took a long swallow. He handed it back and said, "Let's do it."

She wet down the towel with the whiskey but then remembered and whispered to him, "Do you still have those pills in your pocket?"

He gave a slight nod.

The antibiotics for his sinus infection might not be strong

enough to battle this infection but it was worth a try, even if she had him take all that was left.

With his free hand he reached inside his jacket pocket and pulled out the plastic ziplock bag. With it came a pen and he handed her both. It took her a few seconds to realize that it was the one Gwen had given him. His James Bond pen.

She felt a hollow emptiness. Cool as the pen was, an X-Acto blade, a light beam, and a screwdriver wouldn't do them much good. And neither would the nifty GPS without being able to report the coordinates. When she looked at Tully she saw a flicker of despair, and she knew that he realized all that, too.

CHAPTER 65

- - - - - - - - - - - - - - - - - -

"Otis could not have done this on his own," Gwen insisted. "I am not defending him, I'm just saying, how would that be possible?"

"He could have managed to get one of the trooper's service revolvers," Kunze said as he paced the conference room.

"But he hasn't ever hurt anyone before. He's gone to great lengths to *not* hurt people every time he's set a fire."

"His juvenile records are sealed," Alonzo told them without looking up from his laptop. His fingers continued to tap. "There was a reason he was sent to Boys Town, I just can't access it."

"He certainly didn't kill the tattooed biker in the barn," Racine said. "Or the woman they found in the black garbage bag. He couldn't have killed Gloria Dobson and Zach Lester either. He was already in prison."

"Those had to be his friend Jack," Keith Ganza agreed. "Jack was there today. He planned this ambush."

"But who the hell is Jack?" Kunze yelled and the entire room went silent. Even Alonzo's fingers quieted.

Gwen finally breached the tension. "Agent Alonzo, you said this couple took care of other troubled boys."

"That's right. Boys and a few girls. Dozens of them over the course of three decades."

"Is there any way to get those names? Or are they classified?"

Alonzo saw where she was going. "I'll find out." And his fingers got back to work.

Kunze had stopped his pacing and now he stood at the end of the table, his eyes on her.

"I'm sorry, Dr. Patterson." He looked genuinely remorseful. "I should have never allowed you to be on this task force when two people you care about are involved."

"You don't owe me an apology. I had a choice. Besides, if I recall, *you* didn't have a choice. Senator Delanor-Ramos twisted your arm."

"Damn politicians," Kunze said under his breath, and he started pacing again.

"I think I may have found something," Alonzo said.

The rest of them scrambled from their chairs to stand around behind the agent.

"A couple of days ago when I accessed the Iowa farm's land survey to find out property boundaries there was a list of contact names. The executor of the estate was included: John Howard Elliott."

"What about him?"

"He's also on the list I found of troubled teenagers Helen and William Paxton took in. And it looks like John Howard and Otis were at the farm at the same time."

"Holy crap!" Ganza said.

"That's it." Gwen knew that was the connection. "John Howard *is* Jack."

"Alonzo, get back to those Florida properties on that frickin' river," Kunze told him as he grabbed his jacket off the back of a chair. "Let me know what you find out."

"Where are you going?" Racine asked.

"I've got two agents I just sent into a shithole. I'm going down there to pull them out even if I have to do it myself."

SUNDAY, MARCH 24

CHAPTER 66

BLACKWATER RIVER STATE FOREST

Tully was asleep, his head on Maggie's shoulder. She leaned her cheek against him. His hair was damp and sweaty, his forehead was feverish, but he slept peacefully. No groans or fitful jerks. Maybe the whiskey. Maybe the antibiotics. Either way, she was glad he could rest. At least for now.

As for herself? She didn't dare close her eyes but it grew harder and harder to keep them open. The cabin filled with warmth from the crackling wood fire. The storms were dying away to occasional flickers of lightning. The crashes of thunder reduced to a distant rumble. As quickly as they arrived, they exited.

Her stomach growled and she remembered Tully joking that she would regret not having the best waffles in the world. He had ordered the Waffle House's All-Star Special with scrambled eggs, sausage, grits, a waffle the size of a dinner plate, and coffee. Her mouth watered just thinking about it now. She had settled for wheat toast and orange juice. Even the waitress had warned that she would regret her choice. "Oh honey, that's hardly nothing."

The idea that she was thinking about food made her smile. It was something she'd obviously acquired from working so closely with Tully these past several weeks. He seemed to eat out of stress and boredom and anxiety.

She hadn't used all of the bottled water to clean Tully's wound. Now she drank what was left. A few seconds later her stomach was still growling.

"You should have had breakfast," Tully mumbled into her shoulder without moving his head away.

"I don't suppose you have any of those prepackaged honey buns in one of your pockets?"

"I thought you said you'd have to be starving before you'd eat one of those."

"Point."

She felt his "humph" more than heard it.

"Do you hear that?" Jack suddenly said from across the room, startling them.

Maggie thought he meant their conversation, but he walked the length of the cabin with his head tilted to listen and his arms out, palms up, like a preacher getting ready to proclaim a miracle.

Otis wiped at his eyes and rubbed his jaw. The big man had been asleep and looked just as confused as Maggie and Tully about Jack's excitement.

"Don't you hear that?"

He lifted the hatch and opened the potbelly stove. He doused the fire, watering it down until there wasn't a curl of smoke left.

Then he looked from Tully and Maggie to Otis, surprised that no one had even stirred. His eyes returned to Maggie's when he said, "It's quit storming. I've looked forward to this for a long time, Magpie. Don't disappoint me."

CHAPTER 67

Creed scrambled to put his gear back on as he watched the storm clouds move east. Veins of lightning streaked through the black mass that still roared, though the sound had diminished. Under the black mass Creed could see the first light of dawn.

He was harnessing Bolo when a call came in from Agent Alonzo.

"I found it," the young agent yelled before Creed could say anything.

"Otis has a cabin?"

"Not Otis." Alonzo explained what he'd learned about John Howard Elliott and the connection between the two men. "Our guy is John Howard Junior. The senior Elliott owns a piece of land right on Blackwater River. Just on the other side of the forest. Been in the family for years. But the taxes don't list a dwelling."

"It might not," Creed said and the urgency kicked up his pulse. "Some of them are shacks. No electricity. No indoor plumbing. So they don't qualify as a dwelling. Can you give a GPS coordinate?"

Alonzo gave him what he needed. He asked the agent to call the Coast Guard and give them the information they needed to put a helicopter up.

"Cell phone reception's going to be spotty once I get on the river," he told the agent. "So you might not hear from me."

"Wait a minute. Why not wait for the Coast Guard? They should be able to spot the cabin. It's almost daylight there, right?"

Creed grimaced but smiled. "Agent Alonzo, have you ever looked down from above on a forest?"

Silence.

"Tell them my dog will be wearing a bright yellow vest. I don't want them thinking I'm one of the bad guys."

"You got it."

Then before he could end the call, he heard Alonzo say, "Good luck, Mr. Creed."

CHAPTER 68

Jack had given them a head start, just as he'd promised.

It was impossible to run.

Maggie held Tully up. They stumbled and shuffled. She had his arm looped around her shoulder so he could lean on her. But again the handcuffs trapped her left arm against her body, which limited their movement even more.

She needed to get them out of sight from the cabin. Not such a difficult task—it was still dark inside the forest, though she could see the sky starting to lighten. A mist still hung over the river, thick enough to make you second-guess what you saw.

Already Maggie's adrenaline came to her aid, shoving her exhausted mind into gear. Urgency trampled panic, kicking her into fight or flight overdrive. For now it had to be flight. At least until she could get Tully somewhere out of sight and halfway safe.

She pulled them behind the trunk of huge live oak and she gently yanked Tully down into a sitting position.

"What are we doing?" he whispered.

His eyes were focused even if his mind couldn't make his body work as well as he wanted.

Maggie untangled his arm from around her. Then she ripped her hiking boot off her right foot without bothering to untie the laces. She had to roll her sock down almost all the way off her foot to reach the item she had placed in the cuff of her sock. It had worked its way to the bottom of her foot. When she had rummaged through Trooper Campos's gun belt and taken the handcuffs, she had taken the key as well.

Tully saw what she had in her fingers. He shook his head like he couldn't believe it, but then he grinned.

Metal clicked against metal and in seconds they were free of each other. Maggie ignored the raw welt and caked blood on her wrist. She pulled down the sleeve of her shirt and hurried to put her boot back on.

"Okay, what's the plan?" Tully continued to whisper and for the first time he sounded almost like himself.

With his right hand finally free, she saw him touch his shoulder, his fingers anxious to feel the damage. He winced and stopped. His hand hovered over the wound.

"Clean shot through?" he asked her.

"It looks like it."

"Okay. I can do this."

She had witnessed how weak and dizzy he had been on his feet even with her help. He'd only slow her down.

"We need to find a place where you can stay put and be safe."

He didn't respond. He just stared at her. She had expected an argument. Never had she expected this quiet, wounded look. Then it occurred to her. He thought she had taken him up on his earlier offer. He thought she was leaving him behind.

"I'm not leaving this forest without you."

"Sure. I know."

"I'm serious, Tully."

She peeked around the tree trunk. Jack had promised he and Otis would give them a half hour. Experience had taught her that killers don't usually keep their promises. She figured she had fifteen to twenty minutes at best.

"Come on," she said, standing and stretching out her left arm for him to use as a pull-up bar.

He tried standing on his own. Cursed under his breath. Then he grabbed hold and allowed her to help haul him to his feet. He slammed a palm against the tree to steady himself, his lower lip between his teeth.

She found a place for them to cross the river. It took too much time. She was surprised to find the rain had transformed the shallow water to waist-deep. The air temperature was balmy and warm, so Maggie was shocked to find the river ice cold. Tully didn't complain. She made him follow close behind with a hand latched onto each of her shoulders. They waddled liked ducks at an excruciatingly slow pace.

On the other side of the river Maggie hunted for a spot to climb up the bank. This side was the state forest, left wild and undeveloped. They had to wade through water lilies and reeds. Finally Maggie found a downed tree, partially submerged in the river. They could walk alongside it, holding on for balance. She pulled herself up the slippery clay bank, then turned around and helped Tully.

Not far from the river they found the perfect hiding place under another fallen tree. The root ball had been yanked out of the ground, providing a nest of twisted roots that snaked and weaved together. From within, Tully would be able to see out. After they smeared his blue FBI windbreaker with mud, it would be difficult to see him inside.

She handed him the ASR canister that she had also taken off Trooper Campos's belt and stuck inside the cuff of her other sock.

"It'll slow him down." She tried to sound convincing.

When she turned to leave, Tully grabbed her arm. He waited for her to look him in the eyes.

"I know you're going back, aren't you?"

"It's the only way," Maggie said. "If you can't outrun a killer, you've got to outwit him."

He didn't look pleased, but she knew he wouldn't try to talk her out of it. He dug in his windbreaker and pulled out the pen Gwen had given him. It was all he had to offer.

"Put the X-Acto blade into place and slit that bastard's throat."

CHAPTER 69

Creed had put Bolo in the front of the two-man inflatable and the dog was working the air, his huge nose making snuffling sounds. He let the dog help, though he knew exactly where he was going. As he rowed he watched the GPS's screen and followed, taking narrow creeks and winding his way around fresh debris that the rains and wind had set loose.

He'd been up Blackwater River before and was familiar with most of the creeks that forked into it. The river was thirty-one miles long and was one of the best canoe trips in the area. The mist lifted little by little and night lifted into dawn. Streaks of light shot through the trees as daylight broke on the other side of the tall pines. With the sunrise came a fresh hope and renewed belief that anything was possible.

He had changed his cell phone ringer to Vibrate but he had lost all reception miles ago, so he turned it off to preserve the battery.

"Not much farther, Bolo," he told the dog, who acknowledged him with a wag of his tail, but that was the only thing that moved on his rigid body.

A couple more bends and twists and they would be at the property that John Howard Elliott owned. Creed only hoped it wasn't too late.

CHAPTER 70

Maggie thought she heard a helicopter in the distance. Was her imagination already playing tricks on her? A part of her wanted to stay with Tully and hide until someone came to their rescue. The sound of the helicopter made her hesitate and reconsider. Then it faded and disappeared. Replaced by the drumming of her heart.

Jack would expect Maggie and Tully to trip over each other. He'd expect them to be frightened, to get frustrated then get angry with each other. He'd want them to become enemies, so that by the time he caught them they would be so enraged with each other they'd be begging him to kill the other first.

Jack would also count on them running as fast and as far away as they could. Using their allotted time to run for help.

What he wouldn't expect was for Maggie to come back.

When she left Tully she backtracked. It took hardly any time now that she was alone. As the sky continued to lighten and the mist dissipated, she needed to be more careful about taking cover. Crossing the river, she remembered every obstacle and quickly maneuvered around them. By now she was drenched in sweat, and the bone-deep cold of the river actually revitalized her senses.

She was struck by the fact that the cabin couldn't be seen

from the river. Trees surrounded it. Tall long-leaf pines crowded together with not a shoulder-width between them. Other hardwood trees were interspersed. Scrub bushes, junipers, tall grass, and vines grew so thick it made it impossible to walk without them scraping skin or snagging clothing.

Maggie sneaked back to the live oak that she and Tully had hid behind earlier. She hadn't climbed a tree since she was a little girl, but within minutes she was perched high above the ground with a perfect bird's-eye view of the cabin's only door. And she could see the river all the way to the first bend.

She knew that Otis and Jack had taken both troopers' service revolvers along with Tully's Glock and her Smith & Wesson. And Jack already had what she believed to be a Glock. Surely they wouldn't take all five weapons with them. After all, Jack didn't like to use guns. He preferred to cut.

She decided to watch them leave. Then she'd wait. How long? She had no idea. She'd depend on her gut to tell her.

By her wristwatch, it had been nineteen minutes since she and Tully had left the cabin. Jack had promised them thirty. At twenty-one minutes she saw the cabin door open. Her body went still, her back pressed against the bark. She did not move a muscle. A breeze ruffled the leaves around her and sent the smaller branches swaying. Her heart had been banging against her chest the whole time she hobbled Tully across the river and into hiding. But now she found herself remarkably calm, her breathing steady and her mind clear.

She watched Jack point to something on the ground. *Footprints.*

Would they be able to tell that she had come back? Or did it simply look like two frantic people, running one way and then another?

Then the men split up. Jack followed the riverbank. Otis disappeared into the forest behind the cabin.

Maggie checked her watch again. She'd give herself ten minutes. Anything more would be dangerous, but ten minutes was all it should take.

CHAPTER 71

Eleven minutes.

Maggie couldn't find the guns anywhere. Where would Jack have hidden them?

She crawled along the floor, ducking under the windows and staying low. She had already searched every cabinet and cubbyhole in the cabin. She'd looked under furniture, between the mattress and box spring, under the sofa cushions, even behind the chemical toilet. None of the floorboards was loose. The walls were solid. She had rifled through the only two drawers of clothing and patted down folded towels. She picked apart the wood and kindling crate and shoved her hand into the ice chest beneath the carton of milk and packages of ground beef.

No guns.

Twelve minutes.

Maggie scooted under the window that overlooked the river and stole a glance out. She'd never see them return in time to escape.

She tried to remember. It was raining hard by the time they got to the cabin. Neither man had gone out. Otis had brought a duffel bag in with him from the boat. Gray, canvas. She still hadn't come across it. She needed to go through the cabinets again.

Then she heard something. Her body froze and she held her breath. It sounded like a dog barking.

Creed. It had to be Creed.

Relief swept over her before she caught herself. Grace had never once barked. If Creed had found the bodies in the clearing and followed them here, he would never allow his dog to bark and give them away.

And suddenly Maggie's pulse began to race.

CHAPTER 72

Maggie's breath came in quick bursts. All the calm and steady resolve she had built up now threatened to break apart. She started to race from the cabin, then stopped herself.

Was it a trick? Jack claimed to know everything about her. Did he know she was a sucker for dogs? And especially dogs in distress.

Once outside she could hear the barking again. It sounded like it was coming from the same direction she had seen Jack headed. And the dog was frantic.

Instead of following along the riverbank, Maggie stayed back in the forest. Her eyes searched while she darted from tree to tree. The knee-high brush jabbed and poked. It was impossible to walk through the forest and be quiet. Branches snapped. Closer to the riverbank, clay sucked at her boots. Birds fluttered out of her path. Water rushed over a logjam.

And suddenly it occurred to her and she stopped dead in her tracks.

Would Jack have a dog to help track her and Tully? Had the dog already found Tully?

No, the barking came from the opposite direction.

She started walking again, only this time she took careful

steps, watching ahead for movement and frustrated because she still didn't see any. The ground sloped enough that she needed to climb. She kept a steady pace and glanced over her shoulder. Streaks of daylight created shadows as well as blind spots.

Maggie slowed her pace as she got closer to the barking dog. Just over this next slope she knew she'd be able to see the commotion. She slammed her back against a tree, then dropped into a crouch. Urgency fought a battle with caution. The trees came right up to the edge of the river. Keeping low to the ground, she hid behind the shrubs and fallen branches. Now she could hear the dog's sharp bark and growls within a hundred feet. But she also heard rushing water. She eased herself up to take a look over the edge of the riverbank.

Down below she could see an inflatable blue-and-white boat pulled up on a sandbar. Two men wrestled and rolled in the sand while a huge dog barked and snarled from its perch inside the boat. The dog had on a bright yellow vest and harness. And then Maggie realized one of the men was Creed. The other was Jack. Her eyes caught a glint of sunlight off the knife blade in Jack's hand.

She stumbled to her feet and searched for a way to get down the bank. She'd have to cross the river to reach them. A tangle of debris—branches and stumps and roots, three and four feet thick—prevented her from charging down. When she looked up again, the dog had given up barking from the boat and now danced and snapped around the men, but they were locked and rolling in such a tight clench that even the dog couldn't get a bite of its owner's attacker.

Maggie started to yell. Jack wanted her, not Creed.

The gushing water filled her ears and drowned out her voice.

The debris was all along her side of the bank. She couldn't get to the water without plunging down and hoping not to get tangled in it. She sat on the slick clay bank and slid her legs over the edge. She tested her feet, then her weight on some of the thicker branches in the snarl of debris.

Just as she was getting ready to push herself from the bank she saw Otis. He was coming out of the trees from behind Jack and Creed.

The dog whimpered. Maggie saw a spray of blood as the dog jumped back.

"Damn it, Jack. Stop!" she yelled, pushing off and stepping onto the debris.

Immediately wood snapped and cracked, sending her right leg down into the mess of twisted roots, fallen branches, and a snare of twigs and vines. Something stabbed into her calf and she could feel the rush of cold water. She pulled her leg up and tried again. Instead of walking over the tangle, she crawled. Almost to the water, the debris swallowed her again as wood snapped.

The men had not stopped. The dog had joined the fight, again. There was more blood on the sugar-white sand.

She shoved and yanked, back and forth, ripping and pulling at the sticks and branches and vines that trapped her. Her feet kicked and splashed at the water underneath. Over the pounding of her heartbeat and the rush of water she thought she heard the helicopter again.

She was almost free of the tangled mess when she saw Otis jump down off the bank and onto the sandbar. He didn't call to Jack. He didn't seem to notice her, didn't even look in her direction. He walked straight for the men with purpose, but not at all in a hurry. There was an unnatural calm about him.

He came within a foot of the twisted knot of men and dog. Otis was so close he could easily reach out with those huge hands of his and simply pluck the men apart. But instead he stopped and stood over them.

Then he raised the revolver in his hand and fired.

CHAPTER 73

The blast echoed through the trees and everything stopped.

No birds, no breeze, no rushing water. Maggie's ears filled with the beat of her heart and the sound of her breathing.

"Otis, stop," she yelled.

One shot. Only one. Why was he waiting?

Only one because he didn't need to fire again. He had hit his target. Maggie's stomach sank to her knees.

She shoved herself out of the debris, finally free, and staggered in the knee-deep water. The sandy river bottom sucked at her boots. The cold river numbed her senses. It was taking a lifetime for her to cross the forty feet of river. She didn't look down. Didn't check for logs jutting up out of the water. She didn't take her eyes off the scene on the sandbar. Otis stood stockstill over the pile of limbs that hadn't moved. Only the dog had backed away and now stood pointing, alert and waiting, not knowing what to do without its master's instruction.

Otis's hand with the gun fell to his side as he looked toward Maggie. She still wasn't sure if he saw her, though she was thrashing through the water now. Adrenaline and dread kicking her heartbeat back up a notch. Then Otis slowly sank down onto his knees, letting the gun drag in the sand.

"Not right," he mumbled. "Just not right."

Maggie got to the sandbar as one of the men began to stir. The sand beneath them was red with blood. Maggie kept moving. She heard a moan and there was more movement. The dog raced toward the men, sniffing and poking. That's when she saw that it was Creed pushing his way out from under Jack's dead body. The dog had Jack's shirttail in his teeth and was helping to pull the obstacle off his master.

Somewhere in the distance Maggie heard the helicopter.

Relief swept too quickly. She wanted to help Creed but she needed to focus on Otis. He hadn't moved from where he had gone down in the sand. Now sitting, legs tucked under him, the man looked spent. But the revolver was still too close.

"I just wanna go home," Otis said, glancing toward Jack. Almost as if he were telling the dead man.

Creed rolled onto his side, pushing the rest of Jack's body off him.

"Bolo, stay."

The dog immediately let go of the mouthful of Jack's shirt. Bolo sat facing his master, anxiously waiting for his next command. Creed sat back in the sand and tapped his right palm against his heart. The dog bounded to his master, tail wagging. Immediately Creed's hands were examining where blood streaked the side of the dog's tan coat.

Maggie stepped around Jack's body. She could see the back of his head had been blasted away. She kept moving, slowly, not wanting to set off Otis. As she eased her way toward Otis, she came around Creed. She was close enough to touch him, and she dragged her fingertips gently across his back. He looked up and she caught his eyes. They were a blue so deep she couldn't imagine them lifeless. She pointed at Otis, giving Creed a warning look. And she continued her slow movement toward the sitting giant.

"I just wanna go home," Otis was saying, the lopsided grin almost a grimace. "Three meals a day, TV . . ."

She stood off to his side, her shadow casting over him, and he looked up at her.

"Miss Helen's was a real nice place, you know." His tongue darted out to lick his lips and he squinted his eyes. His head tilted like he was thinking about it. "I was calm there. She was good to me and Jack. She was real good to me. Just like Miss Gwen."

"Miss Helen sounds like a very special lady," Maggie said.

Then the smile lifted one side of his mouth as if he had tasted something bad. "She wouldn't like what Jack was doing."

Maggie was sure he had forgotten about the gun, discarded in the sand right next to him. If she picked it up right now, would he even notice? But just as she reached down for it, Otis's hand snatched it up.

And Maggie's heart stopped.

His eyes met hers again, forehead furrowed, anxious but still grinning.

"I just wanna go home," he told her. Then he held out the gun to her, grip first.

"We'll do that, Otis. We'll all go home," she said.

CHAPTER 74

SACRED HEART HOSPITAL

PENSACOLA, FLORIDA

Maggie didn't realize she had fallen asleep until she felt the tap on her shoulder. She was startled to find Gwen in front of her and for a moment she couldn't remember where she was.

"Sorry, I shouldn't have woken you."

Not only had Maggie fallen asleep, but she had managed to curl up into the waiting room's double-set chairs outside of the trauma center.

"When did you get here?"

"Just a few minutes ago. Thunderstorms delayed the flight in."

And now Maggie could see the flashes of lightning out the windows down the hall. Without warning, she smelled firewood and the musty cabin. She rubbed her eyes, pretending to wipe at the exhaustion when she really wanted to erase the image of Jack's smile and his wolflike black eyes. One look at the concern and fatigue on Gwen's face and Maggie shoved aside Jack and Otis.

"They said he's still in surgery."

"Yes," Maggie said, and she patted the seat beside her for Gwen to sit. "But the bullet went clean through."

She saw her friend wince.

" 'Bullet' and 'clean' in the same sentence sounds like an oxy-moron. How are you?" Gwen asked as she reached up and touched Maggie's face.

A nurse in the ER had cleaned her scrapes and cuts, but Maggie knew she probably looked like hell.

"I'm okay."

"I have to warn you. AD Kunze is here, too."

"In Pensacola?"

"He's with the Florida Highway Patrol and Otis." Gwen noticed the look on Maggie's face and added, "He was worried."

"Now I know I'm dreaming."

Gwen smiled but it didn't last.

"I should have seen it," she told Maggie, and suddenly her eyes had strayed to the far windows and the flickers of light. "I should have known Otis was lying."

"Don't be silly. How were you supposed to know?"

"I'm a psychologist, for God's sake. I should be able to tell when someone's lying."

"Jack would have found another way," Maggie said. "Even without Otis. He's been stalking me for over a month. Ever since we found Gloria Dobson's body outside that burning warehouse in the District. He brought me all the way to the Iowa farm just so he could watch me dig up his handiwork. Did you know he was there? At the farm with us?"

Gwen nodded.

"He actually helped us unearth the garbage bag. He watched the CSU tech pull out the receipt he'd left. The one for the orange socks." Now that she thought about it, Maggie laughed, but there was no humor in it. "The bastard went out with us for drinks afterward. And I didn't know. I have a master's in behavioral science and ten years of profiling and I didn't know that a serial killer was sitting across the table from me. And you think you should have known that Otis was lying to you?"

They both went silent. The doors to the trauma center opened and a yellow-gowned surgical staff member came out and then disappeared down the hall.

Gwen laid her hand on top of Maggie's and she said, "Thank you for taking care of R.J."

"Otis saved us. And a great deal of it was because of you."

"Me?"

"You were kind to him. You reminded him of the only person who had loved him unconditionally."

"I guess we all should be grateful to Miss Helen." Then almost as an afterthought, Gwen asked, "Do you think Otis was lying when he said Jack had more dump sites?"

Maggie shrugged. She didn't want to think about that. Right now she needed to concentrate on the survivors, and not just Tully.

Gwen's phone rang. She checked the caller ID and Maggie saw something pass over her face—dread, anxiety, fear—she couldn't tell for sure, and Gwen, aware that Maggie was watching her, quickly gave her a tight smile.

"I have to take this."

"Is everything okay?"

"I'm sure it is. I just didn't expect this call on a Sunday night. Excuse me."

Gwen hurried away too quickly, as if she were running to answer a landline phone at the other end of the waiting room rather than the cell phone in her hand. It occurred to Maggie that Gwen simply wanted privacy. She shouldn't worry, except that initial pained look on Gwen's face left Maggie concerned.

She watched Gwen disappear down the hallway and then she

saw Ryder Creed walk into the room. They noticed each other at the same time. The short distance between the door and her chair seemed to take Maggie's breath away, and she wasn't the one walking.

He had changed clothes, showered, and washed away all the blood and dirt. He smelled like fresh cotton pulled right out of the dryer. His hair was still damp and tousled, and without warning all the intensity she had felt in that Manhattan, Kansas, hotel room came swirling back as he sat down next to her. He looked straight ahead and when she glanced over at him, she realized he felt it, too.

"How's Tully?" he asked, avoiding her eyes.

"Still in surgery." She hated how good it felt to see him, to have him here. And suddenly she found herself telling him, "Thanks for being here."

"I'm not here for you. I'm here for Tully."

She could see him smile and remembered she had used that exact line on him while they waited during Grace's surgery.

"How's Bolo?"

"He's actually doing good. Surface wound."

Creed looked tired. The cuts and bruises on his face looked raw.

"Maybe you can come see him before you leave town. Grace, too." Finally he looked at her and this time held her eyes.

Before she could respond, Gwen was back. Her face was pale, her eyes dazed. She sat down on the other side of Maggie without a word. She didn't even seem to notice Creed. She had the phone still gripped in her hand.

Maggie put a hand on Gwen's arm.

"What is it? Are you okay?"

"No, I guess I'm not," Gwen said. "I have breast cancer."

TUESDAY, MARCH 26

CHAPTER 75

MANHATTAN, KANSAS

This time Maggie had called Noah Waters from the airport. His father had almost hung up on her but stopped when she said, "The man who attacked Noah is dead." But before she drove to her meeting with Noah, she called Sheriff Uniss in Sioux City, Iowa.

He answered with a lecture, telling her that he had been leaving messages for her for two days. Maggie's and Tully's cell phones still hadn't been recovered after Jack tossed them into the forest. The sheriff wanted her to know they had found "Lily the lot lizard"—that's exactly how he referred to her now. He told Maggie that somehow Lily had made it back to the farmhouse but she was still in serious condition now at the regional medical center. When she told him about Howard Elliott, the sheriff was stunned.

"Howard Elliott's been a fine businessman in these parts for over ten years. He's an independent contractor. Has his own truck. Folks say he took real good care of Helen Paxton after her husband disappeared."

Disappeared?

Something about that reminded Maggie of Jack's claim that he had killed his own father when he was a boy. Was it possible he had done the same to his foster father years later?

As soon as Maggie ended her call with Sheriff Uniss, she texted Agent Alonzo:

Skull found at Iowa farm—
check to see if it's William Paxton.

Noah insisted on another walk. Maggie understood he wanted to get out of the house and somewhere that his parents couldn't listen. It had been a week since the attack. He walked more confidently and wore regular shoes. His feet were healing. The cuts on his face were no longer red and swollen. And that wild-eyed panic that Maggie had seen in his eyes was finally gone. But Maggie knew—and she knew this all too well from experience—the real scars would never disappear.

"How do you know for sure it was him?"

She reached into her pocket and pulled out the laminated card the Florida crime scene technicians had found in the back of John Howard Elliott's panel truck. He had built the truck into a custom workshop for his business. As a skilled craftsman, Elliott worked on construction projects across the country. But his vehicle also included the tricks of his hobby.

There were magnetic signs for the outside of the truck that provided significant disguise. Signs that read: ST. VINCENT'S FOR THE HOMELESS, COMMUNITY RESCUE UNIT, and even FEMA. The disguises also included a variety of items Maggie realized would help him look vulnerable and add to his claim of being a nice guy who was "stranded." There was an arm sling, crutches, a neck brace, and even a dog collar and leash.